TRUSTING A STRANGER

"I feel as though you see me for who I am, not for what you expect me to be." Before he could reply, she was sitting next to him, nearly on his lap again, with her skirts crowding around his legs. "This," she whispered, "this is what you make me feel."

She touched her lips to his. It could have been a brush of air across his mouth, so light and delicate was her kiss. The warmth of her lips, her mouth, radiated through him, sending electric bolts along his nerves. He shivered. All the delicate sweetness of her assaulted him, and he wallowed in it, afraid to breathe, afraid to move, lest she stop touching him.

She sat back and stared up at him.

"Despite myself, I trust you, regardless of what your position requires and what your world expects of you. I trust you enough to place myself in your hands, even though I know I should not . . ."

Books by Amara Royce

NEVER TOO LATE

ALWAYS A STRANGER

Published by Kensington Publishing Corporation

Always a Stranger

AMARA ROYCE

KENSINGTON BOOKS
KENSINGTON PUBLISHING CORP.
www.kensingtonbooks.com

KENSINGTON BOOKS are published by

Kensington Publishing Corp.
119 West 40th Street
New York, NY 10018

All Kensington titles, imprints, and distributed lines are available at special quantity discounts for bulk purchases for sales promotion, premiums, fund-raising, educational, or institutional use.

Special book excerpts or customized printings can also be created to fit specific needs. For details, write or phone the office of the Kensington Special Sales Manager: Kensington Publishing Corp., 119 West 40th Street, New York, NY 10018. Attn. Special Sales Department. Phone: 1-800-221-2647.

Kensington and the K logo Reg. U.S. Pat. & TM Off.

First Electronic Edition: May 2014
eISBN-13: 978-1-60183-118-7
eISBN-10: 1-60183-118-8

First Print Edition: May 2014
ISBN-13: 978-1-60183-226-9
ISBN-10: 1-60183-226-5

Printed in the United States of America

To my son

Acknowledgments

To my wonderful agent, Jessica Alvarez of BookEnds, LLC, and to my great editor, John Scognamiglio, and everyone at Kensington.

To the fabulous members of the Compuserve Books and Writers Forum—especially to Barbara Rogan for her phenomenal support, to Sarah Meral for her gracious assistance with German translation, and to Lara Lacombe (who is also a most excellent fellow Book-Ends author) for her eagle-eyed beta reading.

To the online romance-writing, romance-reading, and romance-reviewing community for being so astoundingly open and generous and thought-provoking.

To a conglomeration of people in my life who put up with my demanding, neurotic, control-freak tendencies and help motivate me to be my best self, whether they realize it or not.

To Chris A., who is the kind of best friend everyone should have.

To Cora, to Mary and Paul, and to all of my much beloved family for their endless support in ways too numerous to mention.

Finally—first, last, and always—to my husband and my son. There aren't enough thanks in the world. Even if I say this multiple times a day, every day, I can never say it enough: I love you.

CHAPTER 1

A Vision

A chime sounded, soft but distinct, cutting through the incessant murmur of visitors in the Chinese alcove. When he followed everyone else's gaze toward the sound, all the air seemed to be sucked out of the room. In the expanse between two display platforms, vacant only moments before, stood an exotic creature of stunning beauty. Wrapped in a flowing crimson robe embroidered with lotus flowers and cinched at the waist with a wide belt, the lady stood motionless with her palms flat together over her heart. The dramatic color of her clothing echoed on her lips. Even from a distance, those ruby lips appeared full and soft. Her dark hair, twisted into smooth rolls and held in place with two sticks, contrasted sharply with her powdered skin. The brightness drew attention, but her perfectly placid composure held it. An oasis of serenity in a sea of human chaos.

Only when she finally moved did he remember to breathe. She slid her arms down to her sides, the silk of her gown rippling gently with her movements. When he craned his neck, he could see slim objects slip from her voluminous sleeves down into her hands.

A heavy thump on his shoulder distracted him. "Lord Ridgemont, as I live and breathe. You, an earl. I had hoped to find you here. Of course, the odds that the Great Exhibition's newest royal commissioner would be in attendance were in my favor." The Marquess of Bartwell spoke sotto voce, barely audible above the general din of the grand hall. He almost didn't catch the note of amusement in Bartwell's voice. "Are you real, or simply a wisp of my imagination? Is it possible I have not seen you in a year, coz? Oh, are you as enamored of these exotic performers as I?"

"You know, I expect, that the His Grace the Duke of Carleton insisted I interview the performers personally and ensure they are properly contracted," he replied. His coat constricted his neck and shoulders now. Everything tensed at the sound of the new title, the one that shouldn't belong to him. "Now shut your trap, my friend, and let the crowd enjoy the show."

Busy work, that's what the duke had given him. Put him in the role of nursemaid or, worse, herder . . . as if he were a collie nipping at heels. *I have found no evidence that Far Eastern performers have been contracted formally*, the duke had explained. *I hope I can rely upon you to take the matter in hand. You will recall the scandal we suffered last month regarding that sleight-of-hand trickery. It was quite embarrassing how many visitors he swindled before we discovered him. Every element of the Great Exhibition must be beyond reproach.*

Looking at this ethereal female, robed in vivid silk and framed by the backdrop of black drapes, he could not believe her to be a thief or a cheat. She could not be a menace to anyone, although Bartwell's dazed expression suggested she could be capable of mesmerism. She looked delicate and slight, as if she might be blown away by a stiff wind.

Then she flicked open two large red fans with an authoritative thwacking sound. It was not delicate or slight. This was not a parakeet or a pigeon. Her sharp, precise flashes of movement resembled a raptor, swift and dangerous. She twirled and flipped the fans with a mastery that transformed them, wielding them with more audacity than he had ever seen in a ballroom. A remarkable feat, considering how many ladies had communicated with him quite explicitly and persuasively with their fans across crowded rooms. No mere coquette's device, these fans became weapons, slicing the air and holding her audience in thrall. The metallic clacks as she rhythmically opened and closed them dominated the alcove. She never moved from her spot. Yet the fans danced in the air above her. Blurs of red spun and rippled around her.

Her gestures quickened to a flashing crescendo, and she tossed one fan high into the air. For a moment, her gaze drifted over the crowd before freezing in his direction. If he were prone to fancy, he might say her eyes locked with his. Golden eyes. How extraordinary. Fortunately, he was not prone to fanciful thoughts. The large red fan flipped over and over as it rose toward the ceiling and changed direction, gaining speed on the way down. Her eyes still focused in his direction, she caught the fan neatly behind her, one-handed.

With another sharp thwack, the fans closed. She returned her hands to a prayerful position, fans tucked once more into her sleeves, and then bowed as the audience roared and begged for more.

"Did you see that, Sky? She is magnificent!" Poor Bartwell. So easily distracted by a pretty face.

"You realize," he responded quietly, "that my mother would still box your ears if she caught you calling me by that silly nickname. We are above such vulgarity . . . or whatever term she uses. No one else has called me Sky since we were in short pants. She would likely give you the full lecture on the succession."

"You know I cannot help it. Must I really call you Ridgemont? It simply does not suit you."

It would be best for familial relations if he chose to interpret Bartwell's comments as benignly oblivious. Yes, Lionel should have inherited. Yes, the accident that had taken both his father's and brother's lives last year had devastated the family and thrust him into a role he hadn't anticipated. Yes, Lionel would have been a better earl, having been bred to the position his entire life, and he would have given a great deal for his brother to have lived, for his brother to have taken his rightful place. But fate had deemed otherwise. If Bartwell truly doubted his fitness to manage the earldom, well, Skyler looked up at the glass and metal grid of the roof and swallowed a retort about glass houses. Despite being raised from birth to be a marquess and acceding to the title when he reached the age of majority, Bartwell had yet to take his seat at the House of Lords. He liked his cousin, truly he did, but sometimes the man needed a sound thrashing.

4 • *Amara Royce*

"Besides," his cousin continued, "you may not know this, but while you were off doing your pretty little pencil sketches in America or Greece or wherever you were this time, I became your mother's favorite almost nephew. I think I finally managed to usurp Lord Devin in her eyes." Bartwell grinned widely as Skyler's smile faded.

America. He'd returned to London as quickly as he could, dropping all his projects in Philadelphia abruptly, but he'd still arrived far too late. Meanwhile, Bartwell had been here in his stead to console his mother. And now he was not just Skyler Charles Roderick, second son and engineering student. He was the Earl of Ridgemont.

He let the jab at his design and engineering studies pass. Showing resistance would only prolong his cousin's teasing, a habit that should have faded in childhood. If the man knew of his incipient attempts at designing a flying machine, the mockery would increase beyond reason. While he waited impatiently for the throng to dissipate so that he could converse with the performer, Bartwell refused to leave his side. The woman disappeared into the curtained area behind the displays. He frowned and said, "I must be going. I should take this opportunity to interview that performer and find out who the manager of this troupe is."

"I was hoping you could give me an introduction." His cousin fussed with his cuff links nonchalantly and then looked at him expectantly.

"Do not trifle, Bartwell. Your charms are surely best directed elsewhere. And I have work to do." When Bartwell frowned, he cuffed his old friend on the arm and added, "Come for a visit tomorrow. Perhaps we can go to White's for coffee." Still, the man would not budge. Instead, the nuisance kept tossing unsubtle glances toward the curtains through which the performer had disappeared. Those glances made him more uneasy than they should.

Only authorized vendors and staff could enter those areas. Like the duke, Skyler knew of no Asian performers approved by the Royal Commission. He certainly would have remembered hearing of such a lovely one.

"I really must see if the manager is available."

"I would be happy to assist you, coz."

"This is official Royal Commission business, Bartwell. Word

has spread about that thieving gang of magicians. The few honest ones, unassociated with the criminals, still had to be banned. The Exhibition must not be seen as a center of criminal activity. According to my father's letters, that was one of the Commission's initial points of contention regarding this Hyde Park location—such potentially unsavory elements so close to Rotten Row."

"Then my presence would be a boon. Together we would present quite an imposing front, would we not?"

"Bartwell, you cannot accompany me. I am the official representative responsible for interviewing these performing groups. It would be inappropriate for you to observe." Inappropriate and annoying. He'd forgotten how exasperating his cousin could be, especially when he wanted something. "Besides, you only wish to ogle that young woman. Such behavior would not further my cause. Go find a nice, proper Englishwoman to pester. That one is not for you." He knew his cousin's proclivities too well; Bartwell would be more likely to visit one of the boardinghouses near Fleet Street for female companionship. His stomach turned at the thought, the euphemism a weak shield for how distasteful and destructive such pleasures could be.

Bartwell frowned some more and then said, "Well, then. Dismissed, am I? I doubt my calendar is free tomorrow," he added pointedly. "But perhaps we can meet again soon. Do not be such a stranger."

The man gave one longing look toward the curtains before retreating. Although they bid each other farewell cordially enough, his cousin's stiff posture and the rigid set of his mouth suggested things were not at ease. No matter. If his nose were out of joint, it wouldn't last. Some things never changed. Bartwell had always been prone to fleeting infatuations and mercurial moods.

Meanwhile, he had actual duties to attend to. He straightened his lapels and crossed through the dispersing crowd to introduce himself to this mystery woman. If he were lucky, her employer would be waiting in the wings, which would make his task much easier. The dryness of his mouth could no doubt be attributed to impending teatime. The pulse of his heartbeat in his ears . . . well, a little nervousness was to be expected of a new royal commissioner, was it not?

* * *

The burgundy curtains used to divide many of the spaces in the Exhibition could work wonders of architecture. Two men could easily erect frames and drapes that converted an amorphous space into four distinct and intimate display areas with a central backstage area. And those were the easily movable screens. The larger dividers used to break up the massive wings into national sections created a variety of useful nooks, like the one behind the Chinese exhibit.

When he breached the curtains, he nearly stumbled over a scrawny boy, who immediately scampered to the farthest corner of the makeshift chamber and crouched on the floor next to a large steamer trunk. The child's homespun garments and muddy boots seemed out of place amid the finery of the recent audience. When the boy raised his head, his round face was shadowed by a large tweed cap but was definitely filthy. What he could tell of the child's coloring and facial features resembled that of the fan dancer. Could this be a sibling . . . or perhaps her offspring? He seemed to be about ten or maybe twelve, and the woman looked far too young to have a child this old. Still, he'd only seen her from afar. He knew little of the mysterious Far East; the practices of foreigners could be unorthodox indeed. He nodded to the child and took in the scene.

The room, if such a makeshift area could be given the honorary title of *room*, was lined with crates, a simple wardrobe, and the massive trunk against which the boy cowered. The chatter of the ever-shifting crowd outside this little alcove murmured through the fabric walls, and weak sunlight streamed in from the glass ceilings above. Yet there was no sign of the fan dancer, aside from the faint scent of jasmine hanging in the air.

"Where is the woman who came in here a few moments ago?"

Staring, the boy shook his head. The few sounds he made were unintelligible. *Patience, Skyler, patience.* Communicating with children was not something he did often, nor was it something that came naturally to him.

"The lady with the fans . . ." Ridgemont held up imaginary fans as she had and twisted his wrists in an awkward pantomime. This earned him a reluctant chuckle from his young audience, whose eyes lit with recognition. Gesturing again, he asked, "You know her?"

The boy nodded once, his face quickly turning neutral, guarded.

"Where did she go?"

Again, the boy spoke in an unfamiliar language, almost certainly Chinese or Japanese, while shaking his head emphatically. Really, the Royal Commission should interview all of the performing companies and ensure that they had an English-speaking representative present at all times; in fact, the ability to speak English should be deemed one of the requirements of approval. He supposed this too was now part of his responsibility.

He tried again. This time, he pretended to enter the chamber as the dancing girl, imitating her posture and demeanor, to the boy's obvious amusement. The child actually giggled. He hadn't expected to play the clown so soon or so literally in his role as earl. Then he raised his arms ahead of him, pointed, and asked, "Did she go this way?" He turned slightly and repeated the action. "Or this way?"

Finally, the child became more animated and pulled a silky red robe from the wardrobe. *Yes, her!* His pulse quickened, but he strove to respond temperately. When he nodded, the boy quickly led him to a hidden gap behind some crates and pointed. Peeking through the curtains, he found himself draped in paisley and surrounded by large statues of Indian deities. He stepped out to take a broader look at the crowd around the displays. Given the riot of colors and the constant flow of people, she was well and truly gone.

When he made his way back into the alcove, the child was gone as well.

Bloody hell. Who were these performers? And where was their manager? He wandered around the small room, picking up and inspecting bits and pieces along the way. Figurines, presumably from the Orient, were scattered about. The silk robe lay draped over some crates, and the wardrobe doors stood ajar. This was quite a haphazard group. Unprofessional. As entrancing as the fan performance had been, the Royal Commission would not want to be associated with such shoddiness.

As if pulled to it without conscious volition, he picked up the robe. The red silk confounded his senses, the fiery color confronting his vision while the cool touch of the silk flowed like water through his fingers. And the scent that wafted from it, warm jasmine on a hot summer evening—he found himself drawing deep breaths and had to stop from burying his face in the material. *Don't be an idiot over a bit of fabric. You haven't been a fool for a pretty face yet. No need to start now.* Shaking his head with a self-effacing chuckle, he laid out the robe gently, careful to avoid snagging the delicate fabric.

Hanako's heart banged against her ribs as she crouched in the trunk. She hated being caged up in such a tiny space, but she hadn't many options. This well-dressed, well-spoken stranger would not leave! What could he be doing now? No one remained in the chamber, yet he was still here. His quiet movements suggested a randomness that was at least a little reassuring. If he were really searching for something, he would be ransacking the place much more deliberately, opening and emptying as he went. If she were lucky, his idle curiosity would pass quickly. After several long moments, the flapping of curtains and the receding of his footsteps gave her space to breathe. She waited a bit more before pushing up on the trunk's false bottom.

When she first heard the rustling of the drapes, she had just barely managed to tuck her bright gown into the wardrobe and mask the white face powder with ash. The susurration of the fabric should have been swallowed up in the noise of the Exhibition, but it cut through the background noise as loudly as a thunderbolt. This was why she always shoved her hair into a cap immediately after a performance. This was why she kept this costume on under the kimono.

She had sensed his intent halfway through the fan dance. It was easy to distinguish his attentiveness from the usual avid but innocuous audience. Here was a man with questions. With purpose. She welcomed neither. His eyes bore into her, apart from all the other gazes from the crowd. She'd barely managed to direct her focus back to the fans before she nearly dropped one. As the performance continued, despite herself, she wanted to please him—not the audience, just him. His eyes—bright, almost feminine, almost inhumanly green—shone with an admiration and approval she craved. That she craved it unnerved her. She'd forced herself not to look at him. But she could tell from the determination in his eye that he would seek her out afterward. She did not sense, though, the same kind of lasciviousness or menace that poured off most men who dogged her skirts. His head and shoulders towered above the women around him, and some of the men as well. Admiration suffused his face, but not lust. Even masked lasciviousness was easy to identify now, coming off people in waves. He didn't emanate that baseness. Nor did he display the kind of impertinent curiosity about foreigners that often had her gritting her teeth, as if she represented all Japanese women, or rather all women from the Orient, for it seemed few people even attempted to differentiate the nationalities.

Mr. Broek would have to be told about this gentleman's interest, and he would not be pleased. This was the risk of Broek's ploy; the Exhibition would draw attention that could not be fully controlled or contained. She didn't want any of it.

Last night, through the wall, she'd heard one of the women weeping and others trying to comfort her. Only when Broek's slow, measured footsteps sounded at the bottom of the stairs, like a subtle but undeniable threat, did the crying stop. If she could have, she'd have escaped years ago, even with nowhere else to go. She looked back with a bitter laugh at how subtly and inexorably escape became impossible. She picked up the small jade elephant, rolling it between her palms, feeling it warm from her skin. It had been Takara's favorite toy as a young child. Broek promised her that her sister would not be included in the auction, would go with her under a guarantee of exemption. It would be part of the agreement of sale. A bitter sliver of laughter escaped her—an agreement of sale.

Without any doubt, this young stranger was a gentleman, with his finely tailored clothing and imperious bearing—straight backed but with a languor to his movements that suggested a life of ease. He'd surely been raised for a life of power and privilege, and he wore them both comfortably. His jovially condescending tone likewise suggested he found novelty in her childlike incomprehension. She should have felt relief and pride that her boyish performance was so convincing, but instead she'd struggled not to reveal herself, not to show how very well she understood his intentions, how very little she was impressed by him. She'd wanted him to see the woman behind the facade. A ridiculous, irrational instinct. He was likely just another of the Jade Garden's potential customers—she could not allow herself to forget that. He might even be persuaded to bid.

She tucked the elephant into her pocket and finished sorting through the trunks, packing away the items from the fan performance and laying out everything needed for the next show. Broek changed the arrangement of performances weekly. The new addition for this week was the juggling.

There should be flames or swords, he had said. She'd managed to convince him that such dangerous items would entail undue risk and draw unwanted scrutiny. Not to mention her personal safety. No, he couldn't risk damaging her person when he had so much yet to gain. Now that they'd been in London long enough for word to spread, the bidding would begin shortly, he promised gleefully, as if she and the other women had anything to be happy about.

She tossed the silver balls into the bucket with a clang before reining in her temper. She rolled the jade elephant figurine between her palms, pausing only to swipe hot tears from her cheeks, and then began counting backward from ten in Japanese. *Ju, kyu, hachi.* Then in Dutch. Then in whatever languages came to mind. By the time she got to Spanish, her movements were precise and controlled again. Second basket—dried fruits. Third basket—scarves and cricket balls. When everything was packed away, she picked up the jade carving again, rubbing the spot between its large ears as she considered her options again. Considered what would be needed to free herself and all the women from Broek. *There is no clear path.* But one thing was certain—she would have to act soon.

"So, Ridgemont, what have you learned? Have you been as enthralled by the petite dancer about whom so many of our guests have raved?"

At least His Grace the Duke of Carleton had given him enough time for proper greetings and a coffee before looming over him. After all the accumulated heat of the day, the offices of the Royal Commission of the Great Exhibition of the Works of Industry of All Nations were brutally oppressive. He wished he could doff his jacket for some relief. None of the other gentlemen, dressed impeccably, showed any such signs of weakness. He surreptitiously ran his finger under his damp collar. From the day he'd returned to London, he felt a lack of air. The suffocating feeling was worst in the House of Lords, but it simmered here too.

There have been rumors, the duke told him hours earlier, *of some unapproved performers—most recently, some Orientals in the Chinese section. Every element of the Great Exhibition must be beyond reproach. Make sure they are . . . civilized.*

"I have indeed, Your Grace, seen a charming fan dancer but was unable to locate her or her employer afterward," he said. Thus far, Carleton was the closest thing he had to a mentor, and the duke's influence could be very powerful. "I should mention that the musical contest is flourishing, although Monsieur Berlioz is somewhat temperamental and dissatisfied with the caliber of performers. He is also quite adamant about not performing himself. What else do you know about this Asian troupe?"

"Very little, I am afraid. I have found no evidence that such performers have been contracted. I hope I can rely upon you to take the matter in hand. You will recall the scandal we suffered soon after the opening. It was quite embarrassing how many visitors that circus and their pickpockets robbed before we could prove it. Followed so soon by the death of the tightrope walker, the Commission discussed banning all performers. They are, however, too popular an attraction to do away with entirely."

"Ah, the particulars are unknown to me." *Do not apologize. Show no sign of weakness.* "I read a brief report in one of the papers, but there was no mention of criminal activities."

"Of course, your family would not have been out gallivanting while mourning your father. Indeed, your father was one of our most enthusiastic members. If drive alone were sufficient, his fervor for this little project would have guaranteed its success. Obstacles and detractions did not deter him in the least. Quite unfortunate that he did not live to see his efforts come to fruition."

"Yes, he would have been quite proud of all this and would not have related problems with the Exhibition preparations to me in his correspondence." No, his father did not see faults. His father knew how to pave over faults and obstacles and failings, at least in his mind. Perhaps if Father had been more cognizant of the faults of his steward, the accounts would be in better order . . .

"Were you able to speak with the manager of the Oriental performers?"

Focus, man. He needed to rein in his wandering thoughts. The duke's esteem was a rare gift, sometimes taking years to acquire yet easily lost due to a single misstep.

"No, Your Grace, strangely, the manager was not in attendance. Even the dancing girl seemed to disappear before I could speak with her. In the back, I found a boy who seems to belong to the group, but I was unable to communicate with him."

The duke took a sip of tea and muttered something. *Foreigners* and *language* were the only words he was able to decipher. More audibly, Carleton responded, "That has been a common problem with many troupes for months now. Those *properly* educated can communicate in one of the other standard languages. However, Commission members from more humble beginnings have needed interlocutors at times. It has become even more problematic since the Exhibition opened." His ducal brow furrowed, and he quickly jotted some notes.

The man's tone reminded him so much of his mother's, the old guard of the British peerage. Lulled by the silence and his own ruminations about his mother's thinking, Skyler jumped at the duke's abrupt question.

"Such a loss, both of them. How is your mother faring?" the duke asked. "Does she remain at Harrogate?" It was as if the man could hear his thoughts.

"Yes, Your Grace. I thank you for asking after her. She is tolerably well, as well as can be expected, and it seems that the waters are as restorative as purported."

"Very good. If you would be so kind as to convey my regards to her?"

"Of course, Your Grace. She will be pleased. This has been a difficult time for us all."

"Did you know that your father and I went to school together?"

"I did. While he rarely spoke of his time at Eton, he did mention some of his antics in passing. Daring and dramatic, if fleeting."

"He was quite memorable."

"Always."

"He would have been proud to see the man you've become."

"You do me too much credit. I would like to believe that is true but have not yet earned such an accolade."

"I am certain you will be a great asset to the Royal Commission. You clearly grasp the gravity of our work and the importance of maintaining Britain's reputation. We are the leader of the world, and this is one of our best displays of international leadership. On your shoulders settles the weight of British supremacy."

The weight of British supremacy. That heavy weight settled like a boulder in the pit of his stomach again. Surely the duke meant to be complimentary and encouraging. Surely he was only imagining the underlying threat. Surely the Royal Commission would never make one man the scapegoat if the Exhibition courted scandal again. The tightrope tragedy, the negative reviews, the nobility's distaste for shilling days. The performances were but a tiny factor of the Great Exhibition's success. Surely the noose of public opinion was only in his mind.

CHAPTER 2

A Problem

This time Skyler was prepared. He waited patiently along with the rest of the crowd. He'd missed the rest of the previous day's performances, but now he knew the schedule and waited patiently for the Japanese performance to begin. Only three minutes left to the top of the hour when the next display should begin.

"What do you think it will be this time?" one woman in a massive feathered hat said to another. "Have you seen the tea ceremony? It was mesmerizing." Her companion, diminutive in size and haberdashery, mumbled something indistinct.

"Pardon me, ladies," he said in as official a manner as he could. "I hope I may be forgiven this forwardness, but I am a member of the Royal Commission and would like to know your opinion about this troupe. I have seen only one of the performances thus far. How many are there?"

The smaller woman, wearing a demure bonnet, responded, "I have seen four performances myself, all unique and quite entertaining. My neighbor saw a fan dance recently that she raved about." With both women looking at him fully, he realized the one in the petite straw bonnet was older, perhaps a chaperone. How could any-one not rave about that fan display?

"So you are enjoying the Exhibition?" he asked.

"Oh, it is wonderful! So exotic and magnificent!" the younger lady interjected before her companion placed a hand on her arm.

"Yes, sir," the older woman said. "Many of my friends have at-tended multiple times. We have all seen such amazements, it is nearly overwhelming."

He was surprised to see the boy he'd met backstage come out from behind the curtains. All cleaned up and dressed in flowing silk pants and a short, thick robe, the child bore little resemblance to the dirty urchin he'd encountered. Yet the shape of his face, the blank-ness in his eyes, these were the same. The boy carried three pails, which he placed on the ground before emptying the contents in a semicircle before him: balls of different sizes and colors, wads of fabric, and some thick candles spaced evenly around the half circle.

After the preparations, he took his place at the center of the semicircle, drawing attention and anticipatory silence. The boy bowed deeply, hands at his sides, to the audience.

Then he took up three golden balls and began juggling. How charming. Over the course of several minutes, the child replaced various objects around the circle, usually without breaking his rhythm at all, simply bending down and interchanging objects seamlessly. Such nimbleness and concentration. Yet the audience seemed restless. When using similar objects, he occasionally spun and even juggled the items behind his back, eliciting lukewarm ap-plause.

It took Skyler a few moments to figure out what was missing—the intensity and vivacity of the performer. This child clearly had no desire to be there and had no flair for showmanship. He did what he was expected to do, nothing more. Perhaps he even hated it. Whereas the fan dancer demanded attention and captivated the eye, this little performer shied away from attention and probably wanted nothing more than to hide in the drapes. The manager of this troupe no doubt forced the child to do his duty, but why bother? Street per-formers could do as much, and with more verve.

As the performance continued, the audience gradually thinned. When an entourage turned away en masse, he saw the frantic look in the boy's eye. And everything fell to the ground with a clatter. The head of the entourage, a tall and well-dressed gentleman, turned toward the commotion, a look of disdain on his face. His derision turned to fascination, and the rest of his group followed his gaze. Gasps rose from the crowd as the boy, leaving all the items where they'd landed, reached into one of the buckets and drew out three large, shining knives. Then the child—a child!—held the three knives separated by his fingers, almost like claws extending from his knuckles, picked up one of the colorful scarves, and sliced through it with all three simultaneously. Sharp claws indeed.

A murmur went through the audience, which drew tight again. The crowd stirred at the danger, at the potential for harm. The pack scented blood.

The boy's demeanor transformed. Here was flair. Here was presence.

Skyler's breath caught as the youth tossed one knife high so that it flipped over and over, glinting in the sun, before catching it deftly by the handle. The child repeated the action, adding the second knife and then the third, the blades glowing and flashing. No. This would not do. This was unsafe, not only for the boy but for the audience. God only knew what bad press the Exhibition would get if anyone were seriously injured, especially so soon after the tragic death of the high-wire performer. He tried to edge forward, but the crowd was a solid mass now. More than once, the knives sliced through the boy's heavy sleeves, and as before he caught them by the handles. It seemed impossible he hadn't been hurt. The fabric frayed and fluttered as he gestured. Still, no blood appeared, and his movements continued, constant and smooth.

Skyler pushed toward the front of the crowd but made excruciatingly slow progress amid irritated murmurs. As the child tossed up the knives with increasing speed and ferocity, people backed away but did not leave. Finally, he threw up all three knives at once, remarkably high, sparkling almost like fireworks as they rose and descended. How could he catch all three?

He didn't. Instead, the knives stabbed into the floor around him. When the boy stepped to the side, it was clear that the weapons had triangulated inches from his slippered feet, tips buried into the floorboards. The audience erupted with applause and cheers as he bowed deeply.

When the boy began collecting his tools back into the buckets, Skyler finally broke from the crowd.

As he approached, the child struggled to pull the third knife out of the floor, rocking it back and forth to free it.

"Here, let me help you with that," Skyler offered.

The child backed away sharply before making an awkward bow and standing subserviently a few feet away.

He easily pulled the knife out of the ground and lightly ran his finger along the edge. The blood that welled from the shallow cut was no trick. These were serious weapons, capable of mortal injury, and this was no task for a child. Even more reason for him to pin down the manager—if he could get the performers to tell him who their manager was. He placed the knife gently into a bucket and picked up the container for the boy to toss the rest of the objects into. The child tried to take the bucket from him, speaking again in his indecipherable language, but Skyler would not allow it. These weren't toys, and this troupe clearly needed supervision. If he had to confiscate the weapons, he would.

When he ducked into the alcove this time, the boy scurried to put away the juggling accoutrements, only slowing his frenetic activity to place the knives carefully in a velvet-lined case. He tried to help the child clean up, but every effort was thwarted. It was clear the boy didn't want him near the wardrobe or the trunk. And it seemed his nearness made the child nervous. Where was his employer? Did he even have parents? Why would they let him engage in such a dangerous spectacle? The shredded sleeves of his robe, fluttering as he moved, showed how close he'd come to cutting himself many times during the performance.

He voiced the questions aloud, to no avail. The boy would glance away from his work and shrug or shake his head or just peer at him confusedly. When there was nothing else left to do, nothing else for the boy to attend to, he caught the child's attention. Seating himself on one of the crates, he pointed to himself and said his name, and then he held out a calling card and indicated his name while repeating it again. The boy echoed him awkwardly. "Lord Ridge-mont."

"Yes! My name is Lord Ridgemont. Lord Skyler Ridgemont."

He nodded and then pointed to the boy, who seemed to understand and replied, "Izo."

"Your name is Izo?"

The boy pointed to himself and said, "Izo," and then pointed to Skyler and said, "Ridgemont?"

Here was some meager progress.

"Who is your leader?"

Izo's brow furrowed. When he repeated the question with different wording—boss, father, owner, which made him wince—the boy looked around the little room, a growing unease and panic again evident in his eyes. Tension, but no comprehension.

Enough. He waved his hand to dismiss his own inquiry and held out a folded slip of paper. When Izo simply looked at him, frowning and wary, he pantomimed the fan dancer again. It earned him a chuckle. *Blast it, someone in this troupe must understand English.* When the boy imitated the fan dance, he held out the paper again. This time Izo darted toward him to take it and jumped back as if bitten. This was no life for such a child. He'd seen worse, certainly; this child didn't appear to be starving and seemed to have sufficient clothing. But the fact that no one attended him, no one had even come back here to check on his well-being, no one monitored his performance, not even the enchanting dancer who was obviously related to him . . . this neglect was cause for concern.

On a whim, he dug a coin out of his pocket and tossed it toward the boy, who snatched it out of the air. He wanted to stay, wanted to tell the boy that the knife display was not safe for him, wanted to ask him everything he knew about these performances—about that beautiful woman he'd seen before—but clearly such an attempt would be futile. So he gave a brief nod of acknowledgment and made his way out. He would have to consider more intrusive ways to contact the manager of this group. No one in charge of such performers could hide out of sight indefinitely. If he had to follow the performers home one day, so be it.

Only after the curtains ceased to sway and were completely still did she straighten her spine and set about unpacking her next costume. Again, the disguise had worked, thank the heavens. At any moment, she'd feared this Lord Skyler Ridgemont would recognize her or realize there was something awry. His desire to help was rather sweet, but he could not get too close. Not to her and not to the storage pieces. Their incongruities could be easily missed by casual observers—but the details would not bear up to close inspection. The inner dimensions of the chests would draw questions. From a distance, the shapeless robes hid her proportions well. He'd already spent too much time backstage.

She needed air. Reaching within her thick jacket, she loosened the binding underneath and took some deep breaths. Lord Ridgemont had spoken and acted so kindly. She'd felt that strange pull again, that dangerous impulse to reveal herself. His barrage of questions would have flummoxed her if she actually had tried to answer. When he'd tossed her the coin, she'd wanted to cast it back at his feet. How callous and presumptuous. And obviously so flush with funds that he could afford to toss gold coins at random children on a whim. She couldn't deny the sincerity she'd seen in him— that moment when he'd decided to offer the coin and made it a casual, playful gesture. It didn't seem calculated or condescending. But craving his goodwill would be a mistake. In the same moment, she wanted to kiss his cheek and slap it.

He was more patient than most men when dealing with an indecipherable child. His manner was light, friendly, open. His smile . . . well, it warmed her more than felt comfortable. And those eyes; curse those eyes. Ocean depths a woman could drown herself in. She'd seen such striking blue-green seas off the coast of Nagasaki when traveling with her father. It wasn't wise to trust apparent kindness and generosity. It wasn't prudent to assume that goodness was more than just a facade. Perhaps she only wished him different from the others—from the men who leered and groped, the men who asked what pleasures the Orient hid and sometimes tried to uncover them without permission.

No, Lord Skyler Ridgemont was not to be trusted, certainly not for tossing a . . . gods, a shiny gold sovereign! She turned it over in her palm, marveling at its shine and weight. It wasn't even tinged with grime. Takara would be delighted to see it. Before putting her sister to bed, she would unveil the little treasure, perhaps weaving a story about finding it on her walk home. Oh, she and the other women could do quite a lot with this, make this one coin stretch, if they were careful.

What she could not do was buy a new robe. Celestial mother! The ragged shreds slipped through her fingers. Even as she'd lifted the knives from the bucket, she'd known it would be foolhardy. The bored faces and the people wandering away left her few options. If word got back to Mr. Broek that she'd lost the audience, he'd be furious. Performances as Izo never garnered as much attention as her feminine demonstrations. Better to risk the knives than lose the crowd and gain his anger. The risk proved worthwhile, even if the sleeves of this robe were beyond repair. She'd gotten them all back to attention, and one of the Jade ladies could likely replace the sleeves with relative ease, if she could find extra silk cheaply. The sleeves would have to fit closer to her arms for next time. Surely, with such a response, there would be a next time. *Several promising bids have come in*, Mr. Broek had reminded her at breakfast. *By the end of the Exhibition, we should fetch a fine figure indeed. All told, we shall be quite comfortable, and you and your sister shall surely be under the wing of one of the greatest men of England.* As if *we* would truly benefit, as if this wasn't all intended for his benefit. As if his benign euphemisms could mask the degrading fate awaiting her. She could only hope that she could devise a solution for the women before his plans came to fruition.

One can only climb so high before one runs out of mountain.

CHAPTER 3

A Dinner

"My dearest Lady Devin, you look most resplendent this evening." Unconscionably late, Skyler entered his aunt's dining room determined to brave her censure. He made a grand bow in front of her as she stood to greet him. Long ago, he'd learned how powerful charm could be, and how easily he could wield it. So he did. "My deepest apologies to you and your eminent guests for being so unforgivably gauche. I am stricken to see that I have kept you from your repast."

"Lord Ridgemont, your presence is always welcome," Lady Devin replied fondly, drawing him toward her to kiss his cheek. She whispered in his ear, "Perhaps a new pocket watch is in order, Ridgemont. Surely you know how to tell time, you pup." Then, with a placid smile, she added for all to hear, "Please do take your seat, dear nephew, so service may begin."

His aunt's unorthodox dinners could be relied upon for a motley cast of characters, full of surprise and wit and infinite entertainment. On these evenings, his aunt ignored the lines drawn by the ton and invited anyone she wanted. His father had disapproved of Lady Devin's cavalier disregard for social order. Although Father had no direct control over her as a married woman, he frequently made himself unavailable due to some prior commitment and made his disapprobation glaringly clear. *Dukes and shopkeepers, earls and actors, judges and novelists! You have no sense of propriety, Rose! Your husband should be here to keep you in line, not traipsing the world.*

How Lady Devin kept her temper as her brother raged was a mystery, but she never raised her voice in return, at least not when Skyler and her children were present. Instead, she nodded dutifully and noncommittally and yet went on blithely issuing invitations to whomever she chose. If rumors were to be believed, she'd once had the Prime Minister at the same table as a chimney sweep and his parents. Rumor also had it that her own son, Viscount Alexander Devin, was enamored of a bookseller, a widow, although he had yet to see them together. He'd seen Devin once at the club, seeming remarkably happy and less severe, but there hadn't been an opportune moment to delve into such delicate matters.

This dinner proved to be no exception. If anything, the table appeared to have a more deliberately international flavor than usual. A buxom French opera singer was flanked by a vice chancellor and an Italian merchant. The diva winked at him as he made his way to the seat Lady Devin indicated near the other end of the table.

A small woman was seated near the end of the table, a petite slip of a thing, with smooth black hair in a simple, almost severe chignon at the nape of her neck. When she turned in his direction to speak with her neighbor, he saw a round face and almond-shaped eyes framed with dark, dark lashes. He knew her. A lovely vision from China or Japan or one of those Far Eastern kingdoms. This vision was all the more jarring for her Western appearance: white gloves and a modest navy gown with a high lace collar, and devoid of makeup.

The fan dancer from the Exhibition! The woman who had stolen his breath and repeatedly evaded his scrutiny.

Normally, Lady Devin ensured the common male-female-male-female seating arrangement, so it was strange to find himself placed next to a man, a rather tall, rather blond man, introduced as Mr. Jarlsberg from Munich. Once he took his own seat, he quickly realized that the fan dancer was translating between this Mr. Jarlsberg and a woman he did not recognize. Jarlsberg leaned toward the fan dancer in a way that made his fists clench. How dare the man ogle *his* fan dancer?

Now where had that odd notion come from?

After proper introductions, finally, he knew her name. Miss Hanako Sumaki. And now he knew the musical lilt of her voice. Delicate and soft, her tones made even the gutturals of German language sound sweet. Her facility with both German and English impressed him beyond measure.

When Mr. Jarlsberg mentioned his interest in the Great Exhibition, Skyler took particular pride in the German's admiration of the technological exhibits. When Mr. Jarlsberg asked how the Exhibition was conceived, Skyler explained in German some of the planning and construction he'd learned from his father. When Mr. Jarlsberg asked for comparisons among the different displays, Skyler was able to open the question to the table and draw out some of the highlights. Conveniently, the discussion gave Miss Sumaki a few moments to eat.

He watched surreptitiously as she savored each spoonful of consommé. So exceedingly strange. Why would this unremarkable soup—really, his aunt's dinners were usually so much more impressive—why would a simple broth give her such pleasure, as if she were starved?

A woman beside her, a widow by the name of Mrs. Addison, broke the lull in the conversation by spouting off about some poor orphanage in the city. As the earnest do-gooder wove this unpleasant tale, Miss Sumaki stuttered in her translation. The sad description of two young brothers being separated seemed to strike her mute.

"Please allow me to take over this part of the story, Miss Sumaki," he interjected in German. "One as delicate as you should not be subjected to such ugliness."

She shot him an inscrutable look. He expected perhaps gratitude or relief, but neither appeared. If anything, her furrowed brow spoke of irritation. With him? Still, she bowed her head in deference, and he took over. It was a harrowing tale that seemed to drag on. More than once, he heard a hitch in Miss Sumaki's breath, and her tension only dissipated when the story came to an end, with the jubilant reunion of the boys under the care of the Needlework for the Needy Society.

When the meat course was served, Mr. Jarlsberg found the beef much more interesting than any conversation. So Skyler took that opportunity to begin his inquiry.

"Translation is one of my common employments," Miss Sumaki explained to him in English, as the large German shoveled a large forkful into his mouth. "My employer, Mr. Broek, runs a trade business, and I assist him in various capacities. Since he travels widely, I serve as his translator. At times, like this evening, he hires out my services to his associates. Mr. Jarlsberg is a merchant with whom we have frequent commerce, and we were delighted to learn that we could assist him during his visit to London." She spoke English with a charmingly unusual lilt, the vowels so beautifully rounded and full, the consonants so delicate and spry.

"Hires out your services? And what do those services entail? Are you Mr. Jarlsberg's escort throughout his trip?" His aunt's hospitality did not extend to inviting mistresses, at least not as far as he knew, even if such mistresses served multiple purposes. It was one thing to have an eclectic guest list and another to court scandal. He realized his error, though, as soon as the words passed his lips.

She frowned, almost infinitesimally, but he noticed. She gripped her fork ever so slightly tighter, the tendons on the back of her hand showing. Switching to German, she said, "I am not sure what you mean. I serve only as a temporary liaison, primarily for travelers or international business transactions, as Mr. Broek sees fit. Nothing more. I offer no other services than translation."

Mr. Jarlsberg paused in midswallow. His brow furrowed as a storm passed over his face. When he recovered and could speak again, his voice was gruff and low, but perhaps not as quiet as he thought. "Mr. Broek suggested I could negotiate for additional services."

Her expression neutral, she responded equally low. "As I said, I am only available for translation and, even then, on a limited schedule." Her voice had grown tight.

He could not help but interject. In German, he said, "And thus it sounds as though negotiation is at an end."

When they first had been introduced, Mr. Jarlsberg had the air of a man well aware of his influence over women. Now he grimaced, as if just realizing that others at the table might understand his meaning. His back straightened, his chest puffed out just so, and he smoothed his lapels. It was the kind of male preening Skyler saw on Hyde Park promenades, but Miss Sumaki seemed unaffected. He must have had some mistaken preconception of the evening. He frowned as he attacked his plate again.

Liaison. Did she even realize the illicit implications of the term? Did Jarlsberg? How strange that such an officious title could carry illicit suggestions . . . and in this German's case, apparent assumptions. But onward. Truly, whatever the nature of their business transactions were, he should not interfere. He had more important matters to see to.

"Is Mr. Broek the manager of your performing troupe?" he asked Miss Sumaki, while giving her charge time to recover his composure.

Sky couldn't tell if her surprise was feigned or genuine. Her sharp intake of breath, the widening of her eyes, her glances around the table. Surely she could not have expected to go unnoticed. How many women from the Far East did she think lived in London? She touched her napkin to her lips, dabbing gently and then slowly replacing it on her lap. His eyes followed her hands, his heart beating faster as they moved lower, lower, out of view. Oh, how he wished to follow those hands.

You are in your aunt's dining room, you idiot. For her sake and for the sake of the lovely woman in front of you, don't be an ass. Get hold of yourself, man.

"Yes," she said, finally. "Mr. Broek has arranged the performances. He was disappointed by the dearth of Japanese artifacts on display, understandable as it may be, given the country's policies. He felt the performances would strengthen the authenticity of the displays and provide sufficient context for what might seem like very foreign items."

"Indeed," he replied, thankful that Mr. Jarlsberg was still engrossed in his meal. "It is odd, though, that he would not go through proper channels to arrange the performances."

"I am sure he was unaware of any required procedures."

"Nonetheless, he will need to follow established guidelines for obtaining the Royal Commission's approval. We have received many glowing reviews of your group's performances. Your fan dance in particular is highly praised. It would be a shame to have to shut them down."

"Thank you for the compliment, my lord," she said, dipping her head for a moment and then staring at her plate. "Mr. Broek will no doubt—" She raised her head, interrupted by a loud voice from across the table.

"Chinese. Japanese. Korean. Bah. Of course, they were combined for the exhibit. They are essentially the same." This came from Lord Featherfeld, a marquess waiting impatiently for his father to die so he could take his rightful place as earl. The man had been a blustery, bigoted lout at Oxford and hadn't improved with age.

Miss Sumaki heard. Her grip tightened on her utensils, her delicate skin turning blotchy from the pressure. Her eyes flicked in his direction. Then she lifted her chin. Could the little kitten possibly have claws?

"What a thoughtful question, sir," she said as she caught Skyler's eye. What question? "What has been my favorite place among my travels? There have been so many, it would be impossible to decide. If I had to choose just one, I suppose I found Greece most intriguing. It serves as a kind of crossroads between the East and the West." Her tone was still delicate, but now her voice carried, drawing the attention of the entire table. What was she about?

Lady Devin intervened gently, "My husband said something similar. He traveled to Greece several times. Now that you have reminded me, Miss Sumaki, he told me the story of a Turk who said that the Germans, the French, and the British were all the same. He could never tell them apart."

"What rubbish!" Lord Featherfeld said. Foolish man. "That Turk must have been an imbecile!"

He braced himself. Miss Sumaki might look like the plainest governess, but the fan dancer would not be silenced. It took less than a breath for her to jump into the fray.

"My lord, why do you say that?" Such a simple question, asked so lightly, but the lightness did not reach her eyes.

"My dear girl, you may have traveled widely, but you seem far from worldly. No doubt, one must make allowances for your simplicity. Surely you can plainly see that these three nations are quite distinct. Why, the English and the French are as different as night and day. They have completely different governments, different languages, different demeanors. The French are so . . . liberal and decadent. And they suffer for it. No one with even minimal discernment could ever confuse citizens of the three countries."

"How interesting. Then could the same not be said of China and Japan? The two nations have completely different systems of government, different languages and even writing systems. Geographically, too, they are vastly different."

The marquess faltered and looked around the table for support.

"But, miss, they all look the same. It is impossible to distinguish one Oriental from another."

Oh, no. A warning would do nothing for a man this dense. Besides the blatant idiocy of such a blanket statement and the blatant tactlessness of telling someone that she was interchangeable with anyone of her race, the man was criminally stupid for thinking that any man alive would mistake Miss Sumaki for anyone else. The graceful lines of her body, the satin of her hair, the charm of her face and demeanor . . . and those remarkable eyes, now the color of timeless amber, hardened and polished.

She focused those eyes on the silly marquess with a hardness that could not be mistaken for cordiality. She arched a brow as masterfully as any duke.

"Is it, Lord Featherfeld? Have you seen many? Have you spent time conversing with any?"

"Why, no."

"Perhaps you have made a study of behavior over time, my lord?"

"No, dear girl, I have more important things to do than sit around watching foreigners scramble about."

She ignored that. "Well, then, perhaps you have dedicated some time to perusing detailed studies of their cultures?"

"Again, my time is too valuable."

"Then please do enlighten us about how you have come to such a masterful observation that Orientals are indistinguishable. That kind of broad statement would seem to require extensive supporting evidence."

He stumbled then, again looking around for assistance. None came.

"It is . . . that is to say . . . one simply sees daily . . ." He paused, his throat working, and it was easy to see on his face when he selected a different tack. "I say, it's impertinent for you to speak so. Are women in your culture taught to be so confrontational?"

"No."

"All the better for them, then."

At that, she turned toward her hostess and said, "If you will excuse me, Lady Devin, I would like to retire for a moment. I fear I am not accustomed to such rich foods and need a brief respite to digest."

Lady Devin stood, followed by the rest of the assemblage, and directed a footman to lead Miss Sumaki to the retiring room. Her disapproving glare at Lord Featherfeld suggested he would not be invited again.

Dinner concluded without any further unpleasantness, yet the footman returned to the parlor without her. With growing concern, Skyler noticed that Mr. Jarlsberg was not among the other guests who'd moved into the drawing room. Surely Miss Sumaki's claims about her *services* were authentic. The German wouldn't have the audacity to use his aunt's home for an attempted assignation. If such was the case, he would find them and have them both removed from the premises immediately. As he strode away from the drawing room, his irritation and uncertainty both tugged at him. What did he really know about her morals or her intentions?

CHAPTER 4

An Offense

The halls were deserted. Not even the usual footmen were present, and Skyler made a mental note to speak with the butler about this lapse at the end of the evening. He didn't encounter Miss Sumaki or Mr. Jarlsberg on his way past the ladies' retiring room, but he heard voices farther down a nearby corridor, toward the ballroom that should be closed up. When he approached, he recognized some bits of German, muttered by a deep, demanding voice.

"Lassen Sie mich!" That was her. Miss Sumaki. *Release me.* Her voice was pitched low, almost a growl, and her tone, affronted and decisive, cut clear through him. *"Lassen Sie mich sofort los."*

He rushed toward the sound. Just before he rounded the corner, he heard a flurry of shuffling, followed by a masculine grunt that turned into a fit of coughing and groaning. He paused in a shadowed corner and was able to see down the adjacent hall through the reflection of a fortuitously placed mirror. The German was now doubled over, though still leaning into her skirts. With a rod of some sort in her hand, she pushed him away, and he stumbled to lean against the wall.

"Ich habe Sie gewarnt," she said in German, the sounds grinding

from her throat. And it was true, he could verify that she had warned Jarlsberg beforehand. "You prize your physical appearance and masculine prowess far too highly, sir. I have told you repeatedly that my duties this evening involve only translation. The contract makes the limitations of my services abundantly clear. Do not touch me again or I shall be forced to report your behavior to Mr. Broek."

The man laughed through his obvious discomfort. "You think he will care? I would simply pay him the additional fee for the services rendered. Your charms cannot be so special as to be beyond my pocket. What makes you more valuable than the other Jades? They are pleasant enough. Your skills must be legendary."

"None of that is your concern. He has other plans for me, plans you cannot afford—"

Her voice had risen and then cut off. The abrupt silence alarmed him. Only when he saw her suspicious expression—looking directly at him—in the mirror did he realize that, of course, the reflection would work both ways. If he could see her, then she could see him. He took a breath and rounded the corner to make his presence known to the German, who had straightened up and was reaching for her again but froze when he realized they were no longer alone.

"Miss Sumaki! Are you well? Do you need assistance?" he asked her in English. She looked startled by his query.

"I was trying to find my way back to the party," she replied in German, "but I got . . . lost."

He looked at her hard, ignoring the brute next to her for just a moment.

In English, she added, "Your kindness is appreciated, but I need no assistance. I have the matter well in hand."

The German frowned but seemed to have trouble walking toward him.

"Shall I have this man removed from the party?" Skyler asked, again in English. He pushed the man back against the wall and kept him there with a hand on his chest.

"*Nein*," she replied, in German. "It is time for me to depart. I am sure my guardian will be expecting me soon. I would appreciate it if you could guide me back to the drawing room so that I may bid good night to our gracious hostess."

Despite her neutral expression, he doubted her composure. Her voice trembled. She was shaken by the German's advances but would not admit it. He could not let her go so easily, not after her previous evasions. He might not get another opportunity to speak with her.

"My aunt would be most disappointed if you were to leave so early, especially under such unpleasant circumstances."

"Oh, you must not tell her anything of this dolt's behavior," she said in a rush of English, an unguarded response. Her brow furrowed and color rose in her cheeks. For the first time, she seemed vulnerable, and all manner of protective instincts clamored in his head.

"I believe this *dolt* needs to be returned to his hotel, with speed," he said, noticing that the man had slumped, semiconscious, against a hall table. "You, in contrast, need to enjoy what I am guessing is a rare evening of leisure. With your time split between your lovely performances at the exhibition and your translation, you must have little time to enjoy life." What else might she have to do for this mysterious Mr. Broek? This encounter suggested that she was acquainted with the German, and that this wasn't the first time he had insulted her. Why would her employer allow this contract with this lascivious man? And what expensive plans did this Broek have for her?

She dipped her head, looking diligently at the floor.

"One can find joy easily enough," she said quietly, so softly he could barely hear, "if one makes the effort to look for it."

Breathtaking. The delicacy of her voice, the grace of her neck— a wave of something ineffable swept through him. If only the words rang true. In the silence of the hall, she must be able to hear his heart racing, pounding so hard and fast that the room seemed unsteady. Despite himself and all the warnings in his head, he wanted to lean down and kiss her. Of course, he could not.

"Quite true," he said, his voice rough to his own ears. "You are so young for one so wise."

She grimaced fleetingly. That was as clear a sign as any. It was time to return her to the party before he made a fool of himself or offended her, just like the German. Oh, the German—he released the sot, who slid down the wall, totally insensible, and offered her his other arm. She hesitated.

"Why did you not intercede sooner?" Her question arrested him.

"I beg your pardon?"

"How long were you standing there? Why did you not interrupt?"

"It was . . . I was not . . ." What answer could he give? He had, indeed, been watching for longer than he should have. As a gentleman, he should have made his presence known at once. The fact that he hadn't held some unpleasant implications, which she had apparently discerned.

"I saw you standing there, eavesdropping," she accused, her eyes narrowing. "You hadn't just arrived or stumbled upon the scene. You were waiting. Why?"

"That is true. I watched and waited." No use dissembling when she'd seen him. And what did he owe her really, besides honesty? "I hesitated to interrupt what I thought might be a lovers' tryst." She did not need to know that he not only expected it but had planned to eject them for it. "I waited in order to determine whether the man's attentions were welcomed. When I saw that they were not . . ."

"No," she said firmly. "I had already rebuffed him. You waited even longer."

He shifted uncomfortably.

"Why does the timing matter to you?" he asked in turn. "By the time I arrived, he was no longer a threat to you. You had seen to that. I waited to ensure that my assistance would not be needed. I trusted that you had the matter well in hand, as so clearly you were able to defend yourself."

"It matters because you would have rushed to rescue a woman of your station immediately. You would not have questioned her virtue, nor her need for protection. And you would not have listened from the shadows. You would have charged in to defend a lady's honor, without hesitation."

Although he hesitated to contradict her chivalrous depiction, he could, in fact, think of a prior occasion when the lady in seeming distress hadn't wanted intervention, had rather been quite irritated at his interruption. The experience had indeed made him more cautious, more observant before stepping in.

"I do not question your virtue or doubt your honor, Miss Sumaki." He moved closer to her, holding her eyes with his. "Far from it. I have no doubts about your character."

"You should."

Would she ever cease to surprise him?

"Yes, you are correct again. I should. I know nothing about you, about your family or your upbringing. And yet I perceive you as quite . . . capable."

"So why did you not rush to defend me?"

"Because you did not need me. You were powerful. You were masterful and unafraid. I must say it was a rare and beautiful sight to behold. The embodiment of Shakespeare's 'tempest in a teacup.' What was that weapon you used against him, by the way?"

Her face clouded. He'd meant to compliment her, but something had gone awry.

"Thank you," she said. She closed herself up. In a blink, her troubled expression cleared to placid vapidity. He could not bring himself to press her for a response. "We should return to the party. This dawdling is unseemly. You will see that Mr. Jarlsberg is sent safely home, I assume?"

"Certainly. One of the footmen will see to it." He rang for one and gave directions to convey an unwell Jarlsberg back to his lodgings. During the proceedings, Miss Sumaki stood immobile as a statue, nearly blending into the decor. He wondered at this self-effacing trait of hers. And what it would take to bring her out of the shadows permanently.

When he turned to offer her his arm, she hesitated again, but then placed her gloved hand on his forearm. Sensation danced along his nerve endings at her touch, soft as a butterfly alight and just as likely to depart momentarily. Her touch drew a gasp from him that he swiftly turned into a cough.

Pausing and lifting her hand from his arm, she asked, "Are you well?"

"Entirely, I assure you." He extended his arm again, this time willing himself not to respond to the feel of her. "Shall we?"

Although he didn't flinch, the moment her hand settled gently on his arm again, the strange sensation returned more subtly, a sense of rightness, of serenity amid chaos. Dinner must be sitting strangely, or perhaps there was something funny about the wine. Surely that must explain the fancies that descended upon him.

As the sounds of the group grew more recognizable, voices more distinct, she paused in the vacant hallway, grasping his arm, and said, "I must thank you."

"For what?" Something about her overly bright tone disturbed him.

"Why, for rescuing me from that boorish Mr. Jarlsberg." She smiled up at him sweetly.

"You know as well as I that I had little hand in your rescue. You did that all on your own."

"Well, then, for the clean up afterward. He could have been . . . difficult."

Again, the set of her jaw, the way her smile didn't quite reach her eyes . . .

"Are you quite sure you are ready to return to the party, Miss Sumaki? You could go back to the retiring room."

She gave his arm a slight squeeze, but it was enough to confirm her discomposure. "I am perfectly fine, my lord. I have dealt with much worse, I assure you, and your assistance has been more valuable than I so rudely suggested earlier. Thank you."

"That was the least I could do. Any gentleman would have done the same. I would not wish you or any of the guests to suffer such boorish behavior."

She shook her head. "I assure you that not every gentleman would consider one such as me worth defending." A sharpness slipped into her tone before she masked it with a demure tilt of her head. "I am beholden to you."

"No, not at all." Of all things. The thought of her feeling obligated turned his stomach. "Again, any gentleman worth the term would have behaved thus."

She stepped closer to him. A distant alarm sounded in his head, but the nearness of her, the flecks of amber in her eyes, that scent of jasmine wound their way around his senses, rendering him unable to move.

"No need to look so frightened, my lord. I mean you no harm. Just a simple gesture of my appreciation." She rose up as high as she could reach, leaning into him for balance. He couldn't resist leaning down to meet her, as he wondered what she could possibly mean.

Then her lips brushed against his cheek, light as a summer breeze. His skin burned at her touch, not just his cheek but everywhere. Inexplicably, it felt as though she'd set him ablaze. Her gesture could barely be called a kiss. It was the kind of salute children gave their grandparents. He'd seen more enthusiastic embraces for casual greetings in Greece and Italy. Yet this glancing brush of her lips across his skin moved him more than he would willingly admit.

He turned his head just so and caught her mouth with his. His movement was as much a surprise to him as it was to her. Her sharp inhalation pulled air through his lips, but she did not shy away. Instead, her hands gripped his arms tighter. Hot, mindless desire surged through his core. He marveled at the softness of her hair, the smoothness of her cheek, as his hands explored unchecked. It was as if his body was no longer under his control. When her soft, wet tongue brushed his lower lip, he froze. Too much. The passion sparked by the tiny movement threatened his sanity. He had to regain control for both their sakes. He'd been intent on saving her from this very scenario with the German; he would not turn himself into a villain, certainly not over a single kiss.

As the intensity of the moment faded, they separated bit by bit, their mouths, their arms, until they stood a respectable arm's length apart. Her breath was as labored as his, to his relief. And then a searing thought hit him.

"Was that out of obligation?" he blurted.

She looked at him unflinchingly and replied, "No." She would not elaborate, but her clouded expression suggested a lingering discomfort, perhaps even a little of the loss of control he'd experienced himself. Her face softened for a moment, and he found himself enthralled by her shifting features, as if varying emotions fought for primacy within. She curtsied and then turned toward the door as she whispered, "Obligation had nothing to do with it. But it was a mistake nonetheless."

Brandy and sherry flowed as guests milled about from one compelling conversation to another. No one asked about Mr. Jarlsberg's disappearance. Lady Devin tilted her head questioningly so Skyler whispered reassurances, but the evening was otherwise undisrupted.

The women were particularly interested in the exotic Miss Sumaki, forming what could be perceived as a protective circle around her. "Oh, do show us a bit of that fan dance!" "Could you teach me to flip mine?" "How do you make it sound so strong?"

After perhaps a quarter hour of responding to such inquiries, she went to stand in the center of the room. Closing her eyes, she took several deep breaths, in and out. The room stilled in anticipation.

Then she transformed into a Flower of the East. There was no other way to describe it. One moment, she was small, unassuming, like the dolls his older sisters had grown tired of so quickly as children and laid aside. But then she flicked open a fan, one larger and simpler than those carried by the other ladies in attendance. Its black fabric was devoid of lace and frippery. Displaying the flared fan while holding just the handle end between her thumb and forefinger, she flipped it and caught it again with those two fingers. She then tossed it higher to flip twice before catching it again. What seemed at first like a trivial parlor entertainment proved to be riveting. She spun the open fan around her hand so that it made perfect, hypnotic circles.

He wasn't sure why this performance startled him so. Perhaps it was the vast change in her demeanor. At the dinner table, she had been shy and retiring, almost self-effacing amid the other guests. She spoke only when spoken to and seemed most comfortable when no one noticed her. Her dinner performance had been likewise modest, without the flourishes and drama she'd displayed here. This fan dance stirred the blood. It called to something wild within him. And he realized it was because this time he glimpsed something wild in her. She moved with grace and assurance, knowing exactly what effect she had on her audience. She commanded their attention, she demanded their appreciation, and she hinted at an immense amount of vitality she kept controlled. Her demeanor implied such power could be unleashed, unlocked, if only someone took the time and energy to do so. Oh, he had the time. And he definitely wanted to be the one to unlock the passion she kept so finely restrained.

When she ceased her demonstration, claiming that others deserved more attention, the ladies in the room flocked to her, demanding she continue and begging for her to teach them such tricks. When the women shifted to a discussion of the secret language of fans, he could no longer eavesdrop in good conscience. Any gentleman worth his salt knew that the ways ladies communicated with their fans were part of a realm in which men were unwelcome. Some messages were understood, but others were meant to be part of the feminine mystique. And anyway, he didn't want to destroy his own illusions about the flirtatiousness of ladies' fans.

As the evening wound down, Lady Devin approached Skyler and asked for his assistance. "Ridgemont, dear boy, one of my guests is unaccompanied this evening, and I naturally have concern about her safety. Could you see to the arrangements for her transport? Normally, Alex manages such things."

"Of course, Lady Devin. I could not deny my favorite aunt. Devin is always so capable that it would be a privilege to demonstrate my own gallant competence."

"You boys have always had such a competitive streak. Even Andrew. Just with the two of you together."

"Since she is many miles away and unable to clobber me with a parasol or some such, I must tell you that Amelia was truly the worst of us. She turned everything into a contest, even when she wasn't actively participating."

His aunt squeezed his arm and whispered, "I know. She always got that look in her eye. Undoubtedly, her own little ones shall give it all back to her one day. Now, do go see to a carriage for Miss Sumaki, dear."

"Miss Sumaki?"

"Indeed. I believe she arrived in a hired hack with Mr. Jarlsberg. I would much rather she take a Devin carriage home since she is all alone. She went to fetch her things a few moments ago."

"You may rely upon me, Lady Devin, to see that your guest is sent on her way safely and comfortably."

"Good lad."

By the time he'd sent word to have a Devin carriage readied, Miss Sumaki arrived in the entryway in a voluminous cloak and charmingly peculiar hat. As he explained Lady Devin's concerns for her safety and offer of transportation, she seemed to fold in upon herself, her expression guarded, her responses terse.

"I could not possibly impose upon Lady Devin's generous nature thus. I assure you I am perfectly capable of making my way home unscathed."

"In this circumstance, Miss Sumaki, I am afraid I must concur with my aunt. You might not be aware of the dangers that lurk on these dark city streets. Surely accepting her carriage is no hardship."

She gave an abrupt nod and said, "Of course, I would not dream of insulting such a gracious and well-meaning hostess." But her demeanor suggested anything but capitulation. Although she held her reticule demurely in front of her with both hands, a faint tapping came from the floor, her skirts wavering in time with the sounds. Her fingers twisted the cording of her bag.

Here was one area in which he excelled over Lord Devin: making guests, particularly females, feel at ease. When they were younger, he simply thought Alex shy. As they grew, it became clear that Alex's distant haughtiness was deliberate. Never overtly rude, his cousin still made clear that he had no deeper interest in others, outside his family, than social mores dictated. He, on the other hand, was the friendly one. Whatever was causing Miss Sumaki's anxiety, he could distract her during the few minutes until the carriage arrived.

"If I may ask, Miss Sumaki, how many languages do you speak?"

"Twenty, although my fluency in some suffers a bit from disuse," she replied, her mouth tight. "We have not visited Turkey or Persia for some time."

"How did you find yourself in this employment?"

"My parents were both quite facile with languages. My mother served as an interpreter, and my father was an explorer and trader, an associate of Mr. Broek, in fact." If anything, her tension increased at the mention of her parents, but her response intrigued him.

"I cannot imagine they approve of you working for Mr. Broek so far from home."

"My parents are both deceased, and Mr. Broek became my guardian. It was only logical that I would make my language skills useful."

Heat skated along his neck at her revelations. *Poorly done, Skyler.*

"Ladies here are educated in some classical languages as a matter of course, but twenty seems a bit unusual. And very impressive. Were you formally educated?" Perhaps focusing on her talents could soften the hard lines around her mouth and eyes, ease the tension of her shoulders.

"Not at all, in fact. I have never been schooled as pupils are here. I wish I had been. Instead, my father trained me himself in several languages. He said I took to them like a duck to water, one of his favorite expressions." She smiled fleetingly. "After my mother died, my father and I traveled extensively for his business, which gave me plenty of opportunities to learn and practice. Then, when he passed on, Mr. Broek took me . . . under his wing. I have been his assistant ever since." Her tone was casual until the mention of Mr. Broek, when her entire demeanor closed itself off again.

"You are too serious for one so young," he teased.

"For all you know, I am older than you."

"Impossible! You appear barely out of the schoolroom." He chuckled. She moved toward the glass doors, away from him. "Wait! I am sorry if I have offended you. I was only joking. I did not mean to suggest you are a child."

"How amusing," she said, without smiling. If anything, her placid expression was marred by her infinitesimally furrowed brows. "I have difficulty perceiving humor. What is deemed amusing in one area of the world is most decidedly not in others. The subtleties of British humor sometimes defeat me."

"How old are you, anyway?"

She stiffened and walked away. *The nerve of this man!* She had already revealed more to him than she had intended. He was too easy to talk to, and he homed in on topics that tore at her facade. The crushing loneliness she was usually able to keep at bay now surged full force and took her breath away. His footfalls warned that he was following, even before he grasped her arm. He led her rather unyieldingly back toward the entry. She glanced over at him as they walked but would not deign to speak. He looked . . . irritated. Yet he had no right to be so interested.

"I thought you were well trained in British comportment," he said mildly, belying his firm grip on her. "Surely if you were so informed, you would realize that it is unconscionably rude for a lady to abandon a conversation thus."

Her temper flared. He would dare to school her on propriety in light of his behavior? His condescension raised the hair on the back of her neck.

"A thousand pardons, good sir. Excuse my gross misperception. You see, time and again, your demeanor indicates that you do not consider me a proper lady. Rather impressive, given our short acquaintance. My understanding is that a cut is an appropriate response in such offensive situations."

Abruptly, he stopped walking and released her. "How have I offended?" he asked, incredulous.

"You have to ask?" She matched her tone to his. She stepped back, not caring if people saw. "Tell me, Lord Ridgemont, how often, in casual conversation, do you ask ladies of the ton their ages, as you just asked me? Do you regularly, in their presence, insinuate that they are no more than concubines or courtesans, as you did the first time we met? Do you question, directly to their faces, both their brains and their morals? I would hazard a guess that such inquiries are exceeding rare in polite society." By this point, she couldn't help gritting her teeth, adding flatly, "As is putting your hands on a lady against her wishes and dragging her along like a doll, except perhaps to protect her from imminent harm. Tell me, was a coach or wild animal bearing down on me, such that you had to yank me here to safety?"

His expression shuttered. His eyes, however, turned dark and stormy. More than once during her speech, he'd opened his mouth to interject. And yet, he didn't seem to have anything to say.

She wrapped her arms around herself and considered how to effect her original plan to slip out unnoticed to return to the Jade Garden. Given Lord Ridgemont's solicitude, such a disappearance would be difficult. Still, she dared not risk further conversation with him, dared not risk sharing more about herself than she'd ever intended. She could hear her Japanese accent faltering, falling away, as the thought of her parents raised emotions she could not afford to acknowledge here. She blinked hard to try to dispel the prickling in her eyes. She would not cry now. Not now, not here, not in front of him.

"I'm deeply sorry," he said, interrupting her thoughts.

She shook her head before looking at him. She couldn't have heard him properly.

"I beg your pardon?"

"No, Miss Sumaki, it is I who must beg your pardon." He came to stand in front of her and gently reached out, as if to tilt up her chin. Yet he stopped short of touching her. The moment their eyes met, his hand dropped away, all deference and respectability. "Your censure is entirely deserved. I have been horribly rude. Far beyond the pale. I have said things to you that are completely inappropriate, and I have no defense. Your behavior has been impeccable, and I can only hope that you accept my deepest apologies."

"Of course. Please think nothing of it," she said quickly. She read sincerity in his eyes, even if she couldn't entirely trust it. Her anger evaporated, chased away by sheer exhaustion. Tomorrow would be another busy, demanding day at the Exhibition. "I am sure you'll understand that I must return home. Time grows short, and I must prepare for tomorrow."

"Please. The carriage will only be a moment more, I am sure," he said quietly. Inexplicably, her eyes stung again. "I upset you greatly, and it would be ungentlemanly of me to let you leave without making amends."

She shook her head as she responded, "There is no need. Your apology was more than sufficient. I have suffered far worse insults here in London. I confess I am rather tired and perhaps overly sensitive at the moment."

His hand tightened on hers as his brow furrowed. "In addition to Mr. Jarlsberg, you mean? Who has insulted you? What have they said?"

The abrupt shifts in Ridgemont's behavior made her dizzy. Offensive to contrite to protective? She needed to escape; she needed the blessed oblivion of sleep.

"It is of no consequence. A person on public display in the Exhibition is bound to be the target of criticism. That is the nature of exhibition." She didn't see any reason to mention the private affronts she'd had to fend off from men just like him beyond the Crystal Palace. In the past few months, she'd gained a very clear, unfortunately visceral understanding of what people assumed about an Oriental woman's character. She'd learned quickly to keep a fan or parasol on hand to defend herself bodily. So far, such feminine weapons had been enough to rebuff advances when cutting remarks and other clear signs of rejection had been ignored.

"Has someone hurt you?" His voice rose.

"No," she said, tired and empty. Unwilling to dredge up past events. "Nothing like that. Please, I accept your apology but have reached the limits of my conversational skills."

After a glance through the side windows framing the front door, he offered her his arm. "As if primed for your rescue, the carriage has arrived and is at your disposal."

An odd look crossed her face as she hesitated. "If I might have a moment?"

He bowed and watched her go down the hallway toward a retiring room. He would see her safely ensconced in the vehicle and then cease to think about this young woman who seemed almost too mercurial, too sensitive, too mysterious, too unknowable to be real.

As he waited for her to return, a realization slowly dawned. This was the second time this evening that he had waited for her to return, and the first time was because she was in some kind of danger. Just as he took a few steps down the hallway, about to break into a run, a footman came from that direction with a note.

Many thanks to Lady Devin and to you for the kind offer of transport. I do not wish to be a bother and have made other arrangements.
Regards,
HS

CHAPTER 5

A Midnight Stroll

He rushed out to try to catch up with her, but there was no sign of her diminutive figure along the lamp-lit thoroughfare. A faint rustling in the direction of Lady Devin's garden caught his attention. A slight figure slipped through the shadows beneath the brightly lit windows. Skirting around a rosebush, the figure was briefly illuminated. Aha! He followed, the grass soft and silent beneath him. What could she possibly be doing? Attempting to break into the house? Meeting a lover? He had to laugh at himself for jumping to such outlandish conclusions, but his curiosity burned. A lover was highly unlikely; she'd rebuffed Jarlsberg soundly and shown no interest in any of the other men present. If she'd wanted to steal something, she could easily have taken it while she was inside.

She stopped at the entrance to the garden and looked around, but he was well shrouded in the darkness. She took a few more steps until she was mostly obscured by hedges. Then she seemed to be fiddling with her clothing. After a few moments, she lifted a large bell of fabric. If he didn't know better, he would think she'd lifted her skirts and petticoats away en masse. Then she slid the circle of fabric shut like an umbrella, and a handle even materialized at the end.

If he hadn't seen it himself, the voluminous skirt collapsing inward to almost nothing, he wouldn't have believed it. Her engineered fan at least made sense. All those layers of skirting could not possibly be compressed into as small a space as an umbrella. He would give a great deal to be able to examine the contraption closely. When she moved across the garden's entrance to hang this supposed accessory from a tree branch, he caught sight of her transformed appearance. Dark breeches and a fitted shirt encased her lithe figure. His heartbeat throbbed in his ears at the sight. She could not possibly have changed her wardrobe that quickly. And how had he not noticed those heavy boots in the drawing room?

She picked up the cloak she'd laid across some bushes. With a few quick movements, she had turned the garment inside out. He couldn't decipher detailing, but when she shoved her arms into it, the cloak had become a rather coarse jacket. She looked like a street urchin, like a chimney sweep or chestnut vendor. Performance was her forte, but such apparel had to be masterfully constructed to turn so convincingly from a maiden's cloak to a street urchin's baggy rag coat. She had tucked her glossy hair under a rough cap. If one did not see her face, she could pass for a newsboy, scampering through the streets. Her posture and gait completed the metamorphosis. He crouched behind a statue as she collected her things and shuffled down the street, a hardworking boy returning to his meager home.

His head spun as realization hit home: She was the boy he'd tried to speak to at the Exhibition, the one who hadn't understood English. She was the schoolgirl who gave recitations of ancient Buddhist tales. And she was the old woman who performed the elaborate tea ceremonies. *Fool! She was in front of you all along.*

He couldn't help but follow this changeling. To see her safely home, he told himself. He'd been intrigued by her at dinner, but this was a completely different level of mystery.

Dragon's teeth! She could do better than this! She'd first noticed the footsteps behind her, consistent and subdued, when she proceeded down the nearly empty street. Footsteps, perhaps ten feet or so away, kept pace with hers even when she quickened her steps. She would have thought it an echo, except that her boots made a duller thud against the walk. Then they slowed when she slowed. Not good. She turned onto a busier thoroughfare, took a deep, fortifying breath, and dashed across the street, dodging a gentleman atop a large horse and then darting behind an enormous carriage. Finally, she tucked herself into the entryway of a darkened storefront and looked around.

A tall figure stepped out of the street from behind the carriage, only a few feet away. She crouched low but kept her weight balanced on the balls of her feet. She could run, but it would be so much easier if he just lost her trail. He paused, and she heard a dark curse wing through the air as he looked down at his now-filthy shoes and stomped his feet to remove what he could. Then, as he moved closer, the street lamp clearly illuminated his face.

Lord Ridgemont! She dropped her head back against the wall and sagged. When he'd first appeared at dinner, his golden mane and easy manner had dazed her. In contrast with his frowning or stammering at her as Izo, he swooped into the room, charismatic and debonair, and she was fascinated by his insouciance. Keeping her voice low, her gestures minimal, her eyes downward, she'd futilely hoped he wouldn't recognize her. She'd made herself small, having learned long ago to fade into the background, neutral and timid and unassuming. But clearly fate intended to test her, placing him too close for her to avoid his notice past the customary introductions.

Really, the whole evening could be considered a disaster, at least considering what she'd been sent to do. She could have held her tongue at dinner, she could have spurned Jarlsberg's advances more gently, and she most certainly should have made her escape more stealthily. Why must this man follow her? He had the air of someone on a search, not someone with a destination. His head craned, his eyes narrowed, and he turned this way and that. Her thighs began to ache as she waited. When he slowed and looked at the ground, she thought he'd finally given up. But then he looked around more slowly, more thoughtfully. His gaze stopped in the direction of the storefront.

Gods, grant us enlightenment. She straightened, her legs screaming after hovering over the ground so long. It would not do to be in a subservient position when the enemy approached. Except . . . he didn't seem like the enemy. It was so much easier to be Izo at the

Exhibition, to observe Ridgemont and not have to respond to his inquiries, but talking with him at dinner had been an unusually pleasant experience. She just couldn't allow him to ask her about the
Exhibition performances or about Mr. Broek; she feared she would
want to tell him everything.

Slowly, he moved closer. When his shadow fell across the entry,
she held her breath.

"Miss Sumaki," he said, with a polite bow.

She stifled a groan. He knew. How long had he been following her?

"Good evening, Lord Ridgemont," she responded. "What an
odd time for a constitutional."

"It is likewise an odd time for a young woman to be traveling
outdoors unaccompanied. Indeed, I believe there is never not an
odd time for a young woman such as you to travel the streets alone."

She couldn't see his expression. In the darkened alcove, his
body loomed. A frisson of fear skittered up her spine and set her
scalp tingling. She did not really know this man, no matter how
kind and proper he appeared. She was on the street, in the open,
without protection. She gripped the handle of her umbrella and
took the fan out of her pocket. Without true blades, the fan was a
better weapon when closed. If she had to, she could knock him out
or at least dislocate his jaw. She could do it.

As if reading her mind, he stepped back, out onto the sidewalk,
and said, "It would be only right of me to see you home safely."

He offered her his arm. She was reaching out when she saw her
rough coat sleeve, patched and worn. She knew what she was supposed to look like.

"I assure you, Lord Ridgemont, that your escort is unnecessary.
No one would accost me looking like this." She gestured downward, fully aware of how bedraggled and coarse she appeared. That
was the point. His gaze followed down the line of her body with an
unreadable expression, one that set her on edge.

"Far be it from me to contradict one so wise and worldly," he
replied, "but even if no one could guess your identity, there are
plenty of street thugs who would consider a working boy an easy
target. I need not expose your charade, but you should resign yourself to the fact that I shall see you home."

Her teeth clenched. The pinch of the fan against her palm made her realize she'd held it so tightly that it had dug into her skin, leaving deep grooves. They would fade, but her irritation might not. Irritation and the flutter of a trapped feeling in the pit of her stomach. He could not know about the Jade Garden. Or rather, Broek would decide what and when to tell him about the Jade Garden. But then, perhaps, just perhaps, his awareness of the house would precipitate action.

She nodded, but he didn't move. Instead, he stared at her.

"Who are you?" he asked.

What reply could she give?

"I have no idea how to answer that. I am what you see. I am a performer."

"Even actors do not walk around in character in their everyday lives. You wear this disguise on purpose. You transformed into it as if it were natural."

Not good. Her throat seized.

"You saw me change?" she whispered. As awful as it was to be caught out, she was equally mortified about being observed in such a private moment. In the act of changing costumes, there was always a period of vulnerability, and he'd seen it.

With a curt nod, he explained, "I saw you sneak around the house to one of the gardens, and I was concerned for your safety. So I followed you. I still do not understand what you did with your skirt, how you made it practically disappear into that umbrella. I suppose you would be right out of luck if you happened to get caught in a rainstorm."

How could he tease at a moment like this? And how could her foolish face smile in reply? She felt it, that lightness bubbling up at his words. Damn. Time to move.

"Every woman has her secrets, my lord. If you must insist on seeing me home, we should be on our way. I do not wish to impose upon you any more than I already have, although I would point out that such an imposition was not my intention nor my fault."

"Of course not."

"I certainly did not ask you to follow me. Nor did I ask you to take on the role of protector."

He leaned in and said quietly, "It would behoove you to know that *protector* has some unsavory connotations in my world. Only a woman of questionable morals takes on a protector. It is a lover who provides for a kept woman."

Her discomfort must have shown on her face because he added, "I only explain this so that you may take more care with your word choice in casual conversation."

"I . . . thank you. That's thoughtful of you. Sometimes the implications of your language are a mystery to me. Now, really, I must be going." This delay could be costly. Broek would want a report on the evening, and he would wait for her to return.

"So how shall we play this? To offer you my arm would be incongruous to your disguise."

She bit her lip as the likeliest scenario came to her.

"I can appear to be your servant, following just behind you."

He frowned.

"If you have a better suggestion," she said, "then, by all means, say so. If not, we should proceed."

After a heavy sigh, he took a step back, but then halted. "How will I know which way to go?"

He had a point.

"Perhaps I can walk a step behind you and call out directions when needed."

"Or you could stay a step ahead of me, leading the way. I will admit I would feel more confident if I could see where you are at all times. It would be too easy to lose sight of you on these dark streets."

You didn't seem to have any trouble with that when you were following me, she thought. But then, that reiterated his point, didn't it?

"Perhaps I should walk a few paces in front?"

"No," he said firmly. "If you are too far ahead, I will not be able to talk with you. And you have not yet answered any of my questions."

"Have it your way," she said, as she launched herself out of the alcove at a brisk pace. "You will need to keep up." She moved past him and down the street.

They reached the corner quickly. He hovered in her periphery but said nothing. Before she could step off the curb, she felt a hand on her shoulder and jumped.

"Thomas, watch out for the horses," he said, just before two large, dark horses charged past. How had she not noticed the pounding of their hooves? One passed so close, the edges of her coat fluttered in its residual breeze. He patted her shoulder before letting her go. The loss of him flashed through her before she remembered her place, remembered the role she played.

"Thank you, sir." She choked on the *sir* but bobbed her head. "I'll be more careful. It's not far now." Seeing a safe gap in traffic, she hurried forward, constantly aware of his looming nearness.

"Do you do all of the performances?"

"Yes."

"So you are his sole employee?"

"No."

"Where are the rest?"

"Mr. Broek has multiple business ventures. The Exhibition promotes his primary trade business. At times, he has served as an international liaison. So he has a small staff that works from the Jade Garden."

"Why is it called that?"

"How many questions do you have?"

"I have no idea. It all depends on the answers you give. Some answers prompt new questions."

"I must return. Mr. Broek will be waiting."

"What is your relationship with him?"

"Why do you ask?"

"My inquiries are all in service to the success of the Great Exhibition, I assure you. I do not wish to be intrusive."

"I am not sure I believe you," she said under her breath, and then added, louder, "Yes, yes, of course, you are only doing what you must for the greater good." She heard his sharp intake of breath but refused to look at him. "As I believe I mentioned at Lady Devin's dinner, Mr. Broek is my guardian and has been since my father died. He trained me to be his assistant. Our relationship is a legal and professional one." She could not bring herself to do more than state the facts, empty as they were. Lies would choke her, and sharing the truth was simply unthinkable. He noticed things. He paid attention. He was protective. None of these things was normal. And she shouldn't crave them so much upon such brief exposure.

When they reached the corner of her street, she halted. Mr. Broek should not see him accompanying her. It would raise questions and suspicions.

"The Jade Garden is just a few houses ahead. You may rest assured that you have done your duty. But it is best for both of us if I return alone."

He frowned but nodded. "I shall watch from here to assure myself that you enter safely. If anything is wrong, simply call out." He slipped back into the shadows of a hedge. With the waning moon obscured by clouds, he was invisible. Yet she could not bring herself to leave. *Step away, Hana. Go.* Instead, her body moved toward him. When she rose up on her toes to whisper in his ear, he dipped down to meet her. His breath tickled her ear and neck, sending a hum of sensation along her skin.

"Thank you," she whispered. Then she kissed his jaw, not a feather touch that could be taken as accidental. His whiskers prickled at her lips. Strong. Warm. The underlying hardness of his jaw suggested stability, reliability. He could not possibly know how much she craved these qualities.

A sharp inhalation accompanied the stiffening of his body. His hands seized her shoulders but abruptly fell away.

She nodded briefly and then hurried down the lane, feeling bereft. Suddenly, the night felt cooler, the street more silent, the darkness more menacing. Knowing he watched over her provided a modicum of comfort, but even that tasted bitter. His interest in Broek's business had to be diverted. A shiver ran down her spine as she approached the door. It was already clear that Ridgemont would not be dissuaded; neither would Broek allow himself to be cornered. She would have to take care to protect the Jade ladies from the crossfire.

CHAPTER 6

A Rebuke

"You seem to have made quite an impression on your hostess last night, little flower." Mr. Broek gestured toward the low bench in the corner of his office. Dutifully, she walked over and perched on the edge. Someone had forgotten to sweep the corner, so she spread her skirt as subtly as she could to cover the area. Tsubaki-san would know whose turn it was and chastise her accordingly; Mr. Broek need not be involved.

"Of course, sir. I followed your instructions exactly." Then she clenched her teeth, waiting for him to inevitably continue. Making a good impression was her job, her service to Broek's enterprise, but making too good an impression didn't serve him well. Being too interesting herself drew unwanted attention. It was a fine line, one not entirely in her control but one she'd learned to navigate fairly well.

"Lady Devin has inquired as to whether I might assess the authenticity of some of her japanware." Mr. Broek strolled through the room with a practiced aimlessness. First, he would step to the window, then wander to the fireplace, and finally he would loom over her. In business dealings, others had occasionally mistaken his reedlike build and unassuming demeanor for weakness; she knew better. "Her late husband was apparently quite the world traveler. Her request invites us both to tea tomorrow."

"How nice." Such inquiries were exactly what her attendance was meant to generate. Broek must be pleased by the success. Yet his tone was guarded. Best to proceed cautiously and without obvious reaction.

"She goes on to add, dear Hanako," he said from the window, "that she quite enjoyed your company and wishes you to converse with her while I review her inventory with her butler."

"Again, how nice of her." This was not good news. Accustomed to reading Broek's face, she saw his displeasure and anxiety in the set of his jaw. A private tête-à-tête with Lady Devin might lead to too many questions, too much information about Broek's dealings, too much that he didn't trust her to answer deftly.

"It would not be appropriate for you to become too attached to the lady, Hanako," he said from the fireplace. Even in middle of summer, he maintained a fire in his office. He said it was simpler for making tea at a moment's notice, but she'd heard of his other uses for it. She tensed as he picked up the iron poker.

"We will, of course, attend," he said, as he walked toward her, tapping the poker against the floor like a walking stick.

"Of course," she said meekly. What else could she say? If she balked, he would see it as defiance. If she agreed too enthusiastically, he would see it as ambition or a plan to escape. "May I be excused now?"

"Not yet, my dear. We have details to attend to." And now he loomed. "You will wear the dragon robes. The navy gown was suitable for your role at the dinner party, but your native attire will add to our air of expertise and authenticity."

"Yes, Mr. Broek." Head down, she nodded. Little dots of ash marked his path. *Breathe. Do not look up. Rivers continue to flow.*

"Is there anything else you wish to tell me about the dinner party, Hanako?"

"I recall nothing noteworthy about it, sir."

He grasped her chin and forced her to meet his eyes, bright with icy fury.

"In addition to this lovely invitation from Lady Devin, I received a note from Mr. Jarlsberg this morning, little flower. Would you care to guess what his note said?"

"As I told you last night, he overindulged and became careless. He meant to overstep the standard agreement. I had to disappoint him."

"Not you alone. Jarlsberg wrote that a gentleman from the party interfered and had him ejected. But that you stayed."

Her stomach clenched, and prickles of sweat flared over her skull. The heat of the room was suddenly suffocating.

"I did. Mr. Jarlsberg had accosted me in a hallway, and another guest provided assistance. When I returned to the drawing room after the unpleasantness, the other guests persuaded me to do an impromptu performance. I thought it would be judicious to stay."

"And what of the gentleman who rescued you?" He practically snarled the word *rescued*.

"He is related to Lady Devin and simply acted as her representative. He made arrangements to have Jarlsberg delivered home and then escorted me back to the rest of the party. That is all."

"Shall I add him to the list?" Not the list. He'd stopped giving her updates about the list since their arrival in London. Calling cards arrived daily, but he no longer kept her abreast of how long the list was. Some of the men on it had deeper pockets than others. Her stomach flipped, and she prayed she would be able to make it through the rest of the meeting without being ill.

She shook her head. "No, sir, I did not perceive that kind of interest from him. He mentioned something about the Royal Commission, so it might be unwise to make him aware of this situation." She swallowed the bilious lump in her throat when she ventured, "I assume that Mr. Jarlsberg will stay on the list?"

"Indeed he will, my dear, unless his mouth turns out to be larger than his holdings."

"Is there anything else I should prepare for tomorrow, sir?"

"Your savior will not become a problem, will he, Hanako?"

"Of course not, sir. It was the briefest of encounters. I do not know him. I would be hard pressed to recognize him in a crowd."
Keep looking at the floor. Do not let him see the lie in your eyes.

"We shall see." He tapped the poker against his foot and then returned to the fireplace and set it in the stand. "You may go now. And send one of the girls to clean up this floor—Yuki. I have received a report that her services have been substandard. She will sweep this floor and then take my instruction."

She nodded, not trusting herself to speak. His directive sent another wave of nausea through her. The girl who cried. His *instruction* could be damaging when he was this agitated.

As she walked with a measured pace to the door, careful to appear calm and undisturbed, he shot toward her, caught her arm, and punched her hard in the belly. A gasp tore from her throat as her body seized from the pain. Only his hand gripping her hair kept her from doubling over. He almost never laid a hand on her. What had she done to draw his fury this time?

"Remember your place, little flower. Lies of omission are still lies. Never lie to me." She nodded, blinking back tears, as he continued. "Watch your tongue with strangers. Do not even dream of the possibility of escape. Too much is at stake, and you will not steal my prize from me. And remember that yours is not the only fate in my hands."

Barely able to breathe, she could only nod. She had done nothing extraordinary at Lady Devin's soiree. Nothing. It wasn't her fault that Jarlsberg had had too much drink, that he'd forgotten himself. She had made every attempt to be inconspicuous and unassuming. It was not her fault that her presence inherently drew attention. Broek knew such attention was beneficial to his purpose, had even said as much himself on occasion. *Show your worth*, he said. Yet it was a trap. If her price grew steeper with competition, more would be expected of her. Much more. And now he feared allowing her into situations that he could not control with absolute certainty. Eyes focused on a knot in the floorboards, she tried to settle herself.

He released her and gave her just enough space to walk out of the room. "Make sure Ume is prepared to use the ropes with her client this evening. He made a special request."

She left quietly. Going up the stairs took longer than usual, each step magnifying the pain in her stomach muscles. Broek knew how to hit efficiently—no visible marks and no permanent damage, but enough pain that she would remember he could destroy her, if he chose . . . if she displeased him. She would endure anything—anything—if it meant she could protect her little sister from harm. If it weren't for Takara, she would have run away two years ago, as soon as she realized what a monster Mr. Broek was, what a traitor he was to her father. Now she had to protect not only Takara but all the Jade Flowers he'd manipulated and coerced into his service, and there was no escape.

Of course, Takara would immediately notice something was wrong. When Hanako walked into the common room of the Jade ladies, that little blur of dark-haired energy bounded off a settee for an enthusiastic hug. Takara just happened to direct all that energy in one leading shoulder, barreling forward. That shoulder rammed directly into her stomach, reawakening the stabbing pain in her belly, and she couldn't suppress a tiny whimper. Takara recoiled, taking a swift step backward and cringing without letting her go.

"Did I hurt you, *oneesan*?" Takara asked, frowning with concern.

"No, child, I am perfectly fine," she said, as she mustered the strength to force a small smile. "And how many times must I tell you that you must not call me big sister anymore. We are not in Japan. Call me by my name. When in Rome, dear, we must do as the Romans do."

"I am trying, Hana. Honest. *Oneesan* is how I think of you. It is hard not to." It surely didn't help that the women of the house were all supposed to dress in traditional Japanese attire. The everyday kimonos were made of simple cottons.

"I know," she replied, as she pulled her sister close. She'd been more mother than sister to Takara since their mother's death when her sister was just an infant, but the prospect of talking in front of little Takara about what else Broek's clients expected of the women in bed, what they might expect from the auction, nearly sent her into her own panic. Perhaps deflecting the conversation would work. She had to prepare Takara—and all the women—for the possibility that England would be their new home, and that they would likely soon be scattered like cherry blossom petals tossed in the wind. Trusting Broek's word, Takara, the youngest of the group by far at only age ten, and the only other member who could speak fluent English, at least when she chose, could survive the transition fairly well. The other women . . . their futures were a mystery.

When she released her sister, the girl hurried back to practice writing kanji with one of the elder women, picking up a brush with almost violent clumsiness, to the other woman's dismay.

"Good evening, ladies," Hanako said in English.

"Good ev-en-ning, Hanako," they responded, almost in unison. During the trip westward, she'd been able to teach them a smattering of standard English phrases. Mr. Broek could not find out, though. He would take it as an act of rebellion. So practice was difficult to arrange. Switching to Japanese, she greeted each individually and surveyed their work. She always took some time at night to see how they fared, especially after days when Broek's temper flared. One of the women, Yuki, was uncharacteristically quiet, sewing in the corner—her eyes glassy and unfocused.

"Tsubaki-san, is she unwell?" Keeping her voice low, she inclined her head toward Yuki. The other woman shook her head slowly. "What has happened?"

"Her fate is the same as Sasha's," Tsubaki whispered.

Sasha. Her stomach twisted. There must be a way to save this one. She closed her eyes as she struggled to hold back the memory of Sasha's cries, of the heartless beats of the train pulling away, leaving her abandoned and with child while the rest of the Jade Flowers were locked up tight for the interminable journey. Surely, she would suffer throughout eternity for not doing more to protect Sasha. But perhaps there was something she could do for Yuki.

"Are you sure?" she quietly asked the older woman, hoping for even the slightest doubt.

"Yes. All the signs suggest she is as much as five months along. Soon Broek will notice, or at least the customers he sends will."

Five months! How could she be so far gone without anyone suspecting? As she looked into Tsubaki's eyes, she realized Yuki's condition was not a surprise.

"Why did you not speak of this until now?"

"We were not certain. And . . ."

The woman's tone, hesitant and regretful, chilled her. She could not ask, only wait for the older woman to continue.

"It was three months before I could be sure. Then Yuki asked for secrecy while she tried some traditional methods for . . . curing her condition."

She could not think on that. Would not. Most methods she'd

heard the Jade Flowers speak of were brutal. And usually ineffective. The medicinal broths and tinctures promised resolution of some sort, but they rarely worked. All the more reason there must be a hell to which Broek would eventually be consigned. When they'd left Sasha, abandoned her in Turkey, the girl already had tried and barely survived several of those methods to no avail. She'd been changed, weakened. Yet they left her at the train platform, desperate and destitute, panic in her eyes. The client who'd impregnated her was, per Broek's infernal contract, only liable to pay for Broek's lost income, a nuisance fee that Broek kept. Sickening.

There must have been some other way to save Sasha, but protecting Takara was all she'd been able to see then. So she'd helped prompt the Jade Flowers in their hiding spots, into the massive trunks and baskets, and then she'd stood by Mr. Broek's side as the train pulled away. Stood there watching Sasha's face dissolve into hysterical tears, watching her body collapse to the ground. And no one had rushed to her aid. No one extended a kindness to Sasha on that platform, at least not as far as Hanako could recall. *Son of a dung beetle.* This was why she would not think on these things!

"Can we tell Broek she is ill and unable to do her duty? We are here for the duration of the Great Exhibition, so we may have more time to find a safe place for her."

"He will only accept that for so long, though."

"Then we will work quickly. Perhaps I can find her a position somewhere." But her words held no confidence, and Tsubaki's pitying glance showed she knew it. If it were so easy to find positions in service for these women, she would have done so the moment they arrived in London. But there was nowhere for them to go if they could not speak the language.

"Mr. Broek wants Yuki to go clean the floor of his office."

Tsubaki's brows knotted together, but she nodded.

"While Yuki is unavailable, the other women will have to take her place."

Hanako was too tired to think about any of this. Yes, the other women would have to fulfill any appointments and services Broek arranged, as if they didn't have enough of their own. He wouldn't care about adjustments and replacements as long as the customers were satisfied.

* * *

As she tucked Takara's blanket around her slim form, her sister sat up abruptly. "Tell me something about Mama, one thing you remember about her."

Her sister rarely asked about their parents so, whenever she did, it was hard to resist her. "She had a wooden hair comb you loved. It was in the shape of a lotus blossom, and you always pulled it from her hair. She hated having her hair unkempt, but she never got upset with you about it. She simply laughed and let you play until you tired of it."

"You always make her sound like an angel. But she must have gotten angry sometimes. Didn't she?"

She closed her eyes, and the vision of their parents arguing flashed behind her eyelids—her mother's determination, her father's desperate pleading. *The girls need their mother*, he begged. *We will all lose infinitely more than your father can possibly gain.* The hardened features of *Haha*'s face, the cracking of Papa's voice. Takara should never know these things.

"Of course, sweet pea. But why dredge up unpleasantness? Why not think of Mother at her best?"

Takara batted at her pillow. "Sometimes bad things happen. Isn't it right to be angry about them? Must we just lie down and let ourselves be hurt when we could do something to change it?"

A frisson of fear skated down Hana's back.

"Is something wrong, dearest? You know I would never let someone do you harm."

Her braids waved against the pillow as she shook her head hard, perhaps a little too hard. "No, no, *Oneesan*! I just hear the women talking. Sometimes they cry. They are afraid of Broek-san. Is there nothing we can do for them?"

"I am trying, dear Takara. Trust me. I am trying. This is not something a child should worry about. I will do my best to keep you all safe."

Her sister's mouth quirked; the poor girl was right to be skeptical. Their lives were already miserable. What could she possibly do to minimize the damage, much less free them from Broek? They had no money, nowhere to hide. Impossible. But she would keep her little sister safe.

CHAPTER 7

A Talk Between Gentlemen

Devin's laughter carried through the hallway, drawing some questioning looks from gentlemen near the door. It was undoubtedly strange to hear. He'd been so solemn, so mirthless, even before inheriting the viscountcy. Even more startling than his laughter was the pleasure apparent on his face when he entered the common room. He greeted fellow club members like old friends, which many of them were, but still . . . very peculiar. And obviously, he wasn't the only man to think so.

"Ridgemont!" Devin strode toward him, practically ebullient, and extended his hand. The gesture was so friendly, so alien to his cousin's character, that he needed a moment to comprehend and execute the proper cordial response. "When did you arrive?"

"Here? Just a few minutes ago. In London, a month. I am rather surprised to see you. You have been busy with Lords and orphans and such, or so I hear."

"One must do what one can in the name of justice and innocence," Devin said airily.

"Are you cracked?"

He regretted his cavalier response the moment it came out. Devin's expression went ominously blank.

"Not at all, Ridgemont. This is serious business."

"Settle your nerves, my friend. I am not truly heckling you. I cannot help but wonder, though, given your usual reticence... since when, dear cousin, do you go wading into public turmoil?"

"When defenseless women and children are being debased and exploited and abused."

His cousin meant it. The man who'd never cared one inkling for the world beyond his front door, the man whose only concerns had ever been keeping his castle secure—Devin had broken out into the world with flair and bravado.

"And whom may I thank for your epiphany, coz?" He shouldn't have pushed. Devin had always been so restrained and unflappable, enviably so. Devin was an exemplar of succession. He knew before he completed the question that it was intrusive, improper, and yet he couldn't resist. As soon as he'd arrived in London, he'd heard gossip about Devin's association with a decrepit old shopkeeper. Inconceivable. "You know I am not one for rumors, but I was most surprised to be welcomed back to the club with a particularly suggestive rumor about you and a certain tradeswoman."

"It is important to stay informed about current events, Ridgemont, to go out in the streets and find out what is really happening around us every day. Reading would not harm you either. As for the rest, such rumors are beneath me."

An evasion rather than an outright denial. Given that this was Devin, who never minced words, it was as good a confirmation as any. There it was. Devin had become enamored of not just a bluestocking but one who worked for a living. How in the world had she crossed his path? He nodded and picked up a newspaper left nearby. This was their pattern—cordial greetings before slipping into companionable silence, with the occasional cheroot and brandy. So he was taken aback when Devin broke with convention.

"Cousin, how are you?" Devin asked. "How are you really?"

Who was this stranger? Bodily, this looked like the man he knew, the cousin he knew growing up. But Devin did not sound or act like himself. He looked involved, interested, engaged with the world around him, not simply existing within it.

"I am fine, Devin. How kind of you to ask."

"You have had such upheaval. We were all struck by the loss of your father and brother. I know how difficult it was to take on my father's title, and that was after a childhood spent grooming me for the role. How do you fare as the new earl?"

"I assure you that the Ridgemont holdings are well maintained. Everything is well in hand."

Devin leaned forward, resting his elbows on his knees. "I am not questioning your abilities, Skyler. I have every confidence in you. What I want to know is how you *are*. You have suffered great losses, and yet you have not had much time to grieve. Instead, you have been thrown into a position that can be overwhelming. I want to know how all this affects you. I want to be able to help."

He took a deep breath, holding back the response that shot to his lips. He simply said, "I have no need of help."

It was Devin's turn to recoil, sitting back in his chair as his face flushed.

"That was not my insinuation, Ridgemont. I would think you know me somewhat better than that. Sometimes, in the midst of chaos, a sympathetic ear can serve as an anchor, as an ally."

Truly, his cousin must have lost his mind as well as his heart. This effusive, emotional Devin bore no resemblance to his usual self, none at all. He stared at Devin for an uncomfortable and impolite amount of time.

"What?" Devin finally asked.

"What has happened to you?"

His cousin smiled. Not the silly clownish grin of the besotted, but one of genuine warmth and contentment nonetheless.

"She must be quite something," he said.

Devin's expression faltered. "*She* is. Quite. You have no idea," he admitted. "I am a changed man."

"So when do I get to meet this miracle worker?"

"Our acquaintance is rather convoluted . . . and unstable at the present time." From sunshine to storm cloud in the blink of an eye. Devin, of all people!

"Because of your recent work in Lords?"

Devin shifted in his chair and nodded solemnly. "I was strongly influenced, in the best of ways. Yet now I am in the public eye and advocating for such a fraught moral issue. In any case, I would not dream of having such a good woman dragged through the mud."

"Admirable. You have become lionized in the papers, you know? The Great Defender of the Innocents. Quite overbearing, actually."

When his cousin didn't reply, he quickly added, "You know, I hope, that you have always been admirable. It would behoove me to emulate you."

Devin blurted, "I wish to marry her."

"Pardon?"

"Her. The miracle worker. I want her to be my wife."

"You are in quite a bad state. If my intelligence is to be believed, it would mean ruin." He looked, seriously looked, at the man before him. "Do you realize how scandalous such a mésalliance would be? You just spoke of maintaining 'the highest sense of propriety and decency.' You would be excluded entirely from polite society."

"Ah, would that be such a hardship?" Devin's expression lightened, as if he almost wished for exile. No woman would be worth that.

"Have you considered taking her as your mistress?" he whispered, although he needn't bother with secrecy. Most of the men in attendance were known to keep a paramour, if only for a few entertaining months. Some, like his own father, kept a mistress as if he had a second, parallel life. His father had apparently maintained a series of mistresses for years at a time and provided handsomely for them when he moved on. He'd discovered his father's indiscretions only after he'd taken over the family accounts. It would be easy enough for an unattached Devin to make such arrangements; even if he took a wife eventually, the astute women of their world understood such things. Or so it would seem.

The flare in Devin's eyes told him he'd make a critical miscalculation.

"She deserves better than to be used so cavalierly. She deserves the honor of the Devin name. An accident of birth is meaningless— in fact, she has nobility in her blood. Her father walked away from society for the love of a woman. Why should I not reverse the process?"

"You are in earnest? Does your mother know? Have you spoken with Drew and Amelia? Such a move would . . ."

"Ha! If you think my transformation is not to be believed, then you will certainly be stunned by this. My mother likes her. More than that, Mother not only approves but *advocates* the match. She has attempted more than once to convince *me*."

"You are absolutely right. Stunned is too inadequate a word. My mother must not yet know of these developments, or else she would already have returned to London to object vociferously."

"Your mother is welcome to bluster all she chooses. None of her usual narrow-minded arguments would sway me in this." He relished the idea of Devin having a good, loud row with Lady Ridgemont. Mother incessantly drilled the significance of noble bloodlines and distinctions of rank. In private, she'd even made a few disparaging remarks about the Devin line as "just a vicountcy" but never been ill-bred enough to speak thus in public.

"I do wish you could meet her, Ridgemont," Devin was saying. Then he shook his head as if to clear it. "I am rather surprised that your mother has not paired you off with a lady of quality yet."

"Now I know you have lost your wits," he replied. "I shall stay far from the reverend's noose, thank you."

Devin winked, actually winked, as he eased back in his chair.

"If I have lost my mind, it is entirely worth the trade. She is a rare gem. I suspect that you will find yourself heading toward the altar as soon as the family is properly out of mourning. Mothers will ooze from the woodwork to woo you for their daughters."

"Like insects or sap?"

"Oh, please do remember to use such comparisons with them! It would amuse me endlessly. Surely such talk shall endear you to them immediately."

"Speaking of sap and woods, which I consider an infinitely more interesting topic than marriage-minded matrons, what do you think of the logging being done in the north?"

"Ah, are you thinking of Trevely Forest? I have heard such industry is increasingly successful, but I wonder for how long. Forests like Trevely have stood for centuries. Those trees take several lifetimes to grow beyond saplings. It would be a shame to mow down whole woods, leaving England's bucolic countrysides bare as a baby's bottom."

So Devin was not simply an emotional, female-obsessed sot. He was an emotional, female-obsessed sot with a penchant for preserving open land rather than building profit. Did one need to be a Catholic in order to procure an exorcism?

"My father's land manager, headquartered at Blanchford, thinks we can earn enough from the logging to build a school for the area children. Currently, their studies take place at different houses. This would give them a genuine center for learning."

Devin straightened and signaled for drinks. "I have heard good things about your land manager, but I disagree with this wholesale removal of forest."

"Would you have some time for an appointment tomorrow? Business. Your advice would be most appreciated."

"It would be my pleasure, of course. Come to Devin House at midday. Mr. Foster delivers estate reports to me on Wednesdays, so you may observe. See how he works and how he thinks."

"Most excellent!" He was surprised to feel a knot in his back loosen, surprised to feel such relief at his cousin's assistance, surprised even more to realize that he had felt unsure about his Mr. Marcus's managerial expertise and his own ability to evaluate those most crucial to maintaining Ridgemont dealings.

The movement of Devin's gaze caught his attention.

"Ridgemont, am I imagining it, or does Bartwell look particularly pleased with himself today?"

Indeed. He rubbed his brow. He'd never much liked when these cousins interacted. Aside from balls and parties, his parents had taken to entertaining each side of the family separately. He got on reasonably well with Devin and reasonably well with Bartwell, but time spent together as a group always felt strained.

He still remembered Bartwell chiding Devin for refusing to go riding one day. "Better none of us go than leave someone behind," Skyler had said.

Bartwell replied, "He could take that old mare. That ancient thing could not possibly manage anything faster than a trot, slow and gentle enough for a youngster still in a dress!"

Devin would have been completely justified in retaliating but simply said, "Perhaps another day." Then Devin went on to suggest fishing in the stream, which all their younger siblings could enjoy as well.

Now Bartwell swaggered across the room and gave Devin a nod before addressing Skyler. "What news, coz?"

"None from me, Bartwell. You, however, appear to be about to burst with some revelation or other. Have a seat and get on with it," he replied, sharing a wry glance with Devin as Bartwell drew up a chair. They waited patiently while the new arrival chattered on about the weather and ordered a coffee as he settled in.

Finally, Bartwell leaned in, eyes narrowed and glittering, and whispered, "I just learned that I am the highest bidder in a very exclusive auction."

The man had quite a fondness for objets d'art, although, judging by his acquisitions, he favored them more for their grandiosity than their beauty. The Bartwell family seat was filled to brimming with garish paintings and sculptures, many of which depicted rather gruesome scenes of war and conquest. But such was his taste. And who was to question how a gentleman spent his fortune?

"Do go on," Devin prompted. He really must be light of heart to indulge this boastfulness. "What makes this auction so prized?"

Bartwell grinned in a way that made Skyler's stomach churn. "The, ah, item is very rare and very exotic. From the Orient. Such a specimen has likely not existed in England ever. It is quite lovely and delicate, and it is almost at my fingertips."

Devin might be in a generous mood, but Skyler was in no mood at all. "Save us all some time, Bartwell, and skip the riddles. You make it sound like a bloody plant. What interest would you have in some rare orchid or garden cutting? One that likely wouldn't survive transplantation to such a harsh climate as ours."

His cousin threw back his head as he let out a bellowing laugh that drew the scowling attention of other members. "That's exactly it, cousin! A bloody plant! Ha ha! The rarest of flowers! And it is ready for plucking!" His braying continued long enough in this manner that the senior member present—the Duke of Carleton, for heaven's sake—came to have a word with him. Skyler and Devin quickly excused themselves to avoid witnessing a dressing down, and each made as quick an exit as dignity would allow.

CHAPTER 8

A Test

Broek always acted quickly in matters of business, certain that one must press the advantage. Strike while the iron is hot. And so Hanako was not surprised to find that he had arranged to appraise the Devin antiques before the end of the week. What did surprise her was his insistence that she accompany him. "The presence of an assistant conveys seriousness and expertise," he said. "One must always be conscious of appearances." And so she was again trussed up in British fashion, nearly suffocating from the corset and perspiring from the heavy layers. Just before a footman greeted them at the door of Devin House, she mopped her damp brow with a handkerchief.

"Miss Sumaki, you are looking lovely as ever," Lady Devin said when they were ushered into the drawing room. The dear woman said it without the slightest hint of sarcasm. "It is a pleasure to see you again and to meet your employer at last! Mr. Broek, I do appreciate your willingness to peruse the Devin collection. Our family has so little knowledge of the knickknacks my husband collected along his travels, and it is particularly difficult to find experts regarding some of these pieces." The mistress of the house led them to the library, her slight, willowy figure floating gracefully down the hall.

In contrast, Hanako felt like an impostor, plodding and awkward, stuffed into a body that wasn't her own. When a servant opened the double doors to the library and gestured for them to enter, it took a moment for her eyes to adjust to the sunlight streaming through the large windows.

Lady Devin led them to one of the long glass display cases and pointed out a few British treasures before going to one of the mahogany pillars interspersed among the bookshelves. What clever hiding spots! After sliding open a wooden panel, she laid some small pieces, wrapped in velvet, on top of a glass case. The fabric served as a cushion when she unwrapped some small, intricately decorated cases—inro—unusually fine examples of inro at that. Clearly of Japanese origin, these small lacquered cases were common for carrying small essential items and perhaps a coin or two. What made these examples distinct—and she could already tell they were remarkable, even from a distance—was their artwork. The inlaid mother-of-pearl and the gold leaf were rather standard, but most everyday inro carried mythic scenes. These were far from everyday.

"These are quite pretty, Lady Devin," Mr. Broek stated. He picked up the most elaborate of the cases and examined it with a magnifying glass. "Such trinkets are rather commonplace in Japan."

"May I?" Hanako asked, as she gestured toward the two pieces closest to Lady Devin. When their hostess assented, she picked up the simplest one. It carried the Tokugawa family seal. Such pieces never left Japan. "Mr. Broek," she blurted, "are these not Tokugawa?"

He frowned as he came closer and picked up a near twin to the one she held. "They must be imitative. Cheap copies, I expect."

"Do you have any idea how or where your husband may have acquired these?" she asked Lady Devin.

"My husband had no eye for such things and simply picked up whatever struck his fancy, wherever he happened to be. Perhaps he bought it from a traveling merchant or a street bazaar. Are you saying these are . . ." The question faded in the air, as if she didn't wish to denigrate her husband's judgment by saying he was a fool who purchased the slightest trash and treated it as a great treasure. Especially disturbing, though, was Mr. Broek's excessive shaking of his head, as if disappointed and reluctant to speak. He should recognize symbols of the shogunate, should be cognizant of how very rare and valuable these pieces must be.

Hanako undid the string of the Tokugawa case and began to take it apart. Lady Devin exclaimed, "Oh, my, I never knew they opened! I thought they were simply decorative. How novel!" The inro was empty, although the scent of ginger and other herbs wafted from it.

Lady Devin picked up a few of the others and shook them gently, then tried to open one of them.

"There is a latch hidden in the design," Hanako said, as she pointed out its location. Lady Devin gasped, and her hands trembled as she withdrew a small scroll from the top compartment and then separated the nested containers until a jeweled pendant fell onto the velvet cloth. The swiftness with which their hostess moved was startling; she gathered the edges of the velvet, enclosing all the inro pieces. The items jostled and clattered alarmingly as she returned the pack to the storage shelf.

At first, Mr. Broek watched her intently while her back was to the room. Then his eyes roamed with calculation, which made a fine sweat break out on Hanako's neck. He had recognized the rare inro, and he was making a plan. Such plans of his never meant well.

Indeed, when Lady Devin left the room to speak with a servant, Broek moved closer and whispered, "Hanako, do you have your inro with you? Whatever you have with you would be convenient for a small trade; a little switch, if you will."

"No." Damn him for a greedy fool. "I shall have no part in any deception."

"My dear, that is rich coming from such a one as you, steeped in deception every day of your life."

"I was not made that way. I shall not participate by choice."

"Give me your damned trinket boxes," he said, quietly but with a snarl only she could hear. "I will make the switch."

"No, no," she said at normal volume. "Anyone can see that mine do not match the quality of those. Those are reserved for the inner circle."

Lady Devin returned, and Hana knew what she must do.

"For comparison, let me show you the inro my parents carried. I keep them with me always." She held them out for Lady Devin to peruse, and explained that the carved wooden one had been passed down to her mother, while the painted bamboo one had been her father's. She conspicuously pointed out their flaws: the chipped lacquer, the roughness of the bamboo shaping, the frayed cords. She would part with neither of them—particularly not for some mercenary swindle. And now Broek had no way of switching them. His deliberate stillness and clipped conversation indicated that he saw exactly what she'd done.

"What was it like giving your grand speech in the Lords?" Skyler asked, as they emerged from Devin's study.

"To which grand speech do you refer?" Devin's arch tone was matched by his imperiously raised brow. Such a well-practiced and effective expression. Skyler barked a laugh at his cousin's exaggerated manner.

"You know, the one that was reprinted in the *Times*. The one condemning the sale and distribution of pornographic materials. The one that made you the Great Defender, if your mother is to be believed."

"Spare me. Mother gave me such grief over that. And if you dare remind her, I will spread the word that you are in the market for a wife."

"Do not even joke, Devin. Anything but the hell of a Season being hounded by desperate matrons and their little angels."

"You might find that you enjoy the game."

"Did you?"

"Not for a second. But then, I have not actually played it."

"You know, this may be the most we have talked together since . . ." He couldn't actually recall a time when they'd spoken thus. "And you are trying to distract me but shall not succeed. What was it like waxing eloquent at Lords?"

"It was . . . humbling."

"So many fluffy wigs nodding off?"

Devin smiled. Again. So disconcerting coming from him.

"No, no," Devin replied. "The assemblage did not affect me in the slightest. The gravity of my charge deserved their full attention. My difficulty was that I felt unequal to the task of representing so many innocent victims with the power and passion they deserved."

"You did quite well, and you stifled the blowhards rather handily. I can tell you it was quite a sight: you on the steps of the throne. The hall is a grand sight to begin with, although my father despised the new Gothic style."

"Were you in attendance? I was unaware. Why did you not greet me afterward?"

"I was there only to observe. I stood in the journalists' gallery to avoid notice. You were remarkably impassioned. If I were of a romantic bent, I might even say you were heroic. And fiery, especially when that toad made some claim about art and asked you to provide detailed examples of what you found objectionable."

"He was rather unpleasant," Devin said, "and seemed interested for the sake of tawdry sensationalism, certainly not for beauty and aesthetics."

As they approached the library, Devin frowned at the wide open doors. Lady Devin was having an extremely tense conversation with someone within.

"Lady Devin, my dearest aunt, what an unadulterated pleasure to see you, as always," Skyler said as he crossed the threshold.

"Ridgemont, I needed your obsequiousness today," Lady Devin responded with a smile, genuine but not nearly as ebullient as usual. "Especially when I know full well you act the sycophant only to vex me. Now come, both of you, and meet my guests." She gave no sign of the distress they'd heard in her voice from the hall.

"I did not know you had plans today, Mother," Devin said. As he leaned in closer, Skyler heard him ask, "Is everything well?"

"I have everything well in hand, Devin," she explained, as she straightened and gestured toward said guests. "I engaged an expert to estimate your father's Far Eastern collection. Please welcome Mr. Broek and his assistant, Miss Sumaki."

He'd been so preoccupied with Lady Devin's discomfiture that he hadn't noticed the others in the room. Then he saw her, Miss Sumaki, dressed in a bright red costume. Next to her stood a thin man of average height. In fact, *average* was the word that immediately came to Skyler's mind—average appearance, nondescript suit, bland demeanor. The mysterious Mr. Broek. Finally. His cousin visibly stiffened, which immediately set his own inner alarms ringing. Then his aunt's words coalesced in his head. Before he could find the words, Devin replied, "It is unlike you to allow strangers into the house to paw through our things, Mother. Who is this purported expert?"

He would have to ask Devin to teach him that noble sneer. As Broek explained his background in Far Eastern trade, Skyler longed to know what Broek had said to cause his delicate aunt to utter the phrase "Over my dead body."

Devin persisted, "Mother, what makes them experts on these artifacts?"

Mr. Broek said, in a placating tone, "I assure you, Lord Devin, that I have carefully studied the arts of the Asian continent. I spent the last eight years in Japan, working with Miss Sumaki's father to export goods."

"That you have been exposed to such items hardly makes you an expert." There was the haughty, reserved Devin he remembered. After the death of Alex's father, no one in the house had ever raised their voices to one another. Even Amelia, the youngest of the Devin children, knew how to exert her will with the greatest composure. That was one of the things he'd liked best about visiting them: their steadiness. Now he could not help but share his cousin's sense of suspicion.

"More of an expert than anyone else in this room," Mr. Broek replied "In fact, likely more of an expert than anyone in the city of London. We shall need to return in order to examine the rest of the items. I may bring some of my own pieces for comparison, to gauge authenticity."

Throughout this unpleasant exchange, Skyler could not help but notice Miss Sumaki's avoidance of him. She stood behind her employer, her demeanor conveying a cloak of invisibility, a blank slate. She used that look too often for his taste. She had greeted him and Devin with a perfunctory curtsy and a barely audible, "Good day, my lords." Bile and frustration rose in his throat. The conversation washed over him until Devin's tone turned dangerous.

"While we may appreciate your acumen in business, Mr. Broek, I do hope you understand our attachment to these trinkets, as you call them. Whether they have any monetary or historical value, they carry at the very least certain nostalgic and emotional value. As my mother has made abundantly clear, we are not interested in selling any of these items."

The fact that Mr. Broek wasn't visibly shaking suggested that he didn't perceive Devin's deadly seriousness, although Miss Sumaki seemed to crawl farther into her protective shell and Lady Devin physically but smoothly placed herself between the two men. If anyone ever tried to take something that rightfully belonged to the Devins, Alex would no doubt acquaint himself with medieval torture techniques or other methods of enforcement.

Much later in the evening, Skyler realized what had alarmed him so much about Miss Sumaki's demeanor. She wasn't simply quiet and subdued. She was frightened. And she watched her employer's movements with intense attention, reacting to even the slightest movements, as if she were a puppet on strings.

CHAPTER 9

A Promenade

On One Shilling Days, the atmosphere of the Great Exhibition became less predictable, less sedate, less jaded. Every level of British society could be seen in attendance—from grand dukes and duchesses to lowly shopgirls and bootblacks and cow herders. Sometimes Hanako thought the great variety of these days should make her feel less conspicuous.

Today she felt more foreign than ever. Even among such vast throngs, she was a spectacle. Catastrophe swooped in during her final performance for the day: the tea ceremony. She'd prepared the tea with the usual solemnity and reverence, and yet when she extended a couple of the small paper cups to the audience, an elderly woman in the front had said loudly, "As if any Englishwoman worth her salt would drink such swill! Likely as not to be poisoned!"

They'd brought the delicate cups with them from China, and the supply was running low. After that outburst, no one had taken a sample. It was a rare and sad occasion when the English wouldn't take tea. Even as she collected all the tea ceremony accoutrements onto a tray at the conclusion of the performance, the woman's statement—and its chilling disparagement—echoed in her mind.

When she entered the back room, she was surprised to find Mr. Broek waiting for her. Even more shocking, Lord Ridgemont accompanied him. Both men bowed in greeting, and then her employer—miracle of miracles—took the tray from her and set it down.

"Your performance was as charming as ever, my dear," Mr. Broek said, as if his attendance was commonplace.

"Indeed, Miss Sumaki, if there is any tea left, I would be honored to partake," Lord Ridgemont added.

She made a curtsy and poured for the men. Then she stood, uncertain. She certainly couldn't change into her street apparel, her disguise. Fortunately, she didn't have to wait long for an explanation.

"I believe Lord Ridgemont and I are quite close to an agreement about our contract with the Royal Commission." *Our* contract? "But he has additional questions about your performances that require satisfaction." Satisfaction? Whenever Mr. Broek spoke in public, his words were laced with quicksand. Always, *always*, what he said held tacit obligations and implicit punishments.

"Please, Miss Sumaki, do not be alarmed," Lord Ridgemont said.

From behind him, Mr. Broek scowled. Her face must have shown something of her thoughts. She strove to control her expression, willing herself to blankness. He'd confiscated her mother's inro after she'd thwarted his attempts to cheat Lady Devin. To dangle before her? To sell? To destroy? He wouldn't say. She had so little left of her mother; she couldn't risk losing more. She struggled to maintain docility, at least in Broek's presence.

"I assure you I have no wish to interrogate you," Lord Ridgemont continued. "I simply want to ensure that all of Mr. Broek's performers are being well treated and fairly compensated."

Before she could respond, Mr. Broek interjected, "His lordship has been so kind as to offer you a guided tour of the Crystal Palace. It will be the perfect opportunity for you to converse openly." The command underlying his words was unmistakable. It would be the perfect opportunity indeed for her to convince the commissioner that there was nothing amiss, nothing at all.

"How very kind," she said meekly, casting her eyes downward. "I would be honored by your attention, Lord Ridgemont." Her stomach roiled; if only she could tell this man the truth. If anyone could free her and the Jade ladies from Mr. Broek, wouldn't it be a gentleman with a solid fortune and a respectable name? But there were so many ways in which honesty could fail her, still so many ways the women could be left defenseless, still so very many ways Mr. Broek could punish them all for any hint of defection.

She took Lord Ridgemont's proffered arm, and Broek nodded approvingly and held a curtain open for their departure. She both did and didn't want this. Her hand tingled from the light touch, a sensation that skated through her. She was being escorted by a man of property and propriety. A handsome man. With hair and even eyelashes spun from sunshine. And a solid, muscular arm. *Do not enjoy this. It is not real.* Broek always had hidden motives. His reasons for allowing her to promenade about the Exhibition were clear: a sign of respectability and an opportunity for self-promotion. She could not allow herself to think this was anything more than his puppetry, leading her and Lord Ridgemont on a dance that put them both at risk. How aware was her escort, though, of Broek's intentions?

"So your family traveled extensively?" Ridgemont asked.

She hadn't had any opportunity to explore the grounds before, so single-minded was her work. What she'd seen of the Exhibition was only what she'd glimpsed as she went to her station and what she could see as she performed. Even now, as they wound delicately through crowds filled with billowy skirts, muddy boots, feathers, all manner of life, it was difficult for her to perceive the scope of the grandeur around her. The innovative machines Ridgemont highlighted were dreams of modern convenience. When he repeated the question, she realized she'd been unconscionably distracted and turned to him.

"Forgive my ... woolgathering, I think it is called. This is my first opportunity to see the fullness of this Exhibition. It is ... remarkable."

"On behalf of the Royal Commission, I thank you. That you were too distracted by it to follow our conversation is rather a complimentary testament to its power." He smiled then, a seemingly genuine smile, unguarded and sunny. Pleasure shot through her, from her scalp to her toes. Very odd. And not at all welcome.

"Is there something in particular you would like to see?" he asked.

"I have no idea where to begin. I do not know what is here."

"Then please allow me to show you some of the most popular features, in addition to yours, of course. The technological displays include some magnificent new inventions sure to revolutionize the world. There are also some wonderful examples of the world's greatest treasures. And, if I may be so bold, I think it would be wonderful for you to have your portrait taken using the newest processes. Mr. Broek might find your likeness very useful for promotion."

"That all sounds quite vast and overwhelming. I trust your expertise; show me what most interests you." In truth, already the crowds and the exposure made her a bit dizzy. Performing kept the audience at a polite remove, and disguising herself as Izo gave her the ability to dart about inconspicuously. Now she felt eyes roving over her, bodies crushing in upon her. "I assure you," she added, grabbing onto something else he'd said just to anchor herself, "Mr. Broek needs no additional help in his promotions."

She bit her tongue to keep from saying more. He looked at her sharply but did not pursue the topic. Instead, he talked as they continued through the hall. As they reached the Grand Transept, with its beautiful curved roof, he shifted the conversation in a way that set her immediately on edge. Steam engines: he'd taken her through the display of engines, and talked about how they were revolutionizing travel around the world. And then he'd turned so innocuously.

"You never did say. Did your family travel much?" he asked.

"Let me be frank," she said, with a tone that made him tense. "My family roamed like nomads. We did not explore; instead, we followed the trail of prosperity. My father was a trader and my mother was a translator. He became enamored of her and convinced her to elope." The raw look in her eyes spoke of harsh deprivation before she shuttered it. "My parents made certain that I was trained in a wide range of arts. I have an affinity for languages: indeed, an affinity for mimicry that I must have gotten from them. So they encouraged me to absorb as much local language as I could, wherever we were."

"In what way?"

"When I was around eight, they started leaving me in restaurants or shops . . . just for short periods, mind you. I would need to figure out how to communicate with the locals in order to get assistance."

"That's terrible! They would just leave you to your own devices?"

"I found out years later that they always hid nearby and observed. I was never in actual danger, I'm sure."

"Perhaps not . . . but you did not know that at the time."

"No," she said, flatly. "No, I did not." She shivered, and unsuccessfully tried to mask it by drawing her shawl tighter. Her body recalled the panic that always threatened to overwhelm her, every time, before she conquered it and opened her mouth to ask for help. "Yet I learned very quickly. Necessity is a great motivator. Perhaps not ideal for everyone, it was effective instruction for me nonetheless. After my mother's death, my father used less dramatic methods of instruction."

It was impossible to ignore the way Miss Sumaki's entire demeanor closed down upon itself, like a flower furling itself as night fell. As a man, he wanted to pull back the petals, learn more of her dark, sad secrets, nurture her openness. As a gentleman, he had to respect her privacy.

"We need not continue this particular charade, Lord Ridgemont," she said sharply. "I am sure you have more important things to do than to lead me around."

"You wound me, Miss Sumaki. I thought I was being a more cordial host than to give you such an impression. Have I done something to offend you?"

"Not you, my lord. You do not see?" she said. The delicacy of her voice belied the harshness in her eyes, the tense line of her mouth. "Mr. Broek orchestrated our *promenade* through the Exhibition and the park as a form of advertising. You spoke of my likeness earlier but needn't trouble yourself about Mr. Broek's business. You have an unusual piece on your arm, a species so rare in these parts that it could be mistaken as one of a kind. Those who catch a glimpse will surely want to seek out more."

She gestured to herself grandly. He took in the exquisite vision before him. The red silk robe could not fail to draw one's eye. She was quite a picture of Far Eastern grace. The hard and bitter set of her face, however, destroyed the illusion of serene Orientalism.

"Do not insult yourself." He could not stomach her self-references as an object.

"I meant no actual claim to myself . . . only what people see. No doubt Mr. Broek will be in negotiations very soon."

"Negotiations for what, may I ask?"

"That is between him and those who seek to bargain with him. Tell me, how did these trees come to be part of the building?"

They'd come to a large elm, and he gestured toward a bench at its base. Relief and appreciation shone in her eyes as she sank down onto the seat.

"While some trees were cut down to make room for the Crystal Palace, the ones you see within the structure were here first. The Palace was built around them."

"How fascinating. As if nature could be contained."

"Well, to a degree. What is the Crystal Palace if not an enormous greenhouse? Do you see the yellowing of those leaves on the upper edges?" At her nod, he continued. Her attention focused above, he took the opportunity to enjoy the sight of her graceful neck and rapt fascination. "Some of the trees continue to thrive, but others, like this one, are showing signs of strain. This one does not seem particularly happy with its confinement. I do not know if it sustained an impact during construction or if perhaps it does not get enough light in this location. The trees are all watered regularly and equally."

"That is terribly sad. This poor tree had no control over its circumstances. It could not object to its confinement. It was entirely powerless, unable to move. Has nothing been done to assist it?"

"Arboreal experts have examined it, I assure you. It may yet recover after the Exhibition is done. So far, though, none of the efforts to revive this old gal have succeeded."

"How old is she?"

"That was just a manner of speaking. Estimates say she is only about forty or so, quite young for a tree."

"What will happen after the Exhibition ends?"

"That has not yet been decided. The Palace is expected to remain standing for some time but not permanently. Her Majesty Queen Victoria was quite adamant about returning Hyde Park to its natural state."

"I can only hope that time comes soon enough for this poor specimen."

"Ridgemont, my good man, how good to see you!" The overly jovial voice of his cousin, Marquess Bartwell, startled him.

Miss Sumaki jumped in surprise as well. During this little respite, more than one couple walking by had looked at Miss Sumaki disapprovingly. One or two groups had begun whispering furiously among themselves as they passed. He heard what sounded like "peculiar" and "heathen." If her increasingly rigid posture was an indication, she did not miss a single occurrence. She glanced up at Bartwell once or twice shyly, her face returning to its placid facade.

"How nice to see you, Bartwell," Skyler replied.

Beneath her smooth, silent demeanor, he sensed discomfort. They'd lingered too long.

"You simply must introduce me to this lovely lady, Ridgemont."

Of course, Bartwell would have no compunction about imposing himself. He could only hope to make the conversation brief and cordial so he could return Miss Sumaki to her alcove. As he made the introductions, she stood and gave a respectable curtsy. Bartwell tried to draw her into conversation about London, about the Exhibition, but she gave only the most laconic responses. For some reason, his cousin's behavior put him in mind of a duck dipped in oil, waddling awkwardly and unpleasantly. It was odd when Bartwell asked her about gardening, since he didn't know his cousin to have any interest whatsoever in either agriculture or domestic gardens. Miss Sumaki wrapped her arms around herself, as if chilled, and he decided the tour was at an end.

"If you will excuse us, Bartwell, I must return Miss Sumaki in time for her next performance."

His cousin looked curiously at her, a look he couldn't quite read, except that it sparked an inexplicable and unsettling instinct to sweep Miss Sumaki into his arms and carry her to safety.

As soon as they'd lost Bartwell in the crowd, whatever dam had stopped Miss Sumaki's voice broke.

"You are aware, Lord Ridgemont, that, perhaps even more than being a walking advertisement, your escort today has, in essence, provided Mr. Broek with the Royal Commission's validation, as surely as if it were a written pronouncement."

"That is not what I intended. I gave you a tour as myself, not as a representative of the Commission."

"Still, that is how it will be viewed, is it not?"

He could not contradict her logic. The paperwork was as good as signed, wasn't it? If there were something nefarious in Broek's dealings, there would be hell to pay.

"Why do you not leave Mr. Broek's employ? If you detest it as much as you appear to, why continue with him?"

A bitter crack of laughter escaped her as her face twisted for a moment.

"You make it sound so easy, as if it were simply a matter of choice." She stood and shook out the folds of her robe, and he had a sudden fear she would disappear again.

"You are the most beautiful, enchanting creature I have ever seen," he blurted.

"Do Englishwomen find it appealing to be called *creatures*?" she asked icily. Without waiting for his reply, she added, "I would recommend that you not use such terms, however well intentioned, with women who may not be accustomed to treatment as objects or animals or subjugated, alien organisms. It is rather dehumanizing. It sounds like something your cousin might say."

The chastisement surprised him. Such an insult had never occurred to him before. How lowering. He hadn't intended that connotation but could not deny its unpleasant logic.

"My deepest apologies, Miss Sumaki. I assure you that I hold you in the highest regard. I see you as heavenly, beyond human. It would never occur to me to see a woman in general, and you in particular, as subhuman."

He bowed, then dipped even deeper, remembering the Japanese guidelines she had explained about the depth of the bow conferring respect. "If I could prostrate myself at your feet here in public, I would."

"Oh, do stand up," she snapped, keeping her voice low. "Do not embarrass us both by such ridiculous displays. We have already garnered more than enough attention."

He had always had a gift for making women feel good about themselves. In contrast with his brother's inclinations, he didn't seek to seduce women; he simply had a way of making them feel comfortable, appreciated. His father had often joked about his ability to make women of any age smile and giggle, even blush on occasion. The governess, the ancient cook, his great-aunt Vanessa, whose dour disposition was legendary. He had learned over the years to be attuned to the moods of women. It was frequently as simple as that. A kind word to the harried maid or the gray dowager might be all that was needed to transform her demeanor. Frequently, a sincere compliment making it clear that the woman was noticed would work wonders.

But this woman, with those large amber eyes about which he could write poetry and sing songs, was immune to his charms.

"I must return to prepare for the next showing."

She turned to walk away—again—and this time he reached for her arm, even as his brain chastised him. Why must his control slip around *this* woman?

She stared at his hand.

"Forgive me." He let her go then, the warm silk of her robe slipping out of his hand, leaving him with the inexplicable sensation of an undercurrent yanking him off his feet and tumbling him out to sea.

He followed her to the China exhibit and hesitated as she approached the curtains. Now knowing it to be the equivalent of a dressing room, the impropriety of his previous encounters there with her loomed in his mind. But he hadn't known it was her then.

She disappeared behind the curtains but then returned before he had time to leave. In truth, he'd stood perhaps a dash longer than was normal. Seeing her again so soon, he could not regret it. She held the curtain open and said, "Mr. Broek has left a note. He wishes for me to finalize the Royal Commission's contract with you. Please come in."

Although her demeanor was gracious, the tightness of her jaw and lips belied her professionalism. This kind of intimate tête-à-tête was a mistake, and they both knew it. Broek probably intended exactly that. He should make some excuse, should fetch another commissioner to witness the negotiations, should do anything but follow her backstage.

And yet he followed. His father always said he had more hair than sense.

She crossed the space, picked up a sheaf of papers, and held them out to him.

"Have my answers been sufficient? Would you make the emendations we discussed? I would be happy to sign, and I am sure Mr. Broek would be relieved to have a firm agreement in hand."

"Only Mr. Broek is authorized to sign, not his subordinates." He moved forward just to pluck the file from her hand and then stepped back again to maintain a respectful distance apart.

But then she moved toward him, into him. The feel of her weight against his chest caught him off guard and he nearly stumbled back. He grabbed her shoulders to steady himself and try to separate them. It took him a moment to realize the pressure against his hands was her effort to reach up to him. Her lips brushed his jaw. He lifted his hands from her person immediately and stared at her. The touch of her mouth on his skin startled him, jolted him like an unseen punch to the back of the head. None of their interactions thus far prepared him for her advance. He was stunned by the feel of her. And she stared right back at him, her eyes as wide as his must be. She looked equally shocked. *Just once. Just for a moment.*

He gave in to the unfamiliar waves of heat and electricity shooting through him and closed his eyes. Then he wrapped his arms around her waist and leaned down to meet her lips with his. Her body stiffened; yet her hands gripped his upper arms tightly, and her mouth pressed against his. It took him a moment to comprehend that she was stretching herself up to reach him. He couldn't help himself; a laugh bubbled up from his chest, even as he bent toward her to ease her efforts.

He brushed damp strands away from her face, and her fine hair twined around his fingers and hands. Her sigh shivered through him. Tenderness, care—he'd thought these were feminine attributes, but not now, not anymore. This fierce gentleness, this determination to keep her safe, to wrap around her as a wall of bone and muscle—this was not fundamentally female or male. It was a primal devotion, a primitive cleaving to another living creature. The amazing thing was that anyone who felt this way could go about their business as if there were anything more important in the world than the object of their devotion.

She pulled away, leaving him off balance. Wrenching open a door of the wardrobe, she said, without looking at him, "I am sorry. I should not have done that."

"I am exceedingly glad you did."

"You should know I do not engage in . . . this is not common behavior for me...I am not a whore." She trailed off as she tossed handfuls of fabric on the floor. It seemed impossible to tell one piece from another. If she were looking for a particular article of clothing, this was not the way to go about it.

"I know that," he said, instantly sure of her integrity.

She looked at him sharply, breathing heavily, her hands clenched around red silk. The robe in which he first saw her. She shook her head. "How could you? Just because I say so? No one would believe the word of a girl like me."

"I do." He could no longer meet her eyes. "I know what whores are like. I have seen them on streets, in drawing rooms. I have known friends taken in by the machinations of calculating harlots. There is no such calculation or baseness in you."

"I am no harlot, but you are wrong to think me innocent."

"I would devote a lifetime to learning what you know." He was as surprised as she to hear the words coming from his mouth. Once uttered, though, he felt the conviction behind them.

"You need to leave. I am sorry if I gave you the wrong impression." She met his eyes before hers wandered to his mouth. The fire in her eyes, the subtle increase in her breathing, made his lips tingle. Seeing the flush wash over her face, he had to suppress the wild impulse to pull her back into his arms. When he didn't speak, she added, "Mr. Broek will be pleased to know our negotiations went smoothly. We are indebted to the Royal Commission for allowing us the opportunity to use such a grand venue. He will no doubt return the signed documents to you immediately."

The cool distance in her voice was as good as a dip in the North Sea, reminding him of his position and hers...and the massive gulf between them. He could not risk violating his duty as a commissioner, and he most certainly could not generate scandal about a commissioner dallying with an Exhibition dancer. She might be a better actress than he originally realized.

CHAPTER 10

A Friend

In the solitude of the ladies' retiring room, she sat on a chaise and rested her head against the plump velvet cushions. Ridiculous, really, that the furnishings in a public retiring room were more lavish than any she'd experienced since childhood. Fortunately, the room was deserted as visitors enjoyed the novelty of the penny toilets around the Exhibition. Another ridiculousness. Paying a penny to relieve oneself. These people obviously had more money than they could possibly need if they were spending it so frivolously.

Some days, the performances were more taxing than others. The usual avid curiosity surrounding her was usually tempered by politeness, but sometimes a savage alienation underscored her interactions. She was viewed as a bug under glass, an oddity. And yet again, at times there seemed to be genuine affinity, understanding, a common bond of humanity. Those encounters brought the most strain because they coaxed her into lowering her guard. She could not afford weakness.

"Pardon my intrusion, Miss Sumaki, but are you well? Do you need any assistance?"

It was the woman Lady Devin had introduced her to a few hours before. The two made an unlikely pair: a fine lady and a merchant's wife. A bookseller. Yes, that was it. She had kind eyes. "I am fine, thank you, madam. I simply needed a moment."

"Of course. If you don't mind, I could use a moment myself." The woman gestured to the seat next to her. She nodded, as if her permission were necessary. "I find it difficult to recall the names of so many people gathered in one place. Allow me to renew our introductions. I am Mrs. Duchamp. I run a bookshop on Greek Street, although it is currently closed for renovations." The chatty woman sat at the dressing table and checked her hair in the mirror.

"May I say," continued Mrs. Duchamp, "that, during a previous visit, I saw a girl who must have been your daughter. She was a schoolgirl image of you, and she was lovely."

"I have no daughter," she responded without thinking.

"Oh, well, your sister, then. Quite a charming girl."

She scrambled to compose an appropriate response and found nothing but exhaustion. So she remained silent. A moment of silence that stretched uncomfortably.

"Oh!" Mrs. Duchamp repeated, this time more emphatically. "Could that have been you, then? My goodness, is that possible?"

What good would it do to prevaricate?

"Yes, you are very perceptive, Mrs. Duchamp. I play different roles to add to the variety of the display. The schoolgirl lecture tends to be more popular than one from an adult. People seem to find the childlike version more charming and amusing."

"Please, I insist you call me Honoria. I seem to have stumbled inadvertently upon intimate information about you that you may not have intended to share. It is only fair for me to extend the same level of intimacy to you. And, anyway, how fascinating! Do audiences not suspect you are all of these characters?"

She looked across the room at her reflection in a distant mirror, her image dwarfed by the rich vastness of the chamber. "I find that people in such situations make their own logic about what they see, much as you did. The performers may be siblings or a whole family, so any resemblance is easily rationalized."

"What other roles do you play, then?"

"Some evenings it behooves me to dress as an adult in formal Chinese or Japanese ensemble. The irony is that very few people would stoop to notice the difference between them. No one, in fact, has questioned whether I am Chinese. In the Chinese alcove, it seems rather fitting, as many of the items on display are not genuinely from the celestial kingdom, and some items, like me, are in fact from Japan instead."

"I shall have to revisit with a more discerning eye. How do you know these items aren't genuine?"

"Perhaps I overstate. Some of them may be of genuine foreign manufacture, but I think all of them have come from the collections of private British citizens. I do not know where they acquired them, but there is no guarantee that those are authentic, aside from the hearsay of the owners. My employer is more of an expert; he knows what markings to look for. Some of the porcelain pieces, for instance, are poorly made copies. Likewise, some of the smaller japanware appears to be cheap, worn replicas."

"How did you come to be part of the display?"

"My employer felt it important to provide some semblance of authenticity and . . . warmth."

More silence for a long moment. Too long.

"You are not expected to . . ." Mrs. Duchamp looked at her knowingly as the indelicate question hung in the air. She wondered how such a genteel woman could think to ask, or at least suggest, such a question, how such a woman could even suspect the kind of degradation in which her employer traded.

"I am as much a showpiece as the rest. An exotic bird of paradise on display." She couldn't answer the question honestly, couldn't put into words what she was expected to do. Already she'd perhaps shared too much. It was all too much.

Mrs. Duchamp—Honoria—frowned deeply. "Yours must be a fascinating story. Have you ever considered writing about your experiences?"

"Oh, I could not begin."

"In my business, I do small print runs of important human interest. I believe you could provide an illuminating glimpse into other cultures."

She needed to deflect Mrs. Duchamp's interest immediately. "Shall Lord Devin take over the bookshop after you marry? Is that how British marital law works? Does a woman's business go to her husband?"

It was the other woman's turn to be evasive.

"What an odd question. How do you know of Lord Devin?"

Ah. She recognized the wary look in Mrs. Duchamp's eyes. "I was introduced to him when Mr. Broek and I appraised Lady Devin's miscellany from Asia."

"I gather that your acquaintance with Lady Devin may have led to your meeting her son. I meant to ask how you came to think of such a question associating me with Lord Devin." The woman flushed brightly.

"One hears things." It might not be wise for her to reveal that she'd overheard Ridgemont quizzing Lord Devin about his Mrs. Duchamp. She'd managed to deflect the woman's attention. That was all she needed to do.

"I must say as directly as I can that I have no idea how you came to this impression." Mrs. Duchamp stood stiffly and smoothed out her skirt. "Lord Devin and I have worked together recently; he and the Devin family have been quite supportive in the repair of my shop. But we are not engaged to marry. It is unthinkable."

A pang of guilt shot through her as she witnessed Mrs. Duchamp's discomfort, but she had to use whatever weapons were available to her. She pondered the bookseller's certitude quietly. Rumors were indeed dangerous creatures that grew monstrously out of control. Then a more important thought occurred to her.

"According to British law, if a man takes a woman as his wife, does he then become responsible for any of her dependents?"

Mrs. Duchamp frowned for a moment, clearly rolling the question over in her mind to see if it was a veiled question about Lord Devin before concluding herself free to respond. "To be frank," she said, her voice still tight, "I do not know since I have no such dependents, but some of my married friends may be able to enlighten me."

"Please do not trouble yourself for me. It was simply an idle question."

Mrs. Duchamp nodded, but added, "It would be no trouble, and I find that such specific questions about the law are never idle. If you have need of my help, you have only to ask. You may find it interesting to speak with some ladies from the Needlework for the Needy Society. In fact, I suspect they would find your experience quite compelling. I think many people would."

"Really, I could not write such a story. You see, my writing, it is very weak." At least she could be truthful about that. "While I may have been blessed with what you might call a silver tongue, my hands turn words to dross. My father made sure I could read adequately in several languages, but writing has always been a struggle for me."

"Extraordinary." Honoria Duchamp leaned in close and whispered, "I think a woman's talents should be encouraged, wherever they take her."

Hanako stared at the woman's reflection. Such women, Broek said, were dangerous. They were to be feared and avoided because they made women want what was not good for them. They made women unsteady, he said. Now she understood what he meant. She yearned to take up Mrs. Duchamp's offer of assistance, to give voice to the women of the Jade Garden, to seek the budding freedom promised in the woman's words. But the risk, the punishment if she failed, was far too severe.

"It has been a pleasure speaking with you, Mrs. Duchamp, but I must return to my duties. I do hope our paths cross again. And I deeply apologize for causing you any distress." She stood, gave a proper curtsy, and made her way to the door.

Honoria interrupted her progress with a gentle hand on her arm. "No apologies needed, Miss Sumaki. I too hope we meet again. Please remember that you can always send word to me at the shop if you have need of assistance."

She nodded and forced a friendly smile. "That is very kind of you and very much appreciated." The woman's determined tone at once bolstered and alarmed her. She'd definitely said too much, and she could not risk anyone drawing Mr. Broek's anger.

CHAPTER 11

A Favor

It should have been comical, that unreasonable pile of packages obscuring her face. But everything happened too fast. Skyler had been blithely walking from his solicitor's office to the nearby telegraph station. Too late, he realized this was a popular route for cattle, but he pressed on, paying close attention to the ground ahead of him to avoid all the earthy signs that cattle had passed recently. His downward focus must have been the reason he was caught off guard. One moment, a shop door swung open. The next moment, he was being stampeded by a monstrous pile of packages. His brain registered several sensations at once. The geometric awkwardness of boxes jostling against his arm and neck and face. The surprising force behind them that swept him toward the edge of the pavement. The folds of a skirt tangling around and between his legs. And the scent. That light floral promise of a warm summer night. Jasmine.

"Oh, no! Oof! My apologies! So sorry!" a delicate feminine voice called out hurriedly.

He knew that voice, too. Only some quick footwork kept him from falling to the ground. The packages did not appear to be so lucky. And Miss Sumaki could not regain her balance or slow her momentum on the narrow steps. He immediately rushed to face her, trying to catch and contain the boxes between them, but the top two could not be saved. One flopped on the ground with a light thud, but the other took an unfortunate spin and landed on a corner. The sound of glass knocking and breaking was muffled but unmistakable.

"No, no, no," Miss Sumaki said, as she bent to place the other packages on the ground and retrieve the two fugitives. The one with the glass already showed some darkening as its contents seeped into the wrapper. He knelt to pick up the damaged one, and the overpowering scent of vinegar filled his nostrils. When he held it up to her, she unceremoniously removed her gloves and took the box, examining it with a frown.

"What a pleasure to see you again, Miss Sumaki," he said as he straightened and gave her a wink and an exaggerated bow. The small smile he earned in return as she curtsied pleased him more than it should. "You seem to bear quite a burden today."

As she turned to look at the stack, she said something under her breath that sounded like "Not just today." When she glanced back at him, she said lightly, "We all have our burdens to bear. I am sure some carry them more gracefully than I. You are not injured, I hope."

He leaned against a lamppost to take the weight off his suddenly complaining ankle and catch his breath. This tiny respite also gave him an opportunity to observe yet another vision of Miss Sumaki. Again, she wore Western attire, but the dark blue gown must have been her best dress. This time, she wore a serviceable gray walking dress, the kind that blended in seamlessly with the rest of the workers who passed on the street. Her tidy bonnet was neither too large nor too small but just right for masking her features and not drawing attention. Externally, she was anonymous. But this nondescript appearance could not erase her vividness from his memory. "Not at all! And I can attest to your grace and poise under normal circumstances. Does Mr. Broek not have servants for such duties?"

"In fact, no. Since we travel so extensively, he does not keep many servants." True enough. "The cook does not speak English. It is often quicker for me to procure what we need myself than for Mr. Broek to contact the right vendors and place orders. In fact, this was an emer—" She stopped abruptly and began trying to find a logical grip to lift the pyramid of items safely. "I mean to say that we had waited overlong and found ourselves needing all these items at once."

"Do you need to have the vinegar replaced? I would be happy to fetch another bottle for you."

She looked at him sharply, suspiciously perhaps, before she relaxed and said, "No need, Lord Ridgemont. There is already a sufficient amount in this order."

She'd managed to reorganize the packages in order from largest to smallest, distributing them more reasonably, and he was about to ask how she intended to transport all of this to her home when a nearby set of double doors swung wide open and vaguely familiar voices drifted out.

"Thank you, Mum." A delicate feminine voice spoke with impeccable crispness and aplomb. "Yes, undoubtedly the blue will look better on me for the Cayhill soiree."

A deep masculine cough interrupted this exemplary girlishness, followed by the low, stern tones of Her Grace the Duchess of Carleton.

"My dear, you would do well to recall your lessons." Her voice might have sounded calm and mild, but he knew full well the expectations of rank. A duchess did not raise her voice in public, nor did she stoop to chastise her children in public. A carefully delivered reminder would curtail potential vanity.

"Lord Ridgemont!"

If he was not mistaken, the look on the face of His Grace the Duke of Carleton fleetingly begged for assistance. As the duke herded his wife and daughter closer, that look was replaced by his usual suave veneer.

"What a surprise to see you here, Lord Ridgemont," the duke said. "Have you been introduced to our eldest daughter, Lady Sophia?"

He made a proper bow to both ladies and then glanced uncertainly toward Miss Sumaki. "On my way to the telegraph office, I happened to encounter Miss Sumaki, whose performances at the Great Exhibition have received much acclaim."

Lady Sophia's eyebrows shot up. "Why, I do believe I recognize you! You do those diverting fan dances, do you not?" This earned her a sharp look from her mother.

Miss Sumaki nodded and curtsied but did not speak. Her silence was laced with tension. The ladies complimented her on her performances, even as Lady Sophia eyed the packages behind her. She responded tersely with "Thank you" and "You are too kind" and "It is an honor." Unless his hearing deceived him, her accent grew much more obvious in those few words, more staccato. *What on earth?*

The duke neatly ended the exchange with a reminder to the ladies that they had visits to return during the afternoon. They all performed yet another round of bows and curtsies, and only when the duke and his family were out of view did Miss Sumaki visibly relax, with a loud and meaning-laden exhalation.

"What is it?" he asked, his curiosity piqued. He rushed to pick up the stack before she recovered. If he didn't look at her, perhaps she would feel free to respond. "What disturbed you just now? You can tell me."

"Voicing negativity bears no purpose," she said as she reached to take her purchases from him.

"Please allow me to assist you."

"I have quite a way to go and should be on my way."

As if on cue, the skies opened, and large raindrops spat at them, leaving large splotches on the brown paper wrapping of her packages. She muttered under her breath and then grabbed more insistently at her things.

"My carriage is nearby. Given that you circumvented my previous attempt to send you home safely, perhaps the weather could convince you this time."

As the rain intensified, she took the top few packages, already soaked and dripping, from him and nodded.

"The heavens are very persuasive," she said.

"Come with me." He led her swiftly down the street, thankful that Tompkins, ever attentive, was already pulling down the steps. If the additions Skyler brought with him were a surprise, the driver was too well trained to show it. He stowed the packages swiftly and accepted Miss Sumaki's address matter-of-factly.

"This will not look good, you know," Hana said, watching the faces of passersby as the vehicle pulled away from the curb. She should have objected, should have gone on her way the moment the duke's family appeared, before getting caught in that terribly awkward conversation. Considering the traffic, she likely could have walked faster than this, but the rain came down mercilessly. And she needed to get back to the Jade Garden for Yuki's sake, not that any of these potions could help her with any certainty. "It is kind of you to offer assistance, but I should not have accepted. It would not do for you to be seen with me. For either of our sakes."

"Nonsense," he replied gently. "Rescuing a damsel in distress is at the top of any gentleman's priorities." A wry twist of his mouth undermined his words, but then he removed his hat and tossed it on the seat beside him. "Who the devil cares anyway?"

"You care. And I most certainly care. In your world, women's reputations are their only real currency."

"One ride with the curtains wide open and both of us visibly a respectable distance apart does not constitute a sin against my rank or a moral failing on either of our parts."

She should cease objecting. Under the best of circumstances, she wasn't going to jump out of a moving carriage. Now the street was covered in a layer of thick, dirty rainwater; a hansom going in the opposite direction hit a bad spot and splashed unfortunate pedestrians with filth up to their waists. How rarely she encountered such kindness. It wasn't as if his offer of assistance had sent pleasure rippling through her. It wasn't as if being in such close proximity made her heart beat faster. It wasn't as if she'd remembered him escorting her home or the light kiss she'd left him with. Then she recalled something that had slipped past her in the flurry of stormy activity.

"You remembered where I live?"

He froze for a moment and then relaxed and said, "I recently sent correspondence to your employer, so it was fresh in my memory." He proceeded to study the nearest window, his eyes tracking raindrops, as he said in a suspiciously casual tone, "You were uncomfortable speaking with His Grace the Duke of Carleton and his family. Why?"

This couldn't possibly be the way people of his station spoke to one another.

"Do you always interrogate strangers so bluntly?"

He frowned and leaned forward. "Forgive me. I did not mean to be brusque. On the contrary, I wish to make you at ease. I seem to have particular trouble conversing normally with you."

"How flattering. I thought I did a better job of managing my emotions."

"You are envious of Lady Sophia."

She took a deep breath, relieved that at least he focused idly on the passing scenery rather than on her as she prepared her response.

"Yes, I am. At the moment, so jealous that there is a vile taste in my mouth from it. But no good comes from indulging such ugliness."

"You are infinitely more beautiful than she. I hope you know that."

"I cannot agree. And, anyway, attractiveness is the least of my concerns. Being physically appealing to men is at best a nuisance and at worst a curse."

He let that pass.

"What do you envy of her, then?"

"What isn't there to envy? She has everything to which I could ever hope to aspire. She is everything I am not."

"You are intelligent, well traveled, highly talented, and utterly charming. You are in no way inferior to Lady Sophia, nor to any of the ladies I have encountered anywhere."

"You wield words so expertly, and I do appreciate your kindness. But they show what different worlds we live in. Whatever abilities I may have, I will never have the life she has: the ease, the luxury, the freedom. She has a natural place in this world, a comfortable place that is unquestionable. She is the daughter, granddaughter, great-granddaughter, and so on of nobility. Just like you. I shall never have that."

He seemed about to get up from his seat and then checked himself.

"Are you well?" she asked, startled and concerned.

"Yes, I am fine. A stray shiver, nothing more." But it was most definitely more. His gaze was troubled, his eyes asking some kind of question she couldn't decipher. "I am quite sorry you feel so alienated. And I am sure the duke's family meant no offense."

The carriage halted abruptly, sending her stumbling toward the opposite seat. The heat of his arms around her, his hands on her back, startled her. An impulse to snuggle into his solidness caught her by surprise. He conveyed comfort, kindness, warmth. She hadn't realized how much she craved those things. As she struggled to regain her footing, mentally as well as physically, the vehicle lurched into motion again, and his arms tightened for a moment. She leaned into him, feeling all too aware of his body against hers, all too aware of the simple pleasure of being held with care.

"We must have been at an intersection or some obstruction," he said, as he released all but her hand and she took her seat again.

"Thank goodness for your quick reflexes," she said, sincerely thankful for that brief moment of . . . security. That must be it: the feeling of security, free of any obligation. "I fear I might have fallen out of the door if you hadn't caught me."

"You are quite safe now," he said with a disarming smile.

She didn't realize she'd scoffed aloud until she saw his questioning expression.

"Do you doubt that you are safe with me, Miss Sumaki?"

"Of course not, my lord. I have no doubt you would protect me from harm . . ." Her voice trailed off.

"That does not answer my question. You are completely safe with me." He looked at her searchingly. "You are safe from me."

Could he read her mind? She looked out of the window as she said, "I have no doubt."

"You're lying."

She looked at him sharply.

"You've been afraid of me and of my intentions from the moment we met at the Exhibition," he said.

He could. He *could* read her mind.

"One does not need to be a mind reader to see the signs of your terror," he explained. "You have been stiff as a board since the moment you sat down, becoming impossibly more tense whenever I so much as shift in my seat. And your eyes dart about wildly, as if trying to monitor my every move while simultaneously assessing methods of escape."

His appraisal didn't ease her tension one whit. And she said so. She only hoped that he would not guess the true reasons behind her anxiety. She wasn't even sure she could name them herself.

"I will not hurt you. What has happened to you to set you on edge thus?"

"I should not say this, and yet you already seem to sense my mind. So giving voice to my feelings will likely not surprise you."

He waited. She had the impression that he would wait for her until the end of time, if that were what she needed.

"You bring forth emotions in me that I do not recognize and cannot trust."

He leaned back, which gave her a bit of space to breathe. The sharp intake of breath, the widening of his eyes, the stark surprise in his expression were difficult to contrive.

"Is that so?" he said. "You say I am capable of reading your mind, but I must confess that I had no sense whatsoever of any emotions I might . . . evoke in you. I have no inkling of which sentiments you might mean."

"You make me want to trust you."

Again, surprise. The muscles of his throat convulsed.

He swallowed hard, fighting the tension in his body. She should not watch him in such a bold manner. It made him think of her lips against his throat instead. He had to tamp down his body's wayward reaction so he could fully embrace the depth of her statement.

"I am honored that you feel you could," he said, finally. "You may, you know? If you can trust in me, I would not break that trust for all the world."

"Do not sound so pleased. It is a problem—this inclination. I cannot trust you. I should not want to." Her brow furrowed, and she looked away. So small, so delicate, she was. He really would take on the world for her sake, and he could not even articulate why.

"You make me want to protect you," he replied.

It was her turn to show surprise. She nodded, her eyes growing bright and her cheeks flushing.

"You make me want to escort you around the whole of London, take you on a tour of the Continent, show you all the wonders I know of the modern world. And yet all of it pales in comparison to you."

"You have an enviable facility with words. It is little surprise that Lady Sophia is so taken with you. I imagine you have made more than one woman swoon."

"Lady Sophia is not, as you so amusingly put it, taken with me. You do not know me, but if you did, you would realize how unlike me this is. I do not prattle on at women just for the sake of conversation, nor do I compliment women idly."

"Oh, but you do. I have seen you. And it works."

"I may say a kind word to brighten a woman's day, but I do not flatter them or woo them."

"Is that what you are doing with me? Wooing me?"

That stopped him. The notion of marriage and all it entailed. The earldom added new dimensions of responsibility. He could not simply woo as he wished; he had to marry sensibly.

"No."

"Now that is a statement that engenders trust. Thank you for your honesty. So what is this, then?"

Something else glowed in her eyes at that moment. Curiosity. And something more mysterious. An echoing fire flared within him.

"I have no idea," he admitted as his chest tightened. "Kindness and courtesy, I swear it. But . . ."

"I feel as though you see me for who I am, not for what you expect me to be." Before he could reply, she was sitting next to him, nearly on his lap again, with her skirts crowding around his legs. "This," she whispered, "this is what you make me feel."

She touched her lips to his. It could have been a brush of air across his mouth, so light and delicate was her kiss. The warmth of her lips, her mouth, radiated through him, sending electric bolts along his nerves. He shivered. All the delicate sweetness of her assaulted him, and he wallowed in it, afraid to breathe, afraid to move, lest she stop touching him.

She sat back and stared up at him.

"Despite myself, I trust you, regardless of what your position requires and what your world expects of you. I trust you enough to place myself in your hands, even though I know I should not."

Unable to speak, he stared back at her, mesmerized by the play of the light on her face. So he did what seemed most natural. He leaned down and met her lips again.

This time, something seemed to come apart between them. A gate opened. Perhaps a bonfire ignited. The moment their lips touched, the kiss exploded into something ravenous, something barely civilized. Where this intensity came from, he had no idea. And he was ill equipped to control it. His hand came up to stroke her cheek, but then it wrapped around to cradle her head, to hold her tight to him. The warmth he'd felt from her burst into a white-hot flame that concentrated in his chest and swiftly spread lower.

She gasped and leaned into him; he wrapped his arms around her and pulled her against him hard. He deepened the kiss, ever mindful of the slightest sign of her withdrawal or resistance. But there was none. She opened her mouth to him, her mouth exploring as his did. He almost couldn't breathe with the wonder and fierceness of the moment.

The carriage stopped.

Immediately, she drew away. Tense and flustered, she touched her lips gingerly, which made him want to pull her to him again. Her body heaved as she tried to calm her breathing. He was breathing rather hard himself.

They had arrived at the Jade Garden. A melee of guilt and responsibility stomped and crashed upon that heat in his chest. He could have no respectable intentions toward Miss Sumaki. What were the odds that her Mr. Broek would not notice she'd been quite thoroughly kissed? What risk had he just placed upon her, after so vehemently saying he would protect her? There was no other choice. Upon his honor, he had to accompany her into the Jade Garden and somehow placate her employer and extricate himself without demeaning Miss Sumaki in the process. She thought he had a facile way with language; this would be a fine test.

CHAPTER 12

An Overture

The rain had eased to a fine drizzle. He helped her down from the carriage and made to follow her, but she turned on the walk and swept a deep curtsy before him. A deeply dismissive curtsy. One as masterful as those his mother wielded when she encountered someone distasteful at a ball. Hanako's abrupt shift in demeanor froze his insides as a nasty thought hit him. Was the kiss they shared authentic affection? Or was it just gratitude? Worse yet, was it business? As the memory of her soft lips resurfaced, doubt surged through him. He wanted to believe her, but tendrils of insecurity wove through his brain. She could slip into so many characters. How difficult could it be for her to act the seductive innocent? He could not trust his impressions, could not trust her.

"You have been so kind, Lord Ridgemont. I do not wish to take any more of your valuable time."

Her distant propriety did not bode well.

"I should see you safely to your door, Miss Sumaki. It would be no trouble."

Her expression clouded as she shook her head once, firmly and clearly. Then the remote facade returned.

"I have already delayed too long. Mr. Broek does not need to know I have caused you such inconvenience. He would wish to repay you in some way, I am sure."

"Then this would be an opportune time for me to speak with him about the legal papers for the Exhibition. Would it not?"

She glanced toward the house, her brow furrowed. He half-expected her to bolt toward the door.

"If he is not already expecting you, then, no, it would not be a good time. I will speak with him about arranging an appointment at your office, but he is not fond of impromptu visitors." She said this last part slowly, reluctantly. Her demeanor finally crystallized. She was terrified of Mr. Broek, of what he would do if she displeased him, perhaps even of what he might do if caught by surprise. *This is not your place, Skyler. Leave off now. You will only get her into deeper trouble.* The words in his head were firm but unconvincing. She looked small and vulnerable, so unlike the woman she showed the world, and he would not—*would not*—leave her on the sidewalk. His presence might cause Broek some discomfort, but the man could not possibly do her harm in a stranger's presence. No man would be so base and dishonorable.

"I assure you, my visit will be brief and easy. Mr. Broek and I shall arrange a meeting and avoid all the fuss of intermediate correspondence. Now, please allow me." He offered her his arm.

To his shock, after only a moment's hesitation, she took it. Quite the mimic, she placed her hand upon his arm and proceeded to the door with the stateliness of a duchess—a tiny, perfect doll of a duchess.

He was surprised no footman appeared when they entered. These days, many businessmen who maintained households relied on at least a footman, if only for the sake of appearances. New wealth had many such forms of display.

As Miss Sumaki led him through the house, that timidity returned. While externally she appeared to move with purpose, her inner personality was smothered. He had the impression of a wounded feline curling itself up in a corner. This was not the Hanako he knew, and the change infuriated him. She spoke only minimally, just enough to be polite, as they made their way to the second floor, and she guided him to a closed door and then asked him for his card to give to Mr. Broek. When he dug into his waistcoat pocket for one, he caught the movement of her eyes. They followed his hand as it slid along his torso. It was the first sign of her he'd seen since the carriage—not desire, just a lively alertness. It was enough to give him hope that she was who he believed her to be.

"Please wait here, my lord."

He nodded, but she'd already disappeared into the room, shutting the door firmly behind her. Indistinct voices carried through the wall. Would it be ungentlemanly to rest his ear against the door for better sound? A vision of himself and Devin as children spying at his father's office door caught him. Of course it would. Ridiculous.

When the door opened, Mr. Broek stood in the doorway looking like a proud papa.

"Lord Ridgemont, what a pleasant surprise. It is an honor to have you in my home." The man extended a hand, and he had no choice but to shake it. At least it wasn't an embrace or the salute so popular with some Europeans. Mr. Broek ushered him into the office and gestured to a chair by the desk. "Please, sit. I shall have the cook send up some refreshments."

"By no means, Mr. Broek. Your hospitality is appreciated, but I have no wish to interrupt your day. I was simply in the neighborhood and thought it would be an opportune time to set up a meeting."

"A meeting to set up a meeting? How clever and amusing you Englishmen are. Why wait? My schedule is open right now, which is rare, so we may confer immediately, if that is amenable to you."

At his nod, Broek asked, "How did you happen to be in this area today? Other business?"

"No. When I left the Exhibition this afternoon, the skies opened with biblical proportions. I happened to notice Miss Sumaki picking her way through the muck and traffic on foot. It seemed only proper to offer her safe transport."

"You are too kind, Lord Ridgemont. You must allow me to do you a kindness in return for your inconvenience."

"Think nothing of it. Obviously, the detour gave me this excellent opportunity to get your contract in order for the Exhibition. Do you have the standard form I sent a few days ago?"

"Ah, yes, it is here somewhere." Broek ambled around his desk to rummage in one drawer after another. Finally, Hanako's employer slid a familiar-looking document across the desk at him and pointed at some notes in the margins as he said, "I wish to suggest some additional changes. Only minor revisions."

Minor revisions. Those minor changes required more than an hour of debate before both parties could agree. The tea delivered by the cook, apparently also doubling as the housekeeper and the only servant of the house, had grown cold before they were halfway through the contract. Still, it was now signed. Finally.

"You have no doubt had a long and trying day, exacerbated by this unexpected business. I urge you to avail yourself of the Jade Garden's therapeutic services. Many men of your station find the exotic delights of the Orient refreshing, sometimes liberating, sometimes perhaps even mystical. I would be pleased to arrange a session sure to leave you relaxed and rejuvenated."

Broek's oily manner made his skin crawl. He said nothing incriminating, but then he wouldn't, would he? A shrewd pimp targeting the upper crust would hardly be crude and obvious about immoral behavior. Yet the way he spoke suggested a world of experience darker and more erotic than the words themselves denoted.

"What exactly do you mean by *therapeutic services*? Forgive my ignorance, but I am unaware of the Eastern practices to which you refer."

Of course, this coarse oaf couldn't know his bone-deep distaste for bawdy houses. Whenever such temptations of the flesh struck, a vision of Reginald came unbidden to do battle with them. The quicksilver mood. The sores. The wasting away. The incontinence. By all accounts, Reggie's decline had been swift, unusually so even for such a terrible disease. By the end, most of their Harrow chums had written him off as "that poor soul." During that last awful month, even he had visited his dear friend only once.

And nothing—no one—would tempt him to take such a stupid risk with his own body or mind. Had he misread Miss Sumaki so severely? Impossible that she could be a whore, a cheap trick finely packaged in distant respectability. He was torn. He needed to find out more about Broek's operations. Yet what if it proved his worst suspicions? What if she proved the worst of his fears? Resolution tested and found strong, he accepted Broek's offer . . . but with a warning shot.

"Nothing at all base or untoward, my lord, I assure you. This is no brothel. Easterners believe in the oneness of the physical body and the ephemeral spirit. Miss Sumaki has some lovely traveling companions who are learned in these spiritual arts. The most commonly requested treatment is a medicinal massage, which has been highly praised by clients, some of whom have reported miraculous alleviation of pain and ailments."

"The appeal is undeniable, but it would not do for me to accept any form of remuneration as a member of the Royal Society. You must understand."

"If you wish to avoid any semblance of impropriety, you are welcome to pay a nominal fee. Truly, customers have heaped praises on the Jade Garden masseuses."

Companions. Now he called them masseuses.

"Are these members of your house employees? Are they part of your troupe at the Exhibition?"

"Not precisely, no. They are neither employees nor in any way affiliated with the Great Exhibition. I am sure it must seem odd to an outsider, so I will explain as best I can." He sat back in his chair, tipping until his head leaned against the wall behind him. "I have been Miss Sumaki's guardian for several years. In our travels, she has befriended women who wanted the opportunity to see the world but needed protection. When I learned of their therapeutic skills, a business arrangement seemed the perfect solution. Their services provide for their own keeping, and my trade facilitates the group's travel. If one of the women takes a liking to a town we're visiting or wishes to return home, she is welcome to go her own way. They are not employees per se, and they are most certainly not obligated to me."

"That is . . . unusual. Your generosity cannot be denied. I assume it goes without saying that your staff is professional and entirely irreproachable. As the Royal Commission's contract makes clear, performing companies must be law-abiding and respectable. Thus far, your star performer appears to be admirably ladylike."

"Miss Sumaki is a prize beyond measure. She has many talents. If you wish, I can arrange for her to serve you. Eastern massage may seem rather unconventional to Western sensibilities because it involves the contact of bare skin, but it is very commonly practiced in the East with many beneficial effects. And Hanako has talented hands."

His throat seized. Somehow it hadn't occurred to him that she might actually participate in the Jade Garden's activities. Could the house be as innocent as Broek claimed? He should leave now. The image of her, wrapped in red silk, her hair falling loosely around her as her hands slid along his body, was far from soothing. After the fleeting kisses in the carriage, he would not be able to withstand her hands on him. A surge of passion and some other dark emotion flowed through him. He stood to break the spell.

"I would not impose upon Miss Sumaki. I understand she performs at the Exhibition daily now, and her work there must keep her busy indeed. Your kindness is much appreciated, but I should be on my way."

Broek did not seem deterred. Or fooled.

"Hanako is a consummate professional. Well practiced, I would say. A brief demonstration of Eastern massage would not be especially taxing for her."

He should refuse. He should leave now. But the vision of her, the idea of her so near, so close and accessible . . . he was only a man, after all.

"If you are certain she would be amenable to such a performance . . ."

"I assure you, she would be pleased to serve you," Broek responded firmly.

CHAPTER 13

An Interlude

"Good evening, Lord Ridgemont. I had not thought to see you again so soon." A chill went through her as she stumbled through her greeting. Her disappointment surprised her. She had not perceived him to be the type of man who would engage the Jade Garden's services. When she left him in Mr. Broek's office, she followed her boss's implicit instructions to prepare a massage room, but she never thought he would actually accept. Then, when her bell was the one Broek rang . . . well, that sparked a riot of internal responses: hot and cold, elation and disgust. Now her hands trembled; she pressed them together as she bowed to him and then tucked them in her voluminous sleeves.

Lord Ridgemont entered the chamber slowly, stiffly, almost as if he had to force his body forward by sheer will. Yet his elegant splendor was magnificent to behold. She hadn't had such an opportunity to examine him closely earlier in the day, had instead kept her eyes averted decorously, except when he insisted she face him. The fitted coat, the finely embroidered waistcoat—they spoke of quality and stature. Appearances were deceptive. He could have his choice of ladies, proper or improper. All the times she'd seen him at the Exhibition, she couldn't fail to notice the finely dressed women who eyed him, whether demure maidens who fluttered by him or flamboyant hoydens who steered their chaperones to greet him. How could he be here? Given that Broek gave her this assignment, Lord Ridgemont might not know just how ill the repute of the Jade Garden truly was. She needed to discover how much he knew, how much he expected of her. After their last encounter, this would be a delicate matter.

"And to you, Miss Sumaki." He bowed as if he was in a parlor or public tearoom, not in the bedroom of a pleasure house facing the woman whose attentions he'd just purchased. If he saw her judgment, his expression did not register it. He fiddled with the buttons on his coat sleeve. She took no little comfort in his awkward demeanor; he seemed as nervous and uncomfortable about this moment as she was. She hadn't had many clients—Broek limited her exposure to maintain her value—and yet they'd all been eager, hungry, which was why the rules were so important.

"I assume Mr. Broek has made clear the limits of my activities here." Make the client comfortable. Just another customer. She'd done this before and could do so now. She made herself move toward him, forced a welcoming expression.

He took a step farther into the room and nodded curtly. "He spoke highly of your Eastern relaxation techniques. If your testimonials are to be believed, your hands have medicinal properties." His cheeks turned a bright pink as he added, "And that is entirely my purpose here. He made clear that the Jade Garden is not at all disreputable, and that none of the ladies here should be treated as such."

Good. He knew the limits. It was almost endearing to see his reluctance, contrasting sharply with the avaricious lust and frustration clients brought with them after discussing terms with Mr. Broek.

"Very good," she replied, hoping her tone conveyed efficiency and professionalism. "Medicinal is an exaggeration, I am sure, but I do believe in the therapeutic effects of Eastern massage. I assume he also explained the rules?" His flushed face plucked at a heartstring, and she pitched her voice lower. "I hope you understand I must have explicit confirmation that you accept and abide by the rules of this establishment, the letter and not just the spirit of the house's laws."

Again, he nodded, avoiding her eyes, looking at something over her shoulder, perhaps a lamp or the wallpaper. Yet his nostrils flared as he took a breath, and resolve settled over his features. Resolve and a burgeoning question.

"I am not to touch you. I am to follow your directions exactly. I cannot request additional services from you. If I do anything that displeases you or violates the rules of the house, there is a guard waiting outside to evict me. If I were evicted, I would be banned as a client."

Impressed by his exact recitation, she nodded but realized he wasn't looking at her. Instead, he'd caught sight of the pallet on which he would lie. It seemed impossible that he could grow more discomfited, and yet everything about his posture, his expression, the tilt of his head said he did not want this.

"You understand perfectly," she said softly.

Finally, he looked at her, his eyes meeting hers fully, honestly. He shook his head. "I understand nothing. My presence here is a mystery to me, and I do not even fully understand what *here* means at this point."

She nodded and gestured around the room. "The rumors surrounding Eastern massage techniques tend to veer toward the lascivious. Some Europeans, even some of your fellow Englishmen, make nasty assumptions, but I can assure you that it is a respectable practice without any erotic overtones. In fact, it carries the potential to be a highly spiritual practice, reconnecting a disharmonious mind, body, and spirit."

He nodded but appeared unconvinced, his cheeks reddening anew at the word *erotic*.

"We will do nothing that makes you feel at all uncomfortable. At any point, you may call a halt, and you will be free to leave. In return, I must point out that the rather large Mr. Smith, now stationed outside the door, will be listening carefully. If I call out an alarm, he will be at my side sooner than immediately."

"And I will be tossed out on my ear. Yes, I understand."

"Oh, no, Lord Ridgemont. Mr. Smith believes in punishment as deterrence. He would make you regret your behavior and, if sufficiently affronted, make you regret being born."

To his credit, he did not flinch. He held her gaze and walked toward her. Now she felt a wave of discomfort. This would happen. She retreated to the low bureau in a corner of the room to light some warming candles.

"Mr. Broek has no doubt informed you of basic elements of the massage process. You may go behind that screen to disrobe," she said in as businesslike a tone as she could muster, as if the thought of him disrobing didn't send an unwelcome bolt of heat through her. "As you can see, there is a robe hanging from the screen that you may use."

As soon as he was behind it, she let out a silent exhalation.

"When you are ready," she continued, "please lie down on the pallet and cover yourself with the sheet there. I will give you privacy for this. There is a bell next to the pillow. Ring when you are prepared for me to return." She hurried from the room to wait, pressing her hands tightly together in front of her to keep them from trembling, whether from fear or from desire she could not tell.

The fire in the hearth made the room quite warm, presumably to keep an unclothed client comfortable. Yet he could not stop shivering. His conversation with Mr. Broek had been exceedingly explicit about what was allowed and what was forbidden. He'd gotten the unwelcome sense, however, that even the forbidden was negotiable for a price. "If Miss Sumaki does not perform to your liking, her companions are very talented and eager to please, given the proper motivation," Broek had said. What was that supposed to mean? Bile rose in his throat. Even during the negotiation, he hadn't truly expected Miss Sumaki would be his, his . . . What term would fit her role? He couldn't even complete the thought. He would rather cut off his own arm than offend her, yet here he lay. Naked. Could he go through with this?

Truly, he'd spoken with her employer out of guilt, out of a duty to make sure escorting her home did not cause concern. The contract arrangements served as a convenient excuse. He'd intended to leave immediately after business had been concluded, sure that Miss Sumaki was safe. When Mr. Broek spoke of the Jade Garden's services, he'd been intrigued but dismayed. If Broek had stated outright any depraved or bawdy behaviors, he would have left immediately, would have had Broek and his prostitutes banned from the

Exhibition. But the man was a master of suggestion and implication.

He could not associate Miss Sumaki with the notion of depravity or with such actions. Even now, the idea of her touching his bare skin made him dizzy with a combination of lust, fear, and a smidgen of horror. If she were a British maiden, such contact would never be allowed.

Yet when she first welcomed him into the room, she retained an air of virtue and dignity.

And, dear God, the small confines of the room drove his tension higher. With the memory of their kiss fresh in his mind, a desperate awareness rushed through him as he lay on the pallet and pulled the light sheet over him. His mind drifted to thoughts of her hands on him. He craved her touch, and his cock rose as it sought her attention. *Not now!* The soft slide of the sheet over his skin only exacerbated the situation. *Show some self-control, you bounder.* She wouldn't be able to miss how the fabric tented so obviously.

He tried to lie on his stomach but found it too painful with his erection. So he rolled onto his back and thought of droning Latin lectures at Eton. Perhaps he could quell his physical reaction with unpleasant thoughts. No success. Or the physics lectures at Oxford that had so deeply inspired him. No success there either. So he bent his knees under the sheet, unsure of what he would do once she actually touched him, and rang the small bell she'd indicated.

The door opened with a whisper of grinding hinges. Focusing on a patch of ceiling, he heard the swish of her clothing, the muted clanking of glass bottles, and his own ragged breathing.

"I must admit," he said, to break the oppressive silence, "thus far I do not understand how this could be a method of relaxation."

"No," she replied. More clanking of glass. "It is an unusual and exceedingly strange situation, especially given British propriety. I imagine you must be feeling a bit improper, even a bit vulnerable." There was a hint of warmth in her voice that drew him, but when he looked, she had her back turned, blocking the sight of whatever she was doing to prepare.

"Do you enjoy making customers feel vulnerable?" The question slipped from him, shocking them both. She whirled, glaring at him, her eyes narrowed. Warmth evaporated.

"What do you know of vulnerability?" She crossed to the fireplace and placed a thick porcelain bowl as close to the fire as she could.

"Miss Sumaki, I lay here unclothed." His voice caught. In his discomfort, he almost missed that she'd frozen, too. Her hesitation reassured him that he wasn't the only one floundering through this encounter. But he needed to know why. "Not only am I weaponless, but I have no protection in any form. I am utterly defenseless. You could do anything to me." She took a half step back. "Yet if I were to transgress against you in the slightest, I know punishment would follow."

"You are far from defenseless, sir." She shuttered her expression and strode back to the table. There she gathered two bottles and some linens. "You have the physical advantage, even if you would not choose to use it. You have social advantage, even if you do not emphasize it. You have political advantage, even if you do not acknowledge it. Your frown suggests you disagree, but I am simply stating facts. In this room, and out, you have all the advantages, all the protections of being a man of status."

He schooled his expression. At least the drift of their conversation had cooled his body's uproar. The calming effect was shattered when she knelt beside the pallet.

"Why do you do this?" he blurted. Perhaps it was the bluntness of the conversation or the imposed intimacy of the moment, but he needed to know her reasoning.

"This is part of my job, part of earning my keep." She poured an aromatic liquid into her palm and rubbed her hands together. "My hands might feel a bit chilled at first."

He looked back up at the ceiling, frustrated on multiple levels.

"You should breathe," she said.

"I did not realize I had stopped."

"Do not be nervous. This is meant to be soothing, to loosen your muscles and open your mind."

"Open my mind to what?"

"To the oneness of the universe, I suppose."

With that, she gently stroked his forearm, both of her hands smoothing over his skin, almost petting. Her hands continued their long strokes as they moved up his arm to his shoulder. The sensations paradoxically lulled and excited him, his body unsure what to make of such contact.

"Stop thinking," she said softly.

Impossible.

"I am not sure I can," he admitted.

She lifted her hands and sat back.

"Close your eyes and take a deep breath, then let it out completely." When he complied, she continued, "Now keep taking deep breaths and focus on your breathing. Focus on the filling and the emptying, slow and steady. Let the rest of the world fall away."

"But that's impossible. It cannot just go away."

"It will be there. The world will keep for a few moments. You will be surprised at how the world survives without your mind working for an hour. Now breathe."

He breathed. At first, it felt inane, but then everything went quiet. He heard the tiny crackling of the logs in the fire, heard and felt the steady movement of air in and out of his body, felt the softness of the linens around him contrasted by the underlying hardness of the wooden bed.

"Better." She hadn't stated it as a question, but he answered as if she had.

"Yes, I would not have expected something as simple as breathing could . . . could . . ."

"Give you a handful of peace?"

"Exactly."

He opened his eyes. She was smiling. Warm pleasure coursed through him. He took a few more deep breaths, felt the thin mattress cradle him more fully as he let himself relax. Then her next words cut through his calm.

"If you are comfortable, I am going to resume massaging you now. I should have explained before. My first pass is to unclench your muscles gently. This will facilitate a second pass that probes into your muscles more deeply in order to increase the flow of your spirit. Is that acceptable?"

He swallowed, and her eyes tracked the movement of his throat. Then he nodded.

As she leaned forward, looming over him, he shut his eyes again to brace himself for her touch. He expected the airy brush of her fingertips. But, no, she would not be so tentative. Her hands slid along his shoulders, stroking gently but firmly from the base of his neck outward along his collarbone. Warm. Soothing, yet not. His skin tingled in her wake. Other parts of him tingled as well. *Think of England, man, think of England.*

Her shiver startled him. He heard it in her breathing and felt it in her arms.

"Is something wrong?" he asked.

"Not at all," she said, without meeting his eyes. Her hands still moved over him, but she seemed to be contracting into herself, almost as if she couldn't bear what she was doing. Guilt stabbed at his chest.

"You do not need to proceed, Miss Sumaki. If you are at all uncomfortable, we can consider this sufficient."

She shook her head, which seemed to refresh her demeanor.

"Are you enjoying this, Lord Ridgemont? Is it pleasant for you? Relaxing?"

"Well, yes, but it does not appear so for you."

"Make no mistake, my lord," she said quietly. Her entire body appeared tightly wound. "This is not a social interaction. A physician does not need to enjoy the practice of medicine or even the company of a particular patient in order to treat that patient successfully."

"Ouch." What she said stung, but she'd also scratched the sensitive skin of his inner arm. Her hands stopped, and she whispered an apology. He continued, "That may be true, but such patients are usually in immediate need of care. Your ministrations, sweet as they are, would qualify as a luxury rather than a necessity. You need not do anything that is distasteful to you."

"Your consideration is appreciated, but this is my duty." Before he could object, she raised a hand to his lips, and a hint of oiliness slipped into his mouth. "Perhaps it would be best for you to lie on your stomach. I can work on your back, which tends to be where the worst tension resides."

Her look, distant yet beseeching, convinced him. Something else, too, lurked in her gaze, an emotion he couldn't decipher, except that it sparked something in his gut. He had no desire for her to stop touching him, and he had given her ample opportunity to retreat. If she chose not to, neither would he. He nodded, and she straightened to stand. Without further discussion, she moved behind the screen while he repositioned himself. The warmth of the room struck him again, and a slight sweat broke out on his back and neck. At least now he could lie on his stomach without embarrassing discomfort. He swiped the sheet over himself to dry the unseemly moisture before calling her back. This time, with his face turned toward the fire, he shut his eyes as he heard her kneel next to him and pick up the oil bottle again.

"Just breathe," she instructed. So simple. So that was what he did. This time he didn't flinch when her hands brushed his skin. As they swept along his shoulder blades, his arms, his vertebrae, he just breathed. The subtly sweet scent of the oil reached into the darkness behind his eyes, twined through his senses. He could almost forget whose hands were stroking him and simply fall into the sensation of warm, soothing human contact. Almost. A half-formed question nagged at him.

"Stop thinking," she said, startling him as she removed her hands.

"What?" The loss of her touch felt like a physical blow.

"You were loosening up, almost serene, I think. And then you inhaled sharply and tensed, so much so that your back muscles lifted."

"It is far too quiet," he said abruptly.

"The silence is intended to be soothing. Most especially, in the chaos of these city streets, this is one moment of peace and silence," she explained. "But not everyone easily adjusts to the calm. Some people are so trained to noise and activity that they find the quiet . . . foreign."

"Yes," he replied. "I am so glad you understand." If only he could see her face. Was she smiling, or did she think him unreasonable? "Could you perhaps talk with me? I could use the distraction from my own thoughts."

"Ah. One of the pitfalls. Abrupt silence gives us no place to hide from our demons. Unfortunately, I must admit that talking aloud draws too much energy and attention from my task."

Her task. Was he really just another job for her? He could not bring himself to ask. Before he arranged his thoughts enough to say something innocuous, she offered a compromise.

"I could, however, sing to you, or perhaps hum. I know some children's songs that are easily sung without distracting me. Would that be enough to ease your mind, do you think?"

"That would be lovely." It would certainly be better than the sounds of her hands, of her breathing, of her clothing brushing against the bed.

She began to hum an unfamiliar tune as her hands again moved slowly down his back, gently at first and then retracing their path more firmly. Again, his tension ebbed gradually, and he felt himself sinking into the mat. Then her hands began kneading his back muscles with increasing intensity, and he could not hold back a groan.

"Am I hurting you?" she asked, oddly breathless, as her movements stopped.

"No," he said, struggling not to moan as he said it. "Far from it." He could not bring himself to say more. He certainly could not give voice to the heat that swept through his body as her fingers worked along his spine, nor give her any hint that he pictured her hands working him so firmly elsewhere. Yet she—thank goodness!—did not press him further. She continued to move down his body, rearranging the sheet draping him as needed. As her hands moved skillfully, he suffered a paradox of muscles loosening in some places and tightening in others. When she reached his waist, his thighs tensed. As she gradually moved lower, everything but the area she was attending went taut. His hands dug awkwardly into the mat beneath him. It was almost a certainty that he would embarrass himself if she continued.

"Miss Sumaki," he whispered. "I beg you to give me a moment's respite."

Her hands paused and rested lightly on his bare thighs, the warmth of her skin burning into his muscles.

Dear God in heaven. He was so close, so terribly close. "I am deeply sorry," he said, trying to maintain some semblance of dignity, "but I cannot allow you to continue."

She lifted her hands immediately, but being deprived of her touch only made his desire flare brilliantly, painfully.

"Have I displeased you?" Her voice was hesitant, suspiciously tremulous and small, as if the thought of displeasure caused her distress all out of proportion with the actual moment.

He didn't dare reveal the source of his discomfort. As unorthodox as this encounter might be, one simply didn't discuss male completion with a woman, at least not a good woman. He would not insult Miss Sumaki with such coarseness.

"Not at all, Miss Sumaki. Quite the opposite. Your ministrations have been quite soothing."

"Yet you seem more agitated now than when you arrived."

"I am . . . preoccupied."

"Please. Allow me to finish. I believe you will find the results very pleasant and calming."

He would be finished if she touched him again. Her shifting expressions troubled him, though. She worried her lower lip with her teeth. Warmth and fear warred in her eyes.

"You have pleased me, Miss Sumaki, more than enough."

She shook her head and refocused on him in a way that made his pulse—and his cock—jump. He adjusted the sheet to make sure it masked his bodily reactions and added, "I have taken enough of your time and should leave."

"Please wait," she repeated, her tone more commanding, the timbre vibrating through him. When he looked at her, her gaze moved quite obviously, quite deliberately, to the sensitive area he was trying so much to hide. "I wish it."

The simple statement disarmed him. It shouldn't have, he knew. He should have been stronger. But he sensed the stark honesty of her statement—she did not wish for anything for herself. Until now.

Lying back, he gave himself up to the enchanting bliss of her touch. She made no indecent ventures under the sheet. She didn't need to. As her hands roved over him, softly, and then again more firmly, his body responded more heatedly. One could categorize the endless tension as a form of torture. And when she'd finished with his calves and his feet, when almost all of his muscles felt loose and fluid, her touch again at the nape of his neck was astoundingly soft. And warm. And moist. Only when she moved lower, softly kissing along his spine, did he realize she'd begun using her mouth instead of her hands. No one had ever touched him like this. Before she reached the base of his spine, the sensations built sharply, overwhelmingly. Dear God. Hot pleasure shot through him, and he groaned as he spent himself on the bedding.

She left his side and shuffled to the fireplace. When she returned, a heavy warmth enveloped him—more linens.

"These damp cloths should continue to help relax your muscles and ease your tension. Once they have cooled, you are welcome to dress, and Mr. Smith will show you the way out."

"Forgive me, Miss Sumaki, if I have embarrassed you. I am mortified by my body's behavior."

"You have nothing to apologize for. Call me Hana—Hanako."

The odd tone of her voice made him turn to face her. Her hand was on the doorknob, but she leaned against the wall next to it as if exhausted. Her posture was at odds with the desire flaring in her eyes. He'd been satisfied in more ways than one, but she had not. And, for the second time that day, she allowed him to see her raw emotion. His heart stopped.

"Please remember this one thing," she added. "Remember that, no matter what you may hear about me or about this place, I wanted this—wanted you—and only you."

CHAPTER 14

A Change of Plans

"Hana, blossom, you should set these pieces aside until you can give them the attention they require," Tsubaki-san said gently while taking needlework from her numb fingers. The eldest of the Jade ladies, a quiet little woman, was the closest thing the Jade Garden had to a housekeeper. And a cook. And she was the most skilled with needle and thread, so she oversaw all their work on clothing and other items needed by the household. Occasionally, Mr. Broek accepted special orders for embroidered silk and linen to be used for gowns and tablecloths and other finery. The delicate linen handkerchief Tsubaki took from her was starting to fray at the corner, so severely had she butchered the fabric, reworking the same area over and over.

She kept thinking that she should feel shame and remorse about what she'd done with Skyler, or rather *to* Skyler, about how she'd so clearly moved him in spite of his own intentions. She shouldn't feel intimacy or pleasure or a desire to repeat the event. Between his declaration that he wanted to protect her and his obvious physical attraction to her, she craved more of his attention, more of his presence—which was absolutely something she should *not* feel.

"Yes, Hana dear," Bana-san called from the far corner where she was sewing. Her voice carried so easily. "With your mind so far from earth, you may expect those silks to float around you if you let them go. Alas, they would crash to the ground instead and leave a terrible mess for the rest of us."

The women all chuckled as she felt her face warming. It was fortunate Takara had already gone upstairs to bed. Her embarrassment was overtaken by the truth of their *terrible mess*. The women presented such a composed and unflappable mask when dealing with all that Broek required of them. How they withstood the cheap use of their bodies—when Broek took all the profits, claiming they covered living expenses!—she could not comprehend. Only Yuki still cried sometimes; a pale, delicate young bud of a woman, she was the last one Broek had recruited along the way . . . in Canton, or was it Shanghai? And Ume truly seemed to enjoy her assignments. True, Tsubaki and Bana had been trained as *oiran*, their obedience and acquiescence bred into them long ago, when their families sold them to the pleasure house. She almost wished for that same stoic distancing of their spirit from their performances; such mental skill would serve them well in the days ahead.

These days, Broek made a point of reminding Hana every morning that the auction would be soon, that she and her sister would be in the keeping of a new master *very soon*. Only the gods knew what, if any, restrictions Broek actually placed on the bids—she had no voice in any of it. Even her insistence that Takara go with her when the auction ended held no true weight. She had one measure of control, one expensive and well-hidden measure hidden away that she'd managed to procure at the pharmacy. She would, without doubt and without hesitation, take both their lives before allowing her sister to be ripped from her and subjected to unforeseen degradation and abuse. Picturing the well-wrapped vials tucked under her mattress brought her an ironic sense of calm. She did not have enough arsenic to share with all of the women. If the worst came to pass, she had to see to Takara first. If she could, she would kill anyone who hurt her sister, and Mr. Broek would be first on her list. As unlikely as it would be for her to have such an opportunity for justice, she would not allow her sister to suffer. How could anyone be expected to make such decisions?

"Would you like to share with us what has you so distracted?" Tsubaki asked, lifting her out of the dark depths of her thoughts. The dear woman's hand swept like a dove's wing along her hair, and she had the urge to lean in, to accept the comfort. The usually pleasant matron looked weary and surprisingly gaunt.

"Nothing," she replied. "Perhaps I am just a bit tired."

She could not speak of these things. Her thoughts were a betrayal of them all. And if she focused instead on what had transpired with Lord Ridgemont, how could she explain her chaotic reactions when she could not understand them herself? How could she put into words the sensations that shifted and swirled and inverted themselves from one moment to the next? Guilt. Fear. And still . . . that keen desire to bring him pleasure, growing more intense as she teased him closer and closer to his peak, still made her feel dizzy with power and longing. The sensation of his skin under her hands still made her ache. His welcoming, accepting attitude still stirred an even deeper desire within, one she could barely acknowledge.

Bana laughed as she rearranged her hair yet again. She insisted on tying it in a large knot and securing it with sticks only to have it come loose whenever she moved too quickly. "It isn't a what, Tsubaki. It's a who! Look at her face." The woman hooted. "But we know you cannot be tired for the reasons we would normally suspect." They knew of Broek's plans for her, for her innocence. They were in no more of a position to object than she was. Better to let the conversation sway toward pleasure, as uneasy as it might be, than to dwell on . . .

"Earlier today, I saw Broek talking in his office with a very beautiful man, tall and dashing, broad-shouldered and expensively dressed," Ume interjected. Of all the Jade ladies, she had the greatest appetite for her clientele. On the rare occasions Broek took his own pleasure at the Jade Garden, she was his choice; she was least likely to try to strangle him in an unguarded moment. Hana both admired and feared her for her exuberance. "I don't think attending to his needs would be a hardship," the girl added, her eyes bright. "Were you assigned to him, Hana?"

"You know I do not discuss my assignments." She frowned at

the younger woman, but her disapproval never seemed to make any impact.

"Perhaps it is time you started," Tsubaki said more encouragingly, wrapping an arm around her. "You do look out of sorts. Your mind is so clearly elsewhere, and it is not like you."

"Nothing happened!" she blurted. "I performed the usual medicinal massage! That is all!" Yet his stifled groan echoed in her ears. His back muscles had tightened under her lips before his body shuddered. The faint taste of oil lingered in her mouth. The sensations filled her brain.

"That is not all, Sumaki-san!" Ume retorted. The girl sauntered across the room, her hips swaying with each step. "We can tell by the look on your face! And we know—of all women, we know—that there is much a man and woman can do and still leave her intact, as Broek expects you to remain."

They knew such things, but she didn't. Tsubaki was the one who had first explained the ways to bring a man to fruition with one's hands, and what bringing him even meant. She had no interest in learning more or doing more with random visitors. The Jade ladies knew Broek's expectations for her were different, knew he set stricter rules regarding her. She was the lucky one. And what an awful world they lived in that she was the lucky one, knowing he would at least protect her until he received a satisfactory offer. She would only have to deal with the sexual overtures of one man, not the parade of men who visited the Jade Garden night after night. Her thoughts slid back to Lord Ridgemont. If he could be that one man . . .

Ume kept poking at her with intrusive questions and lewd suggestions, ignoring Tsubaki's warnings and Bana's more insistent scolding. Ume argued, "Sharing a few details would help you to drop some of your inhibitions."

She shook her head and rose to leave. She would rather forgo the company of the elder women than allow herself to be teased and belittled by such a . . . a chit! What a wonderful new word. Chit. Exactly right.

Tsubaki followed her out and up to the cramped bedroom on the top floor, keeping silent throughout the entire trip.

"I do not know what to think, Tsubaki-san!" The words came out in a rush as she started pacing the floor. "It was clear that the massage agitated him more than it soothed him. I tried to maintain distance, to keep the touch as impersonal as possible. But it felt . . . good. In the times I've given massage, it has always, always been a chore, and usually a loathsome chore at that. But his body felt different. So warm and solid. I"—she swallowed—"I wanted to keep doing it, keep touching him. But then his muscles began to tighten, and he shifted on the pallet. It was too much temptation. I wanted to bring him pleasure. And so I did."

Thank the stars that Takara was already asleep in the adjacent room, which was actually a closet but isolated enough from the Jade Garden's pleasure rooms. She could not have said any of this in front of her baby sister.

"*Yokubô?*" Tsubaki whispered. "So powerful, so absolute."

"No, not just lust. *Watashi wa kare o nozomu.* I have never felt desire so strongly, so completely, and never with a man under my hands."

"Desire, attraction, these are natural for the human animal." Tsubaki sat next to her on the bed and draped a comforting arm around her. "Given what fate has in store for us, it is lucky that such desire is fleeting."

"With him, I didn't want it to be fleeting. He didn't do anything to me, and yet I wanted him to. I yearned."

Tsubaki sighed, and an entire expert argument was contained in that sigh. But before she could speak, ominous footfalls thudded up the stairs. The other woman looked at her with concern.

"Hanako!" Broek's surly voice boomed through the door before he wrenched it open. She hoped Takara slept as soundly as usual.

Just inside the doorway, he caught Tsubaki's eye and jerked his head toward the exit. Without a word or a glance at Hanako, she complied. He slammed the door shut immediately and grabbed her arms in a bruising grip. Glaring, he said, in Dutch, in a low, menacing voice, "What exactly did you say to that English upstart from the Royal Commission? What did you do?"

"I did only what you instructed," she replied in a rush. "I performed a medicinal massage, nothing more. Just as I have done all along. Any conversation was related to the occasion." Oh, heaven above, if he knew about her bringing Lord Ridgemont to completion!

"Then why did he ask me so many questions afterward about what happens in this building? About what other services are performed? This is a royal commissioner, and believe me, little flower, if I thought he would welcome the delights of the Jade Garden, I would have made them clear to him from the beginning. But this one is too upstanding, too earnest." His mouth twisted in distaste. He released her abruptly and moved toward the door. Although her first instinct was to rub her arms where he'd gripped her so forcefully that she would likely have bruises in the morning, she knew better than to show him that weakness, knew better than to give him that satisfaction. He already dictated her future and that of her sister and the other women, but she refused to feed into his cruel nature any more than she absolutely had to.

"Nothing unusual happened, Mr. Broek. I swear it."

"You swear it? Quite a serious business, taking an oath. I swore an oath to your father upon his deathbed that I would provide for you and your sister until you could provide for yourselves. I have kept that oath."

At his mention of her father, rage spiked through her. Provide for her and Takara? If her father could see what Broek had reduced them to, how he planned to sell them like any bauble or oddity, the man would have been the last person on earth he trusted with such a responsibility. What sent chills through her was the look of absolute sincerity on Broek's face. *Celestial mother, he believes it all. He has convinced himself that selling us is equal to providing for us.*

But she remembered. The correspondence she'd found from some of the prospective bidders early in their travels to London made clear their less-than-honorable expectations. *So pleased that there are no restrictions regarding elder sister . . . Younger sister would be too burdensome . . . Would have been put off by any marriage requirement.* She shut the other, darker commentaries out of her mind. But the next day, she'd insisted on an addendum that required Takara to remain with her, and that made her exempt of any service to the bidder.

Broek had been infuriated by her demands. He'd accepted her appeal to the welfare of the child, a girl far too young to be subjected to the kinds of lascivious demands a bidder might make— but he'd accepted with his own conditions: her active participation in securing the other women and her performances at the Great Exhibition. To her everlasting shame, she had accepted the terms without hesitation. And she had fulfilled her end of the bargain.

"Given milord's scrutiny, I have decided to move up the auction date," he said in English. "No sense risking discovery while waiting for the conclusion of the Great Exhibition. More than enough suitors have indicated their interest and tossed numbers into the ring that are higher than I anticipated. While you were tending to his lordship's needs, I sent messages out to the top twenty bidders, informing them of the current highest bids for each of you lovelies. I also told them the auction will close in two days' time, the stroke of midnight indicating the end of the second day."

"Two days!" she burst out, the surging panic scattering her thoughts. "You cannot do that! It isn't enough time! No one will be ready!"

He came at her with frightening speed, grabbing her by the chin and forcing her backward until her head ground against the wall. "Not enough time for what, Hanako? Surely it cannot take two days for you and the crones to pack your tiny cases with your pitiful belongings. You may even keep the clothes I have allowed you to wear. Or is it not enough time to say good-bye to your little sister?"

His hand pressing against her chin made it difficult to speak, but she managed to whisper, "You promised she would go with me."

She should have known to brace herself. When the hand on her face lifted, she took a deep breath. The next moment she was sprawled on the floor, and pain covered the side of her face, a sharp pain that made her cry out and then radiated bone-deep through her jaw. She didn't dare look up at him, but he grabbed her hair and twisted his hand, forcing her to witness his fury. He dug something out of his waistcoat pocket and threw it down on the floor in front of her. A small glass vial shattered against the floorboards, and a sickly scent wafted up, making her throat seize. Dizzy, she dropped her aching head to the floor.

"You thought to steal from me? To thwart my plans by dosing yourself and your sister with arsenic? Did you think you would escape me so easily?"

Easily. She closed her eyes and focused on the pain.

"For now, Takara shall go with you as planned. But if you try to steal from me again, if your efforts mar the auction in any way, I shall make sure that Takara not only is separated from you but also goes to the most creative, most licentious, most depraved owner I can find. And I shall be sure to keep you informed of how he makes use of her." He loomed over her as she swallowed a bitter retort. With a cold, heartless smile, he said again, "The auction will be held in two days."

CHAPTER 15

A Claim

When he arrived at the Great Exhibition, Skyler immediately went to the Chinese exhibit to speak with Hanako about their last meeting.

When he lay in bed at night and closed his eyes, he could still feel her fingers sliding over his body, caressing him. Even now, his skin tingled at the thought. And yet, ever since she had slipped out of that room, his memory of her attentions made him twist with guilt and doubt. He needed to speak with her, to find out if she'd felt the same energy, felt the same pull, felt . . . something, anything that would suggest she acted on her own desires and not simply to fulfill expected duties.

But she wasn't in the Chinese alcove. There was no activity and no sign of upcoming performances.

Hours later, she still hadn't appeared. He checked at random intervals, in case the performance schedule had changed without warning. Still nothing. As the day lengthened, his agitation grew. *Stop being ridiculous*, he told himself as he buried himself in the trifles and trials of the Exhibition, fielding complaints from visitors over perceived slights and complaints from exhibitors over . . . perceived slights.

When he reentered the Royal Commission office at the end of the workday, a young clerk hurried to hand him a note.

By a strange twist of fate, now that we have sorted out the legalities and signatures aligning my Jade Flower's performances with your Commission's requirements, circumstances have changed. Effective immediately and for the foreseeable future, my company has ceased performing at the Great Exhibition. The very talented star performer is no longer available. All due regrets for any inconvenience.
Regards,
Mr. Willem Broek

No longer available. Effective immediately.

His mind whirled as he struggled to decipher Broek's message. Every interpretation meant devastating loss. Was she ill? Was she injured? Had she run off with some wealthy visitor to the Jade Garden? Every interpretation sparked a fresh and unexpected rage within him. She belonged with him. She could not simply disappear from his life. From some remote corner of his brain, a voice whispered that he was being irrational, but reason ceased to be a significant factor. He shoved the note into his pocket.

Dusk stretched across the sky as he slipped out of the Crystal Palace. After giving a brief word to his driver, he set off on foot through the park. He simply needed a brisk walk, he told himself. Just some time to think, he told himself. And yet, as he left the park, he knew exactly where he would arrive. When the Jade Garden finally came into view, he slowed. What reason could he give to Mr. Broek for his visit? The fact was that he didn't trust Mr. Broek. He needed to see her, speak with her, directly and without interference.

Who would have thought that he'd actually put those silly lock-picking lessons into practice? He brushed away the fleeting memories of late nights at Eton and friends up to no good. And his impeccable brother's disapproval. No time for that now. A fine sheen of perspiration plastered his shirt to his skin as, tense and alert, he made his way up the servants' stairs. The silence was oppressive and nerve-racking. Had they already abandoned the building? No, the halls were brightly lit.

When he reached the room he remembered, the room where they'd last been together, he heard deep voices coming from the main staircase. Hand on the doorknob, he froze, biting back a curse as he realized he was completely unarmed. Although he could not decipher actual words, he recognized the cadence and intonation of Mr. Broek. The other voice sounded oddly familiar, but then they both receded before he could identify the other man. Releasing the breath he hadn't realized he'd been holding, he became keenly aware of the impossible tension in his shoulders. He rolled his neck and braced himself for whatever he might encounter on the other side of the door.

What he hadn't anticipated was the room's utter transformation. The Spartan pallet he remembered was gone. The austere furnishings had been replaced by a massive bed laden with pillows and draped in soft white fabric. The glimmering sheen of the coverlet implied thick silk. A few candles lit the perimeter of the room, and the scent of wax mixed with a cloying incense. It took a moment for his eyes to adjust from the bright hallway. Clearly, something important was about to transpire here.

A barely perceptible moan from the bed startled him and set his nerve endings tingling with a premonition of familiarity. The bedclothes rippled slightly. Apart from the brief movement, the bed looked freshly made and unoccupied. Only a child could be so swallowed up as to appear invisible in it. Another moan, loud enough for him to recognize that voice without question.

Hanako.

When he pulled back the coverlet, she gasped and looked up at him dreamily. He grabbed the closest candle and stared into her eyes. Dilated pupils. She reached for him languidly, stroking his cheek and then sliding one hand down his throat to his chest. The sensations threatened to drown out his common sense. When he felt her hands grip his upper arms and try to pull him toward her, over her, a painfully sharp awareness of their surroundings and the male voices he'd heard forced him to tamp down his emotions.

"What is wrong, Miss Sumaki?" he asked quietly. "Are you ill? You are not yourself."

She shook her head slowly and rested her cheek against his

hand. He felt, rather than heard, her whisper. When he asked again, she sighed, her warm breath causing his shirt to ripple.

Then she spoke, clear and sad, without looking at him.

"It cannot be you."

The clarity of her words only increased his confusion and alarm.

"What do you mean? Why not?" What on earth was she talking about? Even with her parted lips, wide eyes, and clinging hands transmitting her longing, he couldn't shake a feeling of danger. Her movements were too strange, too imprecise.

"I wish it could be you. I want it to be. Since the first time you kissed me, I have dreamed of you."

At first, a primitive surge of triumph and possessiveness barreled through him. *Since the first time you kissed me, I have dreamed of you.* She twisted in bed, propping her upper body with her elbow but then slipping back down. When he scanned the room, a glass on the low dresser in the corner caught his attention. Had Broek made her intoxicated? Could he have drugged her? What man would want a woman in that condition?

"Miss Sumaki," he said firmly.

Her head jerked up and she looked directly into his eyes for a moment. "I have never felt that before, that need to touch you, that pleasure of bringing *you* pleasure." Then her eyelids fluttered, and her head fell back upon the pillow. She continued, "I must be dreaming right now. You cannot be here in reality. He is coming soon to take what he paid for."

His blood chilled.

"Who, darling? Who is coming? And what exactly has he paid for?" The setting made plain what the transaction involved, but he needed to hear the words, needed to know it was as terrible as it appeared. He needed a name.

"You would call it my innocence or my maidenhead. My virginity." She waved one hand floppily in the air. "Mr. Broek received an offer so high he could not refuse. I would ask you to take me now," she said, as she reached for him again, "just so I could count you as my first, but I would be found out. The gentleman does not trust Mr. Broek." Her head lolled against the pillow as she looked away. "He is handsome, I admit, but he is not you."

She was fading fast. "I am getting you out of here. Now."

"You cannot. We cannot. How did you even manage to sneak in here?"

"That does not matter at the moment. We are leaving."

"No, I cannot!" she burst out, before he touched a finger to her lips to quiet her. When she continued, her voice was so low he only caught bits and pieces. "Broek would be furious . . . *rupture de contrat . . . Verletzung . . .*"

"Selling your virginity is not a contract he has any right to make," he said. His teeth ground together as he suppressed this new spike of fury.

"Of course, it is, silly Skyler," she said, her head lazily bobbing along with her voice, resigned and uneven. "Marriage contracts serve the same purpose, exchanging a woman for something else of value. Land. Prestige. Power."

This was no time for them to get into an ideological debate about marriage. He needed to get her out of this house immediately.

Ransacking a low dresser in the corner, he found a bonnet and a black kimono decorated with cherry blossoms. When he pulled her out of the bed, she slid down to the floor. Only then did he realize she wore only a thin chemise, delicate and elaborately embroidered to draw the eye to specific areas of the body. He swallowed hard and again tamped down a riot of emotions.

Distant voices wafted through the door. With her body practically a dead weight, he pulled her to a seated position, shoved her arms through the sleeves, and hurriedly tied the bonnet on her head. He whispered, "It is time for us to be gone. You must stay silent. Do you understand?"

Her eyes nearly crossed as she tried to focus on him. She nodded jerkily and made as if to stand, but then landed back on the bed, frowning. "Wait," she said. "The others . . ." He pulled her up again, but she shook her head and began mumbling, "I cannot leave Takara . . . must stay . . ."

He stroked her hair with one hand while tilting up her chin with the other. He had no idea who or what Takara was, and there was no time to find out. When her eyes met his, she quieted. He said, "You are not safe here, and I shall not allow you to be harmed, especially not for Broek's profit."

"No, no, no . . ." she whispered, her voice trailing off. Then her head drooped, and she slid to the floor. He lifted her unconscious body in his arms and silently made his way to the back stairs.

"My lord!" Tompkins pitched his voice low, but his tone was shot through with disapproval. "Sir, this is highly improper!" He stood away from the carriage door, his arms tight at his sides.

"Please do open the door, Tompkins. As you can see, my hands are occupied."

"I shall not be a party to whatever this iniquity is."

Damn and blast. Even if Skyler could wrench open the door somehow, he would need help to hold it open and pull down the stairs so he could get her inside. Deep breath. Honesty.

"Time is limited, Tompkins, but here is the situation: this is a rescue. This young lady was in imminent danger. I believe she has been drugged."

Tompkins reached for the latch but stopped and looked at him doubtfully. It was insulting, really.

"Look here: you have known me since I took my first breath. Do you honestly think I would be capable of anything nefarious? Do you honestly think I would do a lady harm? And, really, Tompkins, do you think I would risk making you an accomplice?"

That seemed to convince him. He pulled the door open wide and set down the steps for entry. He even guided the way, protecting her head with his hands.

"Now the question of the moment, my lord, is where do we take her? Honorable as I'm sure your intentions are, she cannot, simply cannot, be housed at the Ridge. Your mother would dismiss the lot of us in disgrace."

He felt, rather than saw, the man frowning in the darkness. Tompkins wasn't wrong. Fireworks, cannon, the explosion of a full armory would be nothing compared to his mother's reaction if word got back to her of such opprobrium. It would likewise be dishonorable of him to put Hanako's standing at risk. Tompkins trusted his motives, but the other servants might have doubts, might make ugly assumptions about her. On top of that, his interest in Miss Sumaki was abundantly clear to Broek. It would be easy enough for him to suspect and come knocking at the Ridge.

Honor. What honor is there in any of this? He shouldn't have to stumble around like a bumbling thief in the darkness to protect an innocent. Only then did he recall his cousin, newly crowned Defender of the Innocents. He would know. Better yet—that woman who'd helped him, the one Lady Devin seemed to adore.

"Take us to Devin House. Lord Devin may have a connection who can assist this poor young woman." Lips pursed, the driver gave a curt nod and shut them inside.

"I need your help, Devin." Every moment she was in public view increased the chance of her being caught. He had no time for pleasantries. "Please, you must come with me immediately."

Thank the heavens for strong blood ties. Without hesitation, Devin gave his footman some instructions and then said, "I am at your service."

When they reached the carriage, Tompkins was still scowling but opened the door as usual. Gesturing for Devin to enter first, Skyler asked, "Any trouble, Tompkins?"

"None, my lord. Your guest still appears to be breathing."

Devin didn't seem to hear the exchange, saying instead, "Ridgemont, I assume this is an emergency, since you would never darken my doorstep at such an—" He froze in midstep. Bracing himself against the carriage, he said without turning, "What in hell is going on here?"

Skyler closed his eyes for a moment, said a quick prayer, and then answered, "She was in grave danger. She is in this insensible state because of her employer. I do not know what it is, but I suspect she has been drugged with laudanum or perhaps a more potent dose of opium. He had terrible plans for her this evening. When I found out, I could not stand idly by and allow her to be harmed. You might say that I am the hero in this scenario."

Devin snorted before climbing the rest of the way into the carriage and sitting across from the prone Miss Sumaki.

"So what do you need me for?"

"The woman you worked with to recover those children's photographs . . ."

His cousin stilled and eyed him warily. "What about her?"

"Do you think she would take Hanako in and hide her until I can figure out a more permanent solution?"

"Hanako?"

"Miss Sumaki. Do not look at me that way, Devin. I have done nothing inappropriate. Well, nothing nefarious. I am concerned for her and happened to use her given name. I am not besmirching her honor."

Damn his cousin for raising that infernal brow and gesturing with that condescending flourish, tacitly pointing out that the situation threatened to ruin whatever reputation she had. Damn his silent judgment.

"Alex, I swear to you, nothing untoward has happened. She needs help."

"I cannot guarantee that Mrs. Duchamp can shelter her. It would be a risk. But if anyone can, it will be her."

"Could you give her address to Tompkins? Once you have done that, you are free to resume your evening. The sooner I get her to a safe house, the better."

"I am going with you."

He bristled at the implication. "Do you not trust me, cousin? Do you really think I would come to you like this if I had immoral intentions toward Miss Sumaki? Why would I bother?"

Devin brushed him off and responded in a clipped tone, "Nothing of the sort, Ridgemont. I simply wish . . . to make sure you get there safely."

Once they were on their way, his cousin's expression turned almost soft and distracted. Devin did not comment when he sat next to Hanako and let her rest against him. And he found his own desperate concern for Hanako eased by Devin's presence.

When Mrs. Duchamp opened the back door, it only took her a moment to assess the situation. With a swift, sweeping glance at the bundle in Skyler's arms, she nodded silently, stepped back, and gestured for him to enter. Without hesitation, Mrs. Duchamp firmly shut the door behind him and quietly said, "Follow me."

As he followed her up the stairs, his relief was palpable. Hanako would be safe here. The room Mrs. Duchamp led him to at the back of the house was small and spare but tidy. She pulled back the coverlet on the narrow bed, and he laid Hanako down gently. Mrs. Duchamp sat gingerly next to her and felt her head, then tucked her in as one might do for a child. He hovered over the foot of the bed to confirm that her breathing was deep and easy.

"Thank you," he whispered as he straightened and turned to Mrs. Duchamp. "I am sorry to disturb you so late in the evening, but Lord Devin assured me that you would be willing to offer Hanako shelter. He insisted that this would be the best place for her."

"Lord Devin?" she said, startled. She rose from the bed like a startled deer. "He told you to come here?"

"Yes. I explained Hanako's situation in the broadest of strokes. Unequivocally, he recommended you. He said no one could provide more reliable assistance or care."

"Is he . . . did he accompany you?" The strain in her voice, her glance toward the hall—something about Alex unnerved her, but he wasn't sure how to interpret her reaction. Alex was so clearly enamored of her, but he had a viscountcy to consider. Her feelings were a mystery.

"He directed my driver here and is waiting in the carriage."

She looked toward the window, her expression unreadable.

He cleared his throat. "Mrs. Duchamp, this may seem unconventional, but I am concerned for Miss Sumaki's safety and would like to stand watch over her tonight. Considering her state when I found her, I do not wish for her to wake in unfamiliar surroundings without an explanation. You could serve as chaperone." Devin had tried to convince him otherwise, but the man didn't know Broek. He had to admit he didn't either, but that was exactly why he could not leave Hanako and Mrs. Duchamp undefended. It should be impossible for her employer—her erstwhile employer—to figure out where she'd gone. But if he did somehow find her, there was no predicting what he was capable of.

Mrs. Duchamp nodded at him absently and made her way to the window as if dazed. She said, "It is thoughtful of you to treat her with such care. I have seen her at the Great Exhibition, and she seemed quite vibrant. We've spoken before. Perhaps tomorrow, if she is willing, you both can share more about this situation with me. I have friends who may be able to extricate her from whatever trouble threatens her." As she spoke, she gazed down toward the street and touched a hand to the glass. In the reflection, wistfulness swept over her. Interesting.

"Thank you, Mrs. Duchamp," he said softly. "If you will excuse me for a moment, I shall give instructions for my carriage to take

Devin home and return for me in the morning. I shall have a basket prepared and delivered as well, so that we do not impose overmuch on your hospitality."

When she turned to face him, her eyes glistened. "Do not trouble yourself. This is no imposition. I am well accustomed to such emergencies and would not have you go to any special efforts. There are sufficient food stores in the pantry for all of us. Miss Sumaki will be safe, and you are admirable for wanting to keep the watch. Tell Alex . . . tell Lord Devin . . . never mind." She shook her head, as if to clear it. When she looked at him again, she was the placid, competent businesswoman he'd met at the front door. "Please give Lord Devin my regards."

He nodded, distantly fascinated by the way her subtle agitation so exactly mirrored Devin's. He touched Hanako's hair just once— he couldn't resist—before going downstairs to send Devin on his way with an irrationally hopeful plan for Hanako's future.

CHAPTER 16

A Haven

Hanako was still sleeping when Skyler returned to the tiny room but moaned as Mrs. Duchamp touched a damp cloth to her forehead. Everything about her seemed compressed and fragile, stirring an almost primitive protectiveness deep within him. His jaw clenched as he thought about what had brought her to this plight.

"Do you have any sense of what is wrong with her?" Mrs. Duchamp asked. "Do you think she needs a physician?"

He shook his head, but doubt jabbed at him.

"I believe she has been drugged but do not know exactly what concoction she was given," he said. "My impression is that it was done to lower her inhibitions without causing her permanent harm."

"If that is the case, then she should recover by morning without any medical intervention." The older woman's mouth pursed and her expression hardened. "Who did this?"

"I found her at the Jade Garden, which is run by her employer, Mr. Broek. In addition to her performances at the Exhibition, she apparently provides therapeutic massages there." He hesitated. When he'd revealed to Devin what Hanako had said about being sold, his cousin was disgusted but not especially surprised. Still, to describe such a vile transaction to a respectable woman . . .

"Has he hurt her?" Mrs. Duchamp's voice was low, but her eyes blazed with fury.

"I do not think so. I believe I arrived before the intended events took place."

"Good." She began to pace the room, her expression distant, distracted. "The Needlework for the Needy Society has encountered young women in a similar condition, incapacitated in order to subject them to the uses and abuses of others. In addition to stupefying the victim, laudanum is believed by some to work as an aphrodisiac. It is a reprehensible practice occasionally used on new girls in brothels." She frowned. "In fact, I ought to see what else I can find out about this Jade Garden." Her voice dropped, and she ceased to address him, but her motions grew livelier, almost violent. She paused only to add, "On occasion, a body may react poorly to laudanum, especially if the dose is too large. She is such a tiny woman."

He nodded and admitted, "That she remains insensate for so long worries me."

"She seems to be breathing easily, moving occasionally, and speaking somewhat. As long as she remains animate, if not specifically conscious, she should be fine eventually. But she needs watching."

"I could not leave her in this state if an entire cavalry tried to tear me away."

That caught Mrs. Duchamp's attention. "Good man." She felt Hanako's cheek and tucked the blanket around her more securely, then moved toward the door.

"Wait, Mrs. Duchamp. You cannot mean to leave us without a chaperone."

The woman looked at him kindly and said, "You brought Miss Sumaki here intending to protect her virtue. I trust you shall. My presence would be superfluous."

It was not the response he expected, and it left him . . . nervous, especially in light of Devin's parting advice. "When a vulnerable woman shares with you her deepest desires, desires she believes only you can fulfill, it is easier than you can imagine to lose your head."

He'd sworn to his cousin, "Upon my honor, I shall do her no harm." And he'd tried not to be insulted when Devin appeared unconvinced.

When Mrs. Duchamp moved toward the door, he took a step forward, saying, "Surely it would not be proper."

She turned to him with an odd little smile and replied, "The value of propriety is inordinately inflated. I prize compassion and respect more. And the nearly paralyzing emphasis that people of your rank place on keeping unmarried men and women apart is almost amusing." Her eyes looked at some unseen spot in the distance as an indecipherable ripple of emotions swept across her face. More softly, she added, "I see honor in you. You would not do anything to cause her harm. I can tell your instincts and your judgment are sound. Trust yourself."

Unconvinced, he nodded politely. Mrs. Duchamp could not imagine how much time he had spent unobserved with Hanako, and ought not to have any inkling of how terribly his instincts went awry in her presence. Flashes of their previous encounters shot through him at inconvenient times, leaving a shameful arousal in their wake. But seeing her so helpless, so out of her wits, devastated him. Carrying her up the stairs and into the bedroom had made him think the unthinkable, want what a man in his position could not possibly want. He wanted her *with* him . . . in the light of day, without shame or scandal. And, as Mrs. Duchamp had said, he did value propriety—but not for his sake. For hers. She deserved to be treated like the rare gift of womanhood she was, not as some exotic freak of nature or tawdry bauble to be traded.

Yet Mrs. Duchamp had, without a moment's hesitation, opened her house to them. He would not impose upon her hospitality more than necessary. He bid her a good night and watched as she gently shut the door behind her.

After standing over Hanako and watching her rhythmic breathing for longer than he would care to admit, he settled himself awkwardly into a nearby chair, the rush seat creaking as he sank onto it.

"You." Her voice was so quiet that he'd almost missed it. "Please. *Watashi o nokosite inai.* You cannot leave me." She curled into a ball toward him, as if her body contracted to take up the least space possible.

"I would not dream of it, my dear." Her brow furrowed, and he longed to smooth it with his fingers, to massage her concern away. But he had no right to touch her, any more than he already had this evening.

"I may be sick."

At that, he leaned forward, gripping the arms of the chair to keep from standing, to keep from taking her in his arms. "Should I fetch a doctor?"

"No. Just ... is there a bucket or a basin ... something?" She faltered and looked away, but not before he caught how her eyes glistened too brightly and blinked too quickly. Her body slowly curled into a ball. The sight stabbed at him. Still, Devin's warning made him keep his distance. He fetched the basin from the washstand and placed it by her head. She stared at him, as if struggling to make sense of what was happening.

"You?" she whispered, suddenly more alert. "Why are you here?" She tried to sit up but couldn't, and her face conveyed rising panic. "Where am I? What is happening?"

"Rest now. You are in a safe place where no harm will come to you," he said. When she shook her head against the pillow, he added, "We think you have been drugged. It will wear off soon. Until then, *rest*."

Frowning and struggling to respond, she drifted off to sleep again. Despite his best efforts to keep watch faithfully, so did he.

Her scream jolted him awake. He popped out of the chair like a racehorse at the gate and heard footsteps running up the stairs. As Mrs. Duchamp rushed in, his brain finally grasped the essentials of what was happening.

"I think she is dreaming," he said with a sigh of exhausted relief.

Their hostess seemed almost to deflate, all the bravado and purposefulness draining from her. An honest moment of frailty.

"Yes, that makes sense," she said. "Vivid, sometimes disturbing dreams can be a result of opium use. They should do no harm, at least no physical harm."

"I do apologize for so much of an imposition, Mrs. Duchamp. You had no cause to help strangers like us under such mysterious circumstances."

She replied, "An incapacitated woman in need of help is cause enough. What concerns me greatly about these circumstances is that where there is one such victim, there are usually more."

A rare woman, indeed. Two rare women so far out of his experience. He pressed her to return to her bed, and she did not protest. He did not allow himself to fall asleep again.

"Lord Ridgemont?" Hanako said suddenly as she sat up, confused and alarmed. Weak-limbed, she tried to rise from the bed but fell back and closed her eyes. She still looked too pale.

"I am your servant, Miss Sumaki." He stood and bowed. The formality felt odd but essential. Here he was, at the bedside of a beautiful woman without supervision; yet it felt anything but wrong. He needed her to see that he felt as much, if not more, respect and esteem for her as he would for any woman in his social circle.

"Where am I? I fear I am going mad. I cannot think. Terrible memories. Something horrible is about to happen, but I do not know what. I do not know what to do. I can barely move." Her words came quickly.

"You are safe here. This is the home of Mrs. Honoria Duchamp, who runs the bookshop downstairs. It should be nearly impossible for Mr. Broek to figure out where you are. I am here to help, whatever you need." Words were all he could offer, and they felt miserably impotent. At least her delirium appeared to be lifting. But then she began to weep. What else could he do? How could he not slip onto the bed next to her? How could he not take her hands in his and then wrap his arms around her? He whispered words of comfort into her hair. She lay quiescent for a few moments and then strove to rise again.

"I have to go back. My sister is there, defenseless. He must be furious." She gripped the covers to her chest and looked around wildly. "Where are my clothes? I must go!"

"Miss Sumaki," he said, adopting a tone he hoped was calm and soothing, in sharp contrast to the concern that roiled through him. "I received word yesterday that you would no longer do performances at the Exhibition, that you'd been contracted elsewhere. The suddenness raised suspicion, especially after our last meeting." *Suspicion* seemed like a safer word to use than jealousy or possessiveness. His actions would likely convey his feelings well enough. "I broke into the Jade Garden and found you lying senseless in one of the bedrooms. What exactly did I rescue you from last night, Hanako?"

She lay back and closed her eyes, but he noticed that she did not release his hand. He needed to hear about the sale when she was conscious and alert, needed to know that what she'd revealed last night was true in the light of day.

"You had become too inquisitive," she whispered, "and you would have uncovered the auction soon enough. So he closed my auction yesterday, a month early, and I was to be claimed last night."

"What kind of auction?"

Her gaze, steady but anguished, met his. "You can guess. There were others as well, but their . . . bidders could not arrive with such abbreviated notice."

"Bloody, bloody hell." Others. Frustration surged through him, and pain radiated through his jaw as his teeth ground together. He'd never seen any other women, but he'd suspected secrets behind Broek's circumspect demeanor. He stood abruptly to alert Mrs. Duchamp, but Miss Sumaki's hand gripped his. She stared up at him, as if a great, frenetic energy struggled to escape.

"I must return," she said. "They will suffer horribly because of me. So horribly. I cannot allow that."

"I shall fetch Mrs. Duchamp. She seems to have some experience with this sort of thing. I believe she can help."

"Could you see if she might lend me something to wear? I should not relay the request through you, I realize, but time is short."

"Of course. But you must realize I cannot allow you to go." He laid her kimono on the bed.

She pushed herself upright and leaned forward, her body tense and her eyes alert as she stared at him.

"You cannot allow me?"

"You have not sufficiently recovered from last night. As you say, your Mr. Broek will be furious, and you are in no condition to face his wrath."

"I have to go back there!"

"You shall not!"

When he would not move from the side of the bed, she slid to the other side and stood gingerly, bracing herself against the wall. She held up her free hand when he tried to block her path to convince her to rest. He kept his eyes trained on her face, not allowing them to drift down to the seductively thin silk.

"If you will not speak to Mrs. Duchamp, I will do it myself!"

"I told you I would. If you would just rest, I will go right now."

"But I need to leave! I need to go back to my sister!"

"And I told you I will see to it."

"You cannot keep me imprisoned here!"

"You are not thinking reasonably. You are still suffering the effects of whatever he drugged you with and not yet at your full strength. Let me help you, you stubborn female!"

"I do not need your help, you bloody overbearing male!"

"Your accent! It has disappeared. Your speech! You . . . bloody?" The realization knocked him sideways. "Even your accent has been an act?"

"Of course it is an act," she said, still fuming at him. "Everything is an act. I am my father's daughter. But I learned quickly what an audience expects of me. That Japanese accent is like any other language to me. I use it when the situation calls for it." Through the tiny window, light dribbled across the sky. Now she was coherent and alert, bitingly aware, and infuriated.

"Why?" he asked. "Why use it at all?"

"By now you should see that my entire life is a performance, that every moment is constructed for some audience or another. When people look at me, they want to see an Oriental spectacle. Speech is as much an integral part of that vision as clothing or face powder. They want the illusion of a shy, delicate Asian flower."

"So you have been playing roles constantly, just shifting between different ones as needed? Are you ever simply yourself? Are you your true self with me right now, or is this yet another persona?"

Her eyes flared at that. How quickly their moment of sympathy had passed.

"What would you have had me do? At fifteen, should I have walked out, an orphan with nothing and no one? Leave my sister to Broek? Surely I would have found gainful employment and affordable housing immediately, before being thrown into what passes for an orphanage. Surely I could trust Broek to care for my sister more if I left." Her anger was a palpable presence in the room. And he loved her all the more for it. "At eighteen, should I have left with only my translation skills to support me, in hopes that I might not find myself walking the streets or in the poorhouse? Again, leaving my sister to fend for herself against Broek. Or should I turn my back now, when it would mean that those same women and children I've been trying to protect for the past five years would be left help-less in an alien world, unable to speak for themselves?"

The massiveness of her burden penetrated his consciousness. He reached for her, but she pulled away sharply. "Do you know what would happen if I walked away now? He might be prosecuted, per-haps, but they—they would certainly suffer. They would be moved from their current prison to an even harsher one, and they would be entirely unable to communicate or defend themselves. No one would consider or care that they were coerced into this life. Yes, I am complicit, but what else would you have me do?"

"I do not know!" His frustration burst through. "I just want more of the real you. Irrational and selfish as it may be, I want you to have been real for me." Could he trust her? What did he really know about her? In their short acquaintance, she had always employed a facade, always masquerading up to perhaps this very moment. It was impossible to know the core of her, the truth of her. His mind drifted back to her drug-induced haze the night before. She'd shared some truth then. Her intelligence—that was real. Her anger—that was certainly real. Her fear, her vulnerability—not the daintiness she used for show but the powerlessness that she struggled to mask—those were starkly real, too. She didn't want to need him, didn't want to want him. And she sure as hell didn't want to rely on him or anyone else to support her. But she needed help.

Or was this only what she wanted him to see, to think? Was she just toying with him, playing him like a puppet? There was only one way to find out. Trust. She trusted no one. Based on her experience, she had no good reason to. He would have to prove that she could trust him. She wouldn't play him for a fool. As his mind reached this momentous conclusion, she spoke again, "Imagine, for just a moment, that you had not been born into the world in which you were born. That you weren't born into a world where the slightest gesture summons obedience, where the blocking of your shoulders doesn't demand respect, that nothing was given to you just because you wanted it."

He wanted to object, but that was exactly the life he'd been born into. So he remained silent.

"I do what I must to survive and to protect my own in a world that does not want me."

"I want you, Miss Sumaki." *More than you could possibly imagine.* He said it so bluntly that he feared she'd retreat, that she'd think he only meant it physically. When she wouldn't look at him, he knew he'd used the wrong words. "I didn't mean . . . I don't just want—"

"Hana," she whispered, a mere breath of air as her eyes met his.

"What was that?" He leaned in, clinging to a tendril of hope.

"My name, my real name, is Hana. Hana Makado Johannsen. My father pronounced it Hannah. My mother's name was Sumaki, so I use it for her. You, Takara, and Broek are the only ones who know. And I cannot leave my sister, Takara, in Mr. Broek's hands, not even for a few more hours."

"Hana Makado Johannsen. Hana." He savored the light vowels on his tongue. "That is a beautiful name. Uniquely you." She hadn't recoiled from his admission, thank God. He slid his hand to cup her cheek. When her eyelids fluttered shut and she leaned her head into his hand, he was undone. His entire world condensed into this moment, this sensation, of her face resting upon his hand. She trusted him, he felt, trusted him not just with her name but with her soul.

He was sure she felt the tug between them as strongly as he did, as if some invisible cord tied them together, pulled them closer. Her shallow breaths ruffled the whiskers on his cheek, generating a remarkably pleasant tingle along his skin, radiating through him. Her large eyes, still slightly dilated, mesmerized him. As her lips brushed his, light as a butterfly's wings, and the delicate taste of her teased his senses, all rationality dissolved into an all-encompassing mantra: "I want you, Hana, and I will do whatever you need."

CHAPTER 17

A Request

When the door swung open and banged against the wall, the anger in his cousin's eyes could not have been mistaken—anger trained very obviously on him, and Skyler's already sorely stretched temper flared sharply. Mrs. Duchamp followed closely behind Devin with an expression of bewildered concern on her face as she looked back and forth, from Devin to him. Even when he addressed Devin directly, his cousin ignored him and spoke instead to Hana. When Devin looked at her, his eyes softened immediately, turning worried and gentle. Ah, yes, that little shift conveyed so many accusations. The lack of trust stung. *I am not a brute, you know.* It was too much. He couldn't believe Devin had the audacity, barging in like some armored knight to defend a fair maiden without a clue of what was truly happening, or what his own behavior and intentions were. Apologizing for him.

"What is it, Devin?" Lord Ridgemont asked with alarm. "Has someone come for her?"

Devin quite obviously ignored him. "Miss Sumaki, are you well? Last night you arrived looking quite sickly, nigh insensible. I hope you are recovering without ill effects and my *cousin* is not causing you distress."

She nodded and mirrored his cordial, neutral tone. "I am improving quickly, my lord. It was most kind of Mrs. Duchamp to shelter me in such an extreme situation." She clasped her kimono closed at her throat, but otherwise she looked at ease.

"My cousin should know better than to tax you. I apologize for his behavior."

"See here, Devin!" Skyler interjected. "I have not been taxing her, and you have no call to interfere."

His cousin still stared at Hana, as if seeking clues, breaks in her facade.

He could have kissed Mrs. Duchamp when she answered his query. "No, Lord Ridgemont, no one seeks Miss Sumaki yet. We heard some commotion from below and rushed up to assist."

He thanked her with a nod and turned back to glare at his cousin. Blood pounded in his ears as Mrs. Duchamp went to Hana and they began speaking in low tones. If Devin thought him dangerous to Hana, then the man could go hang. He had nothing to apologize for, no reason for Devin to think so poorly of him.

"You, Ridgemont, sought asylum for her here." Devin finally deigned to address him. "I am at her service. In taking Miss Sumaki under her roof, Mrs. Duchamp is vouching for her protection. Judging by the sounds we heard from below, she deserves some measure of defense from you."

Measure of defense? From me? You presumptuous ass! He was about to say as much when Mrs. Duchamp touched Devin's arm lightly and gave him an oddly intimate warning look. Remarkably, Devin stepped back, and his demeanor eased. She then took a seat on the narrow bed, gesturing to Miss Sumaki to join her.

"Lord Ridgemont," Mrs. Duchamp said, "of course I know your behavior is impeccable. Your reputation as a perfect gentleman is unassailable."

"You may think so, but clearly my own cousin has his doubts. Not that I have ever given him cause." He'd once been able to count on Devin not to dismiss his abilities, his character. Everyone else had brushed him aside, the child no one had expected, the afterthought. But Devin always had treated him as an equal, until now.

"The men of your family obviously take their responsibilities quite seriously, as is right and proper. I'm guessing you also both take your failings to heart and can be that much more demanding of others because of it." Devin gave Mrs. Duchamp a searching look, one that made Skyler feel uncomfortably intrusive. "What I am saying is that each of you needs to trust that the other is acting under the best of intentions and toward the same end. Do not allow impulsive emotions to distract you." Then she turned and spoke with Hana in low, indecipherable tones.

The two women conversed for a few moments; he could hear only fragments, such as Takara's name and others he didn't recognize. Meanwhile, he and his cousin continued to stare at each other warily in silence. A dim corner of his brain recognized his childishness, but, in fact, Devin's treatment and assumptions hearkened back to his childhood, when he could do no right in the shadow of his brother's excellence. The women's tête-à-tête came to some mysterious understanding that ended with the ladies hugging, and then Hana stood and faced Devin, drawing his full attention.

Skyler's breath caught. It was Hana and yet not Hana. He'd seen this version of her before. It was the transformation he'd seen at the Crystal Palace; more than once, in fact. Immediately, she'd turned from an unassuming wallflower into a force of nature, demanding one's full attendance. In such close quarters, her unexpected radiance stunned him, knocking his irritation with Devin out of his head.

"Your gallantry is deeply appreciated, Lord Devin," she said, her voice lilting in that way Skyler found so disarming. "It is quite touching, in fact, that you would be willing to come to the rescue of someone like me."

Skyler took a step toward her, about to argue the ridiculousness of referring to herself so poorly, but when she looked at him and raised her hand to stop him, he could not disobey.

"As I was saying, Lord Devin, your care is appreciated. But it is entirely unnecessary." She gestured expansively, her manner decisive and commanding. "As you can plainly see, Lord Ridgemont is no threat to me. He is as attentive and respectful of my wishes as you are. I apologize if our discussion became heated and . . . disruptive. It seems your cousin and I have strong views, as well as strong voices. We likewise share a reluctance to concede a point."

She gave Skyler a wry glance, as if daring him to deny it. He would be a fool to object now.

"I assure you," Hana repeated, "that Sky poses no danger to me."

Devin glanced over at him, his eyebrow raised. Her use of his given name—no, his nickname—was not easy to overlook. Mrs. Duchamp coughed delicately and moved toward the door. Her conversation with Hana must indeed have been momentous. She did not seem at all surprised by Hana's words or her attitude. Instead, she caught Devin's attention, and an entire conversation appeared to take place in their eyes.

"Without a doubt, I am safe in his presence," Hana continued. "Therefore, I respectfully request that you leave us to resolve our conversation privately."

Skyler froze. Every cell of him froze. The air in his lungs froze. Did he truly hear what she seemed to declare? She knew the rules of propriety, and even though they'd already broken so many of them in action, only the two of them knew the truth. But now she might as well have just told Devin and their hostess that they were going to rut like rabbits. Were they going to? His blood surged at the very thought. He needed to get his head straight.

Devin looked heavenward, as if saying a swift prayer. His cheeks turned a bright pink as he glanced behind him at Mrs. Duchamp, already in the doorway.

"Forgive my bluntness, my lord," Hana added. "I simply mean that Lord Ridgemont and I have some delicate matters to discuss. I did not mean to make you at all uncomfortable or to, in any way, suggest anything untoward between us."

"You are blunt," Devin responded. "Fortunately, I have recently become accustomed to outspoken women. I have, in fact, come to admire one very outspoken woman quite deeply. I admit I am relieved to learn that my belief in Lord Ridgemont's honor is deserved."

Damn it all, Alex, you should not have needed such proof. And he couldn't help but see the irony: nothing had happened last night. Devin's warnings had made sure of that. And yet Hana had declared her intentions. And they would resolve their conversation *privately.*

CHAPTER 18

A Compromise

She turned the key firmly, thrilling at the muffled snick of metal against metal, thrilling at this moment of self-determination. Mr. Broek would punish her for her disappearance. She knew, without the slightest doubt, that he would assume the worst, assume she'd been ruined, and therefore get her off his hands for the highest payment he could get as quickly as he could get it. For all she knew, he'd postponed last night's transaction, as he'd called it, just until she returned, and she'd immediately be shipped off to her new owner. She could not begin to consider whether he would try to separate her from her sister; he'd always promised they would stay together, but he hadn't exactly been a man of his word thus far.

This one thing—this fleeting moment—was within her control. Mrs. Duchamp had revealed the true nature of the Needlework for the Needy Society, a group of women devoted to uncovering social injustices, and made clear the resources that could be used to assist the Jade ladies. Hana didn't really believe that their help would be successful; they didn't know Mr. Broek's nature as she did. But Mrs. Duchamp's reassurances had given her one thing: a keen awareness of the opportunity before her. Hana had so few choices. Recognizing her own desires was a heady thing. Even if she could not free herself and the Jade ladies from Broek, her body and mind belonged to her alone. She would choose this one time who to share it with. Just the thought made her dizzy. She gripped the key tightly against her chest as she turned to find Sky standing in the center of the room.

Without conscious thought, she was suddenly leaning into him, her arms thrown around his shoulders. His eyes widened in shock, and his body braced to counterbalance hers. Those eyes, so icy blue, she could immerse herself in their brightness.

"Well, that answers my first question," he whispered, his breath dancing along her cheek as he stared down at her. His arms wrapped around her gently, hugging her waist.

"What question was that?"

"Did you just say to my cousin, my very proper cousin, what I think you said?" His whole body stilled, waiting.

"What do you think I said?"

"Unless my English-to-English translation skills are truly piss poor, I believe you just declared to a viscount and a highly respected businesswoman that you intend to engage in inappropriate behavior behind closed doors with a man to whom you are not married."

"Your translation skills are passable." Upon her confirmation, his hands began to roam.

"Furthermore, given the fact that you very scandalously locked the door to prevent anyone from interrupting and presumably prevent either of us from leaving this room, and also given the fact that you are pressed so very indecently up against me"—at which point, he pulled her body even tighter to his, every inch of them touching from knees to chest—"I must conclude that you intend to have your way with me."

His words startled her into laughter. His body shook as well, his laughter rumbling through her, bombarding her senses. Yes, she would take this moment, this bubble of freedom and joy, and revel in every second of it. He thought he was making a joke. How very sweet. She didn't bother to reply with words. Instead, she tightened her grip around his neck and pulled him down to meet her.

The softness of his lips against hers prompted a quiver deep in the pit of her stomach. So delicate. So gentle. He was always so careful with her. But this moment called for grander measures.

She pushed him away. His face clouded with confusion. "I— Hana—I did not mean to—I am sorry—"

She stopped his stammering by pushing him back again, and yet again, until his legs bumped into the bed rail. "More precisely, I intend to seduce you."

"Lord in heaven," he whispered. "I thought you were only joking. What about Broek? What about the other women?"

"Mrs. Duchamp assured me that wheels are already in motion to watch the house for any signs of women being moved, any sounds of women being harmed. I trust her."

"But . . ." He trailed off. The confusion returned to his face. His eyes were wide again, but fiery with barely restrained lust. She would remove those restraints.

"Breathe, Sky. Just take a moment and breathe." It touched her to watch him comply, to watch his chest expand and contract as calm inched its way through him. She wasn't sure when exactly this determination had come over her. Perhaps it was when she realized that she had to return to Broek, that she would never have this opportunity again. Or perhaps it was when she woke and saw his face in the dawn light, a glowing guardian angel keeping watch over her. "For now, forget everything beyond these walls. Breathe and be here."

He closed his eyes, and the tension slipped from him.

"Listen to me, Sky. Breathe and consider what you want most at this moment. Think carefully. I know what I want, here and now. And I want to share it with you. But you need to choose this moment for yourself."

He opened his eyes, now pained and struggling. "We cannot, Hana. I refuse to hurt you. I refuse to demean you. You are a rare gem, and you deserve to be treasured, not used and tossed aside like some trinket." His hands had returned to her waist, holding her steady and already setting a distance between them.

With one hand, she stroked his hair, such a beautiful golden softness, while she laid her other palm against his cheek.

"You would never cause me harm. In all your actions, you have treated me with more esteem than I have ever known. But we both know that you cannot *have* me, cannot keep me. What happens when my new owner claims me, we cannot predict. So what I want, what I need here and now, is to give you the only thing I can. You make me feel valued . . . and recognized as someone more than a showpiece. Let me have that. I need you to love me with all the care you can give me, here and now. I need this before I give myself over to a future in which I am just someone's plaything."

His expression turned stormy, preoccupied as he stared at her. She could almost see the twists and turns in his mind.

"Stop," she insisted. "Don't think. Don't try to plan. You cannot afford me, and you should not try. Just breathe and be here. Just a few moments, that's all we need."

"Understand this," he said, his jaw taut. He gripped her arms tightly. "I want you more than I want to continue breathing. I want you with everything I am. It is taking every ounce of training in discipline and comportment not to take what you so, so generously want to give me. But I cannot do that to you."

God curse the man's infernal propriety. If words would not sway him, then she would use actions. This was her one chance, and she would not be denied by his misguided sense of honor. Slowly, she pulled at the tie of her robe. His gaze dropped to her fingers as his breath caught.

"If you were in my position, facing a lifetime of bodily servitude, would you not want to know just once what it felt like to be connected to someone you actually wanted? Would you not want just once to experience honest passion? If you could only truly give your body once before it ceased to be your own, would you not take that opportunity, regardless of how the rest of the world might judge you for it?"

Light as it was, her clothing felt suffocating. The knot finally popped apart, and the edges of her kimono slid open.

"No, Hana, it would not be right. I am trying to protect you. I am trying with all my might to do the right thing. If I were to take advantage of you now, I would be no better than Broek or the man to whom he tried to sell you. I cannot treat you so villainously." He tried to step from between her and the bed, but she grabbed his arm.

"Listen to me! You would not be taking advantage." She pressed herself against him and reached up to pull his head down toward her. Her robe slid off one shoulder, and she shrugged to drop it off the other, until it drooped at her elbows. She saw his struggle not to look, saw his reluctant glimpses down her body. "You are the hero in this pathetic tragedy, Sky. Last night you came to the aid of a damsel in distress, but this damsel does not get a happy ending. Do you understand? So she has to scrounge for whatever tiny treasures she can find. One such treasure is you, here and now, you. Please?"

He rested his forehead against hers. His hair tickled her face. She would remember that later . . . the tiny prickling of her skin as his grip tightened around her and his eyes bore into her.

"I would rather die a thousand deaths than hurt you," he said. "I will find a way to keep you safe."

If only the steel in his voice were enough to overcome the realities of her situation. In truth, he could not rescue her. No one could. But within this narrow future to which she was condemned, she had one small freedom, one choice within her control. And she chose him.

"There isn't time for all that. We have right now. Help me make this a moment that can sustain me in the face of whatever comes next. I need this. I need you."

Holding her face gently in his hands, he closed his eyes and breathed. She would cherish this, too—his slight frown, his long lashes, his earnest determination. When he opened his eyes, he stared down at her and caressed her cheek. So sweet. Then his hand slipped behind her neck and pulled her toward him.

"I was doomed from the start. I should know better than to deny you anything. You are a force of nature."

So very sweet. She trembled at the intensity of his gaze. And then their mouths entwined. With unexpected boldness, he swept his tongue along her bottom lip. When she gasped, he deepened the kiss. Heavenly goddess, there was magic in his touch. She trembled as his mouth became more insistent, one of his hands cradling her head while the other cinched around her waist. Yes. She dropped her hands to free herself of the kimono and started to drag up her chemise. They had so little time!

He pulled back and stilled her movements. "Shh. I cannot resist you. I will give you whatever you need. Now it is your turn to breathe. To be here, now, with me." His hands covered hers, brushed them away, and then roamed lightly over her hips. Her own whimper surprised her. His gentleness eased her near panic and made her aware of the sensations bombarding her. The warmth of his fingers seeping through the fabric, the shivery chill of his breath against her neck, the gentleness of his touch. Always gentleness. But she couldn't rest, couldn't stop, couldn't quiet the clamor of her body.

"Just here. Just now," she said, as she quickly unbuttoned his waistcoat, not stopping to savor the fine fabric. She went up on her toes to press herself against him.

"It isn't fair," she said.

"That covers quite a lot. What is not fair right now?"

"It isn't fair that I cannot reach your lips. You have quite an advantage in height."

"I promised I would give you what you need." He bent his head, leaning in so close they shared the same air. "Take what you want."

A fierce panic seized her—*too much, not enough, no time*—but she shoved it down. Breathe. She took in a breath and took his lips, not gently but not frantically. When his tongue teased past her lips, the world heated. Only when he reached up to loosen her grip did she realize how tightly her fingers grasped him. "Easy," he whispered against her mouth. Then she realized how much better it would be to touch him, to feel his skin without anything between them. Kissing him forever would be heaven, but it wasn't enough. The hardness of his back, the hair on his chest tickling her skin, it was all uncharted territory, and she wanted to explore every inch. Wanted, too, to be explored every bit as thoroughly.

Everything about the moment fed a tight buzzing in her head. Every touch pushed her higher, toward some end she could not imagine. When he stroked one of her peaked nipples through the whisper-light fabric, the sharp sensation was indescribably intense. She gasped and clutched at him.

"Breathe," he said.

"You first."

He chuckled and bent down. Then he blew gently across her breasts, making the chemise ripple along them, and she could not suppress the noises that escaped her.

"Clever," she whispered. "Two can play at that game, you know. The Jade ladies talk."

"Oh, dear God, I do not want to know anything you have learned from them."

"Yes," she murmured. "You do. Just a few things."

Whether to stop her from talking or to stop himself from

dwelling on what those things could be, he returned to her mouth, effectively silencing her. Not enough time. She pulled away, yanked up her chemise and tossed it on the floor by the bed.

"I do not want us to hurry this," he said as he sat stunned in the chair by the bed, the chair he must have spent the night in. She couldn't think of that now, couldn't face the delicate emotion that welled up at the image of him keeping his vigil—for her. "You are too beautiful. This is too precious."

She blinked hard against the welling up of tears. "It is, but there is no time. I need you, all of you, now!"

"You have me," he replied as he removed his boots and then his breeches and then his undergarments methodically, never taking his eyes off her. Under other circumstances, she might suspect he was teasing her. "You have all of me. Why not take a moment to enjoy it?"

"Oh, I shall. I am enjoying every second of you," she said as she pulled him down with her. That he came willingly, crawling over her to maintain the closeness of their bodies, drove her passion higher. The fluttering in her stomach turned on her, though. The pure excitement gave way to nervousness. What was she supposed to do to please him? What could she do to ensure that this meant as much to him as it did to her?

As if reading her mind, he said, "Everything you do drives me wild. Everything. You have only to look at me to see proof of how you move me. Only touch me to find out how hot and needy you make me."

So she did. His chest felt firm, tense, hot. Every breath made their bodies brush against each other. She would not look down, though. Could not. Even without looking, she felt the hot hardness of him against her waist. And she knew, at least theoretically, what that meant.

"Are you sure you don't want to hear at least a little of what the Jade ladies have discussed? I think you would find it . . . tempting." She slid one hand down his chest, marveling at the textures and sensations, and paused at his waist.

He growled. Actually growled.

"No, I do not want to hear any of the tricks of the trade. Whatever we do here, I want it to be honest and sincere, just between us. No masquerades, no performances." And then his lips came down again, harder, more insistent, even more demanding of a genuine response than were his words.

And, oh, how her heart pounded at his fierceness.

"Yes," she mumbled against his lips. "This is honest," she said, as she slid her hand down. Could she? Just a light brush of her fingertips against his hard length. He shivered and groaned. Oh, yes, she could! She wrapped her fingers around him and stroked, amazed by the combination of hard and soft, delicate and yet rugged. He dropped his forehead to rest against hers as his hand captured hers.

"Nothing could be more so. But if you keep touching me like that, dearest, I shall not be able to continue."

He raised her hand above her head, pinning it there for a moment before his slid down her arm, following the line of her body. "Shh," he said. "Stop squirming."

"Easy for you to say. You said yourself, no masquerades. That should include no games, no teasing. We can make better use of our time." Her own panting and writhing should have embarrassed her, but there was no time for self-consciousness.

If he would not take matters into his own hands, then she would. She slid her hand down from over her head, brushing past his, to graze her aching breast. She couldn't help but whimper and arch as she stared up at his face. So many expressions flitted across it—surprise, comprehension, lust.

"I can do better," he whispered as he shifted his position. When he kissed her busy hand, she stopped breathing and gave ground. Then his mouth closed over her taut nipple, and she moaned. *Oh, heavenly stars! How is it possible to feel this good?*

As if he'd heard her thoughts, he muttered, "I have never imagined anything this good. I could do this forever and consider myself a lucky man."

"There's more, you know." Already she loved how such simple words could make him quiver, not to mention how much she loved having their bodies pressed so closely that she could feel him shaking.

He lifted his head and looked at her, his gaze uncertain. No, that would not do. She raised her head, putting all of her desire, all of her frantic need, into the kisses she scattered on whatever parts of him she could reach—his jaw, his neck, his shoulders.

"Please," she whispered. "I need this. Whatever lies ahead, please let me have this to hold on to."

He didn't respond in words. Instead, he moved above her, nudging her legs apart with his knees.

"I know what you need, sweetness. I do not know if I can truly give it to you, not in the way you deserve, but I shall give you whatever I can. I was made for this moment."

His fingers gently explored her, making her gasp in amazement as the sensation ramped up an urgency she'd never known. When his arms flexed, she realized her nails were digging into them, but she couldn't make herself stop.

"Please. I cannot wait," she said between gasps. "I do not even know what to ask for, but I cannot stand this torturous anticipation."

He froze and stared down at her. Horrified concern showed on his face, throwing ash onto the flames of her desire. She stared back. What had she done to displease him so terribly? Was he disgusted by her wantonness?

"What is it? Did I do something wrong?"

He slipped his fingers from her and loomed over her, propped on his elbows. He opened his mouth as if to speak and eventually managed, "You are untouched . . . intact. This is . . . important for you. I should be gentler, not come at you like some kind of barbarian invader."

"Gentle sounds lovely." She rolled her hips against his. "Just do not stop." To punctuate her command, she wrapped her hand around the hot length of him and stroked once more. His shiver of pleasure transmuted through her skin, as did the groan he emitted into her shoulder. Yes. So she guided him to her entrance. Thicker, hotter, harder—oh, gods, his cock—replaced his fingers, nudging at her entrance, dipping in just a little before he froze above her.

"My God, Hana. You're so soft, so tight . . . so hot." He gritted his teeth, and his shoulders, his neck, his buttocks, even his stomach tensed has he held himself over her, trying to go slowly. But his body wanted more; his hips rocked gently as his arms shook from the strain of holding himself up and not thrusting into her as she suspected he wanted.

"More," she said. He obeyed by inching farther inside, and the feeling of his hot, slick skin against hers, inside her, made her dizzy. She could feel every inch of him . . . from the inside . . . and it was glorious.

"Are you—have I hurt you?" Concern battled with passion on

his face. She could feel the same battle in the tension of his muscles. Everywhere.

"No. A pinch only. It is nothing. Please. More," she prompted again, her body jerking against his until he was seated in her as far as he could go, until their bodies were practically fused, skin to sensitive skin.

"It feels so strange," she said with a moan.

He paused. She grabbed at his back, desperate for more of that intimate friction.

"What do you mean strange? Should I stop? Does it hurt?"

"No, no! For the love of the stars, do not stop! I feel invaded, overwhelmed, but it is marvelous."

He thrust, and the sensations radiating from where they were joined grew exponentially.

"Yes," she cried, her hands gripping his body. So hard. So large. How had she never felt this before?

His hips began to pump faster, harder, and he groaned and shivered some more. After just a few more thrusts that left her breathless and on edge, he spat out, "I cannot hold out. I've never felt anything like this."

CHAPTER 19

A Mistake

The quickening of his pace sent a frisson of alarm up her spine, cutting through the inexplicable sensations inside her. *No, no, no.*

"Wait!"

She struggled to separate their bodies, to no avail. Her bucking and pushing only made him groan more deeply and suddenly stiffen, deep inside her.

"You must take care—!" she said, panic overcoming her heady desire.

"I love you," he shouted as he stiffened. She felt the liquid heat of him filling her as his hips thrust almost involuntarily before his body came to rest on hers. She cried out and shook violently, but not from ecstasy. Whatever nebulous pleasure and rapt fascination she'd felt evaporated as his body relaxed.

She shoved him away and slipped off the bed, holding one of the sheets to cover herself.

The look on his face—pleasure mixed with growing confusion—made her want to hit him, even as she recoiled from the thought. She'd felt the sting and worse of hands on her. Damn him for his lack of control. Damn her for letting it happen. When she grabbed for clothing and stepped away from the bed, he reached out to her. She avoided him.

"What are you doing? Come back and let me hold you, Hana."

She shook her head and began dressing.

"What has upset you? Will you not even look at me now?"

His voice resonated with a pain that matched her own.

"What did I do that was so wrong?"

She could not look at him. Yet he would not be silent, would not fade into the wallpaper or furnishings as she so wished she could. Her fingers shook terribly as she tried to find the armholes of the kimono.

"This was a mistake," she said finally. "You are not to blame, but we should not have."

A rustling of the bedclothes, quick thumps on the floorboards, and he turned her toward him. He was still naked, devastatingly naked.

"No. I refuse to accept that." His eyes glittered, unblinking. "What we just shared was not a mistake. I have never felt anything like that with anyone. I have never wanted to share my body like that with anyone before. More than that, I wanted to bring you pleasure, be as close to you as any two people can be. And it was good."

Silenced by the fierceness of his gaze and trapped by his looming body, she could not look away.

"It was good for you, wasn't it?"

She nodded. After all, that feeling of him inside her was so, so good, so elementally fulfilling. To deny it would be to deny her own soul. As furious as she was with him, she could not deny that she wanted him still, again, more. His finely muscled arms and broad chest made her warm and weak all over again. But she could not make that mistake again.

"Good is not enough," she said quietly, as she tried to pry his hands off of her. "You and I do not belong together. You know what I am. You know my fate. You should have left me at the Jade Garden when you found me. Now Broek will be beyond reason, especially when he learns I am no longer a virgin."

"Is that what has you so upset? That I took what he would sell?"

She opened her mouth to argue that he could not take what was not freely given, that she gave herself by choice. *Focus on the objective, Hana. You have to go back.* So she held her tongue.

"He can go to the devil," he continued. "You are not his to sell, no more than you would be mine to buy. But now he will see that he has no sale to make. You belong with me, Hana, and I will not let him take you." He wrapped his arms around her, and she could not resist leaning into his body, taking comfort in his warmth, taking sparks of pleasure in the slide of his skin against her face.

"You have no jurisdiction over him."

"I shall marry you," he said simply, definitively.

She bristled at his imperious tone. "No, you shall not. I would not accept."

"You already have, my love. You just did—in that bed." He pointed at the disheveled cot. "But that is not to the point at this moment. Now," he said, his low voice rumbling through her, "tell me what really upset you."

"How presumptuous you are! As if you know my mind or my life. There was no proposal of marriage in that bed, and there was certainly no acceptance of such an imaginary proposal. There was . . . *fucking* . . . the simple indulgence of animalistic drives. It could not be anything more than that." She jerked away, but he held her fast in his embrace, her head tucked under his chin. She felt his chest expanding and contracting quickly, heard the rapid, furious exhalations through his nose, until he calmed himself enough to respond.

"Hana, you must help me to understand. You know I mean you no harm. Be honest with me. What happened? When we . . . at the end . . . I was not sure if you were struggling to get closer or to push me away. And then you erupted into a pocket volcano. Why?"

Feeling his solidness, hearing his voice vibrate through every place where their bodies touched, she felt again that communion of thought between them. This tsunami of conflicting emotions left her battered and clinging to his voice, an anchor in the tempest. He needed to put some clothes on.

"It was that moment . . ." she began.

He loosened his grip enough to lean away so that he could peer down at her face. The concern on his face made her ache.

"Say again, my love?"

"That moment, at the end. When you . . ."

"What, Hana? What did I do wrong?"

"Your seed," she whispered, her face aflame. "You should not have. We should have taken . . . precautions."

With a huge exhalation of relief, he held her head gently between his hands, and his whole body seemed to loosen and mold itself against hers.

"Darling, you have nothing to fear. I told you I want to make you my wife. If you were to become with child, we would marry immediately, and it would be legitimate. Next week, if not sooner. I will take care of you in every way."

She pulled away and closed her eyes. The image of her mother flashed behind her eyelids, and her knees buckled with the visceral memory. But the vision gave her the conviction she needed to face him.

"You do not understand." She looked at him unwaveringly and moved away from the bed. "I will not have children. We should have taken more care because I cannot bring a child into this world."

"You are barren? How could you know? It would be impossible to tell with a virgin. If you were barren, why would we have to take precautions . . ."

"No. Listen to me. I have no reason to believe I am bodily unable to have a child. I am saying I *will not*. I will not bring any child from my body into this world."

"What do you mean? Why not?" He frowned. She felt anger and frustration simmering beneath his confusion.

"You have no idea what it is like to be me, to be an outsider everywhere, to be looked upon as an oddity wherever I turn. My father was the only home I ever knew. Even when he lived, he could not be at my side constantly. Could not protect me every waking moment. And when he was not there, the threat of torment was constant. From my earliest memories, I was subject to laughter and mockery from children—in Japan because I was not truly Japanese, everywhere else because I was a foreigner. As I grew older, I was subject to leers and gropes from men of all walks of life, men who jeered about what my most useful talents must be. At best, I would catch looks of awkward pity from well-meaning strangers.

"I speak twenty languages. Yet for most of my life, people have assumed I am incapable of understanding them, that I lack the intelligence to learn their language, or perhaps that I lack the brain capacity to function as a member of their society. They have speculated about me and insulted my blood in my presence, assuming I would not understand. They have nodded indulgently at me and bid cordial greetings, asking in extremely slow, loud tones about the weather where I come from or about the shape of my eyes. There is always an impasse, one not of my making. I have done everything in my power to be pleasing and amenable, to make myself acceptable. None of it makes any difference."

He reached for her again, but his sympathetic expression clawed at her insides. She wrenched herself out of his grasp and backed away.

"I will *not* condemn a child, my blood, to suffer such an alienated existence. It would be monstrously cruel to knowingly subject someone I love to that fate. Bad enough that my sister will suffer it!"

The gravity of the moment knocked him breathless. To never have children. He realized suddenly that he'd already pictured miniature copies of Hana running around the estate, their estate. Pictured them laughing and happy, dancing at Hana's feet.

"The Jade ladies have instructed me in various ways to prevent . . . unwanted consequences. There are devices . . . and teas back at the Jade Garden. I must imbibe some of the tea immediately."

"What happens when we marry, Hana?"

She scoffed. "Do not be fanciful. You cannot marry me. If you wish to entertain the impossible scenario that we wed, I would not provide you with children. I shall not change my position on that. You must understand. And you could not afford me anyway."

He stumbled back onto a chair. He wanted her children. And his family line needed an heir. Heaven only knew what Her Majesty would think of an earl who was one-quarter Japanese. His mother would be apoplectic. Well, she would be, regardless—whether he took a foreigner as his wife or declared that he would not produce an heir. Both together would certainly cause his mother to file for lack of competence.

"But . . . I love you," he said.

"So you said."

"And I thought you loved me."

"I . . ." She paused and took his hand. "I don't have the words to describe what I feel for you." She raised his hand to her lips and kissed his palm. The simple gesture sent a pang through him. She wasn't accepting him; she was saying good-bye.

His fingers twisted in her grasp as he reached for her chin and drew her face toward his. "Marry me."

"Do not be ridiculous. I know your society's ways as well as you do. You cannot marry me."

"I am Ridgemont. I can do whatever I choose." Damn his mother. Damn society. Men had married actresses and opera singers before and survived.

"No, and it is unbecoming of you to lie to me so brazenly. You must marry a woman of your station. If I were a daughter of royalty, of stature, perhaps my strangeness could be forgiven eventually. There would still be difficulties, but perhaps they could be overcome. This cannot be."

"It can be. We can be together."

"I have been sold to the highest bidder. I have no choice in that. And you could not marry me anyway."

"Broek's auction goes against British law and basic human decency and would not be upheld in court. You are under no obligation to honor his transaction. I could become your protector. You would need for nothing. And bloody society be damned, I can marry you. It is within the law for me to bind myself to you in marriage. Bloody, blasted society can say whatever it wants about the match, but no one can legally keep me from taking you as my wife . . . if you choose."

If only she could believe him . . .

"I cannot have this conversation now. My sister needs me, and I have already delayed too long."

"Even if we didn't marry, I would set you up in an apartment of your own. Whatever needs you and Takara had would be met."

"Hear me, Ridgemont! Even if I could manage to get Takara away, defying Broek now would leave the other women at his mercy. How can I escape the fate reserved for them and live with myself? I must go. I should have gone as soon as I woke."

"Hana," he said quietly, waiting until she looked up at him to continue. "I do not regret what we shared here today. Do you?"

She turned away.

CHAPTER 20

A Guarded Response

"Hana," Skyler said quietly. "I do not regret what we shared here today. Do you?"

If only she knew how to answer. Being joined with him had felt perfectly natural, perfectly right. But already thoughts of the future loomed, and guilt at her loss of control nauseated her. How could she have forgotten herself so badly that she had sacrificed even her duty to Takara for her fleeting pleasure? The fact that Broek thus far had shielded Takara from the Jade Garden's dealings didn't mean he could be trusted indefinitely, especially not when enraged. The room began to spin as her mind spiraled into the murky ugliness of all the possible consequences of this one stolen hour.

A discreet knock saved her from answering Skyler's question. Mrs. Duchamp called through the door, "Miss Sumaki, I brought you some clothing that I hope will do. They were left behind by my assistant."

Skyler threw on his shirt and grabbed his pants before darting to crouch on the far side of the bed. She opened the door just enough to accept the small pile of clothing from the remarkably unruffled woman. "Thank you for your kindness, Mrs. Duchamp."

"Of course, whatever you need," Mrs. Duchamp said blithely as she pulled a pair of scissors out of her pocket. "Unfortunately, the skirt will be long, and I haven't the skill to shorten it, but I am certain Mina wouldn't mind if you alter them."

"Again, thank you." Hana bowed to her. "We shall emerge shortly."

Mrs. Duchamp turned to leave but paused and touched her shoulder. "I mean what I say. Whatever you need, my friends and I will do all we can to assist you."

Hana could only nod as her throat clogged with emotion at such kindness. She quietly shut the door as her gracious hostess turned to descend the stairs.

She and Skyler finished dressing in silence, a silence that grew heavier, more awkward and significant, more painful with each passing second. The ferocity with which he dug his boots out from under the bed and yanked them on indicated that he had deciphered her unstated answer. Did she regret what they'd done? As beautiful as it seemed while it was happening, how could she not?

"I must return to the Jade Garden immediately," Hana whispered, as she finished tying an apron over the borrowed skirt, which was far too long, as Mrs. Duchamp had warned. She took the scissors to the hem, cutting a strip several inches wide to make the skirt wearable. "It was a terrible mistake for me to delay so very long," she added. "The women will be punished because of my disappearance. Takara—" Again, her voice deserted her. She twisted clumsily as she made her way around the hem, not caring about the ragged edge. All she needed was to be able to walk—and run—without stepping on her clothes.

"Do your regret what we did, Hana?" Skyler sounded accusatory, but then the pain in his gaze stabbed at her heart. She'd wanted him to be the one, she'd been the one to insist, the one to push. And it was too late for recriminations. She would never be able to see him again, so she owed him an honest answer.

"I cannot regret what we shared, Skyler." She went to him and stroked his cheek, staring into those clear blue eyes that warmed when she touched him. "But I should not have stayed. My sister . . . I sacrificed her for a moment's pleasure. The women—I have no idea what Broek is subjecting them to right now because of me. How could I be so selfish?" Even as she said it, she wanted to savor the reassuring hardness of his jaw, the warm roughness of his stubble. Need rose, sharp and insistent, and she felt shame. She had to go. "I have stayed longer than I should and must return."

His brows rose, and he pinned her hand against his face with his own large palm. "You cannot return to the Jade Garden, Hana. You will never go back into that abyss of immorality. You must know that." He spoke gently but firmly.

He could not mean to talk to her as if she were a child being scolded. Heat tingled along her scalp and spread along her skin.

"Do you not understand? I must go for my sister, for all the women being kept there. I must!"

"No. You must never go near that hellhole again. The women need saving? I shall fetch them for you. I shall free them and bring them back here to you."

He looked so determined, so sure of himself, that she wanted to believe him.

"You? Do you imagine yourself some chivalrous knight?" She gave a sad, unpleasant laugh but didn't miss how his nostrils flared. His hands had balled into fists. "This is my task, my quest, if you wish to be romantic about this. I must face this dragon myself."

"I understand that they need to be saved. But you? Back in that pit? I cannot allow it!" He positioned himself between her and the door, his bulk filling the space so that she could not even reach the knob.

"Allow it?" she said. Her teeth snapped together on the *t* sound. How dare he dictate to her? The surety on his face prompted an equal, opposing conviction rising within her. "You have no part in this. And you most certainly have no right to allow or disallow anything I do."

Redness spread over his face, his neck, even his ears. If one could spontaneously combust, he very likely would. His eyes blazed with possessive fury, and, as much as she wanted to defy it, she also feared how it resembled the fury she saw in Broek. She held her breath for a few moments until the feral light in his eyes faded. He was still angry, but the unreasoning, animalistic fury was quickly extinguished.

Sounds of the street coming to life floated in through the window. Carts creaking, wagons clattering by, vendors unpacking their crates and boxes and calling greetings to one another.

"I believe," he said, finally, "this morning means I have quite a major stake in this."

Then she said quietly, "I have a way in. I will secret the women out as quickly as I can." She hoped her tone was so moderate, so reasonable that she could convince him. She might even manage to convince herself. "Please," she said. "The other women are still there. *My sister* is still there. Would you honestly have me abandon them to whatever Broek has planned for them?" She blinked hard as her eyes watered. "I cannot do it."

He came to kneel before her and took her hands. All he could do was shake his head.

"Can you not see?" she whispered. "I would rather be a sacrificial pawn than a queen who survives because of the sacrifices of others."

"You need not sacrifice. I will fetch them." He kissed her palms one by one and then enveloped them both in his hands. It was the sweetest touch she'd ever felt. Every touch from him was the sweetest.

"You cannot free them, Skyler. You have no sense of the damage Mr. Broek is capable of. Even if you could overcome him, Takara would never go with a stranger. And even if she would, what then? You cannot open some kind of station for wayward women in your own home. What could you possibly do?"

"Simple. I shall expose Broek. He shall be justly imprisoned for his crimes, and you and the other women will be freed of this life."

"Simple? Freed? Now who is being naïve? What can you imagine would happen to these *oiran*? How are they supposed to live? Where are they supposed to go? They have nothing; Broek has seen to that. They have literally the clothes on their backs. They don't know how to speak English or write it. While they have passable feminine skills, like needlework and drawing, they have no reasonable way to support themselves outside of that house."

"You're saying they should go on living like this, suffering Broek's exploitation, because they have no other choice? You would rather consign them to selling their bodies than have them risk freedom in poverty?"

"Yes! No! I do not know! You make the options sound so simple. Utter poverty is far from simple, and right now those women at least have each other. To be thrust into one of your workhouses, unable even to ask for help or understand what others say . . . yes, it would be worse than what they have now."

He wrapped his arms around her, wanting to stretch his whole self around her like a shield, and was thrilled when she didn't pull away.

"But, Hana," he said, "if he plans to sell them, they may still find themselves alone and abandoned on the street, used and discarded and facing the same awful fate you wish to forestall."

"I made Mr. Broek promise me that the women would be taken care of and that my sister would go with me. He promised me."

Possessiveness thundered through him, frightening in its intensity, at the implication that she would go with whoever bid on her. He grasped at rationality. "What in your history with him gives you the impression he will keep his word?"

She opened her mouth to respond but then drew back. Unseeing, her eyes darted back and forth as she went through some mental inventory or calculation.

Taking advantage of her hesitation, he added, "Mrs. Duchamp knows people who can help, and I am certain she could find a safe house for them somewhere. What if we ask them? Give them the choice. If they decide that they are willing to risk the unknown rather than continue in this terrible servitude, then I will proceed. If they choose to let Broek dictate their future, then that is their choice."

He lifted one of her hands to his mouth and kissed each finger gently before replying, "You shall not return to the Jade Garden . . ." She took her hand from his, tried to pull away from his embrace. ". . . *alone*. And I will gather as many reinforcements as I can before we make any moves. Devin will help, I know it. Mrs. Duchamp obviously has allies who seem to specialize in this sort of thing. You shall not return to the Jade Garden without me."

Hot tears slid down her cheeks as a dizzying mix of relief and dread filled her. She *would* get them out. But it would not be easy.

She looked at him warily, but her shoulders lost their stiffness. Her face changed as she moved toward him, softening. In her eyes, hope shimmered. It was a look he wanted to see often: every day, every moment.

"Agreed?" he asked softly.

When she nodded, relief flooded him.

"They will be safe here at Evans Books for a short while as we figure out a more permanent solution. I am certain Mrs. Duchamp would be happy to shelter them here. She would likely be glad to have some company after living alone for so long," he added. And his demeanor lightened further when he said, "And I shall keep Mr. Broek occupied while you marshal your troops. You shall hurry but be safe. And silent."

She stretched up to kiss his cheek and just managed to graze his jaw with her lips. He lifted her off the ground so they could kiss properly. She blossomed for him. It was swift but deep, as if she, too, wanted to burrow into the kiss and never come out. When he set her back on the floor, he smiled broadly and then gave her another quick kiss on the lips before saying, "I shall confer with Devin immediately, and then we storm the castle!"

Off he went, his pace nimble, a vision of hope and determination.

She listened to his departing footfalls briefly before making her escape. As she moved down the hall on silent feet, she held her breath for any sound of movement. Too early for the store to be open and unlocked, she was certain she could manage to make her way down from a second-story window. The back of the house faced an alley. In the early morning, who would be watching it? Through the most sensible door, the room was full of crates. She tried not to think of them as a bad omen. She shut the door behind her without a breath of sound and inched her way between the crates to the window. A curse escaped her as she saw the lane bustling with people. Servants and delivery persons crossed to and fro.

She jumped when the door creaked open behind her.

"Miss Sumaki, how on earth did you find yourself in here?" Mrs. Duchamp spoke as one would to a skittish horse. Her father had used that voice often in their travels when dealing with wary animals and even more wary merchants.

"I did not mean to intrude, Mrs. Duchamp. You have been most hospitable. I needed to . . . relieve myself . . . and was unsure where to go."

"Oh, dear! I had not considered . . . I apologize." Her brow furrowed. "The house has not been quite right since my . . . since Mina left. I have a housekeeper come in daily, but she isn't due to arrive for a few more hours. I should have made sure things were maintained for you." She hurried out and up the stairs. It was mortifying to think of that woman handling . . .

"Wait, Mrs. Duchamp!" She caught up just as the older woman reached the bedroom door. "Do not trouble yourself. I am well able to look after my messes. Simply give me some direction on your household procedures, and I shall do the emptying myself."

"Nonsense! You are a guest."

"You already handle more refuse and detritus, if only figuratively, than anyone should have to. Please. I would feel simply awful."

Mrs. Duchamp acquiesced but added, "You should ready yourself to leave soon. Lord Ridgemont and Lord Devin estimate that you should depart for the Jade Garden, escorted by Ridgemont, at the hour mark. If there is anything you need, I am downstairs."

Hana nodded as her stomach flipped.

From the hallway, Mrs. Duchamp added, "You are no longer alone, Miss Sumaki. It may be difficult to embrace assistance when one has struggled alone for so long." She sounded as if she spoke from experience. "But learning to accept help, learning to trust in the strength of others, does not diminish your own power. It makes you stronger."

She certainly hoped Mrs. Duchamp was correct. They would need all the strength they could muster to lay siege to Broek's stronghold.

CHAPTER 21

A Complication

The Jade Garden looked so innocent and unassuming in the light of day. One would be hard pressed to imagine the depravity that lurked within. It matched with all the other houses on the street, with its nondescript stonework, its iron railings, its bland, rectangular windows. Passersby likely could not distinguish it from any of the other houses around it.

Yet Skyler was keenly aware of how very different this house was when he knocked on the front door and was ushered in by a large, gruff boulder of a man. He could only assume the man was some kind of guard, a new addition. How many like him were now patrolling the house? He prayed that Hana would not run into one. When they finally reached Broek's office, the human boulder pushed the door open without knocking and gestured for him to enter.

Broek stood by the window. Likely the man had seen his carriage pull up in front of the house. "Thank you, Vernon. Please stay nearby in case we need . . . refreshments." Given Hana's drugging, he resolved not to drink anything Broek had to offer.

"Ridgemont! My bosom friend and favorite cousin, what brings you here?"

The voice from the corner stunned Skyler. Bartwell? What on earth? Could he be relied upon to assist in overpowering Broek? A strange glint in his cousin's eye made him pause and reconsider the situation. A hollow nausea swept over him, although he could not quite explain it.

"Bartwell? Is that you? What on earth are you doing up and about at this hour?"

His cousin and Mr. Broek exchanged a knowing look, one that raised his anxiety even further, before gruffly answering, "Business."

Broek took his seat behind the desk and drew a file from the top drawer. Then he knew, even before either of them spoke again. He knew exactly why Bartwell was there and what he expected to gain. He knew, too, that it would take little time for his cousin to comprehend why he himself was there.

"I could ask the same of you, Sky. Business or pleasure?"

For a moment, he wanted nothing more than to beat the smirk off Bartwell's face, except perhaps to see Broek languishing in prison or, better yet, burning in the fiery pit.

"Ah, nothing of note. I have more Royal Commission minutiae to discuss with Mr. Broek regarding the performances. I am quite sorry to interrupt."

"Not at all," Bartwell said. His voice held a tone of self-congratulation. "In fact, your presence is timely. Mr. Broek and I were in the midst of an important business transaction, but he seems to be unable to fulfill his side of our bargain. Perhaps you can be of some assistance." His cousin gestured toward the other seat before the desk, no doubt a request for solidarity.

He shook his head. "Pray, do not allow me to disturb you." Alarm skittered down his spine. Where was she now? How much progress had she made? This new variable twisted their plans.

Broek sputtered momentarily before saying, "Surely, Lord Ridgemont, the paperwork can wait one more day. While Lord Bartwell is your relation, he may underestimate the sensitivity of our business arrangement."

"On the contrary, Broek," Bartwell said dismissively, "I would prefer to have a witness at this point in the proceedings, one who may attest to your failure to fulfill the transaction."

"Do you really wish your cousin to know the details of our exchange, as unflattering as those details may appear?"

"I wish to have what is now rightfully mine."

Skyler's blood chilled as the vague impressions in his head coalesced into harsh reality. Echoes of his cousin's braggadocio about an auction, about some rare plant, ricocheted in his mind. It couldn't be his cousin. Hana had said the bid was exorbitant. Where would he get that kind of ready money? More importantly, Bartwell, *his cousin*, would not stoop to such degradation of a woman, essentially buying a slave for his sexual pleasure. Or would he? No. Impossible. He forced himself to unclench his fists as he glared at his cousin. A vision of Hana spread out beneath him came to mind, and every cell in his body longed to crouch over her, like a tiger or a bear, growling *mine!* She'd shared so much of herself—her abominable past with Broek, her fears, her bravery. He could not let her go. He tried to school his features to neutrality, but it was too late.

Broek had been watching. When the man caught his eye over Bartwell's head, dawning comprehension crossed his cold, cruel face. So did a flare of rage.

"You," Broek accused, his face turning red as he stood abruptly. "Lord Ridgemont, I must admit that this is an exceedingly inconvenient time for you to call, since just last night I was the victim of a robbery. Breaking and entering as well, I believe." The tall stick of a man slowly walked toward him. "If I may be so bold, I do not believe you are here to discuss contracts. I think you may know something of last night's events. Where is she?"

His cousin looked at him in confusion, then at Broek, and the moment of awareness was as sharp and sudden as if a lightning bolt had struck him. Rising to his feet, he said, "You are the reason Miss Sumaki is not here? What have you done with my prize? Where is she?"

"Your prize! Do you hear yourself, Bartwell?" He could not believe the man who stood before him shared his blood. "You are speaking of a woman, of a human being, as if she were nothing more than a trinket."

"Oh, far more than a trinket . . . I would not pay fifty thousand pounds for just any trinket."

"Fifty thousand pounds? Have you lost all sense? Is that the funding your steward was going to use to seed all your villages for the late harvest?" Unless he was sorely misinformed, the loss of fifty thousand pounds would devastate the Bartwell holdings, which were currently not as impressive as the lineage implied.

Bartwell's face hardened as he closed the distance between them. "What do you know of my estates, Ridgemont? What business is it of yours? Do you really dare to question me about my affairs? You, who have been an earl for all of six months? You would do better to go back to drawing and leave the work to real men."

"Your schoolboy quarrels will have to wait," Mr. Broek interjected.

Before he could respond, Broek was inches away, and Skyler felt a cold, sharp prick at the corner of his jaw. A ribbon of fear shot through him as he recognized the bite of a blade against his throat.

"I think you know a great deal. You have taken something of great value from me, and I intend to make you suffer for it." Broek looked over his shoulder toward the door and made a jerking motion with his head. A moment later, the doorman and two similarly large ruffians had him pinned to a wall while they tied his arms behind him.

"Where is she, Lord Ridgemont?"

"You are the one who shall suffer, Broek . . . for your crimes against these women."

Sharp pain blossomed from his gut, and it took him a moment to realize that Broek had punched him. He could only be thankful that the brute hadn't used the knife that still gleamed in his hand.

"Do you really think he took her, Broek?" His cousin's voice sliced through the pain.

"Oh, I am certain. It is written all over his face. He took her, and I am equally certain he then *took* her."

"What do you mean? He . . . they . . . she is no longer . . . you think he took what is rightfully mine?"

When had his cousin become such an ass? Suddenly his head banged against the wall, the red-hot pain along his jaw competing with the insidious throb of his skull as both men crowded in upon him.

"You bastard," Bartwell screamed in his face. "I bought her fair and square. Untouched. She was mine to take, mine to break open." His cousin's fists came at him faster, his anger working into a frenzy. He would have laughed at this pathetic excuse for a man . . . if he could breathe. His nose must have been broken at some point, and possibly a rib as well.

"Enough, Bartwell!" Broek commanded. "We still need him able to speak. Now, Ridgemont, I assume you have had a chance to consider the error of your ways. Where is she?"

"I do not know." That was true. She should be in the house by now, but he had no idea exactly where.

Broek looked disgusted and turned to his guards. "Take him upstairs. Find out what he knows about Hana's whereabouts. Find out how much he owes me."

"You cannot abduct me," he argued. "People know where I am and will note my absence."

"Your own cousin, the quite upstanding Lord Bartwell here, shall corroborate that you left here under your own power, safe and whole. Only you have the ability to determine if that turns out to be true."

Unable to use his arms, Ridgemont resisted the guards futilely as they shoved him, stumbling and battered, up the stairs to a cramped room, possibly a closet. No furniture. Just fists and boots and pain. *Where are you, Hana? Get out, get out! Oh, God, I don't know where she is.* His last thought before the world went black was that he hoped Hana had a knife with her.

He jolted awake and couldn't help the groan that escaped his throat at the sudden movement. Virtually every part of him throbbed and ached. Even opening his eyes was a struggle. He heard shuffling outside the door, and heavy footsteps. His wrists burned from the ropes still binding him, and he struggled to his knees. There was a distinct chance he would not leave this room breathing, and he was determined to face whatever came standing upright. *Please, God, let Hana be safely away.* As he rose, watching the door, a whisper of a sound behind him made him whirl, eliciting another unbidden groan as the pain stabbed him again.

There, at the now-open window, stood a tiny figure, even smaller than Hana, clad entirely in black, including a mask covering the intruder's face and hair. Even in the dim light, the figure's golden eyes shone, startlingly familiar.

"Who are you?" he asked in a whisper, pain knifing through him as he tensed.

The visitor held up a palm. The footsteps beyond the door paused, and he held his breath. When the movement outside continued, the stranger moved behind him, and he felt the ropes slip away from his wrists. He rubbed at them, wanting desperately for this little person to speak, to identify himself, to tell him where to find Hana.

The nimble fellow was already back at the windowsill by the time he realized what was happening. He rushed close and whispered, "Is Hana safe? Has she gone?"

The figure looked at him with eyes overflowing, glowing amber eyes just like Hana's, and shook its head. Braced in the window frame, his little savior lifted both hands, holding one of them palm up while the other pointed to the door and then walked a path across the other hand to a room one floor down at the other side of the house.

He nodded. "Has she been hurt?"

Those eyes filled up again, but this time all he received was a shrug.

Then he whispered one last time, in barely a breath, "Are you Takara?"

His mysterious little savior bolted out of the window without answering, but he was certain. He leaned out to find her, but she was already halfway up a pipe leading to the roof. He dared not call out; he could stand another beating from Broek's guards, but he would not endanger Hana's sister. When he turned back toward the barren room, a long slim object on the floor drew his eyes. It was a fan: actually, two fans together, Hana's specially constructed fans, and there was a key tied to one handle. They were heavier than they looked.

With his new tools in hand, he was able to catch the guard at the door by surprise. One sharp, solid knock on the head with both fans in one hand rendered the man unconscious. He tucked the body into the small room, ripping a strip of the guard's shirt for a gag and locking the door behind him. Then he followed the visual directions his mysterious little savior had given him.

He heard the moans halfway down the hall and ran the rest of the way. In his panic at the sound of Hana's suffering, caution fell away.

He fumbled to open the door with his key as a punch slammed his forehead against the heavy wood. Hell, he would not lose consciousness again. Holding Hana's fan like a bat, he swung it at the brute's head with all his might. The crack of the man's jaw was audible. At first Skyler was impressed that the man didn't scream, but then his huge bulk stumbled back and slid down the wall. Behind the incapacitated man were a handful of women, all dressed in bright kimonos, a few carrying fans like Hana's. The one who'd struck his assailant stood up from her lunging position and bowed to him.

The scuffle was enough to alert Broek that something was wrong. Two more guards stormed out of the room, and the lock of the door snicked shut behind them. The Jade ladies swarmed, an astounding sight to behold as fans whirled and slashed, making their strategic defense look as delicate and benign as a butterfly. They didn't show the same grace and skill as Hana, but they left him in awe.

When he finally got the door open, Broek was holding Hana in front of him, one arm locked around her neck. The bastard had hit her. She whimpered, and tears left sooty tracks down her cheeks. He had once heard of a man going blind with rage but thought it was a matter of hyperbole. At this moment, the entire world fell away, a gray blur framing his singular vision. He saw nothing, heard nothing, felt nothing except Hana—her brilliant eyes wide with fear and pain, her voice broken. He needed to calm himself and act rationally to remove her safely.

"Damaging your merchandise seems rather shortsighted, does it not, Broek?"

Broek snarled, "You've already done the damage. Were there justice in this world, you'd be tried as a thief, a poacher!"

"There is justice in this world. In fact, I believe it is roiling directly behind me. I could not steal something you did not own."

Broek roared as he yanked Hana's hair and pushed her forward.

"Who do you think fed and clothed these strumpets? Who made all the complex arrangements to transport them here? Now all my work, all my efforts, are for naught. I heard them out there. Your duplicitous cousin has withdrawn his bid. This city is ruined for me now, and those rampaging cows behind you are worse than useless to me. I will extract what I am owed in blood!"

Truly the man had lost his mind.

He gripped the closed fan tightly behind him. When he met Hana's gaze, her fear dissipated. Without altering her stance or her movements, she stared at him with alert, calculating eyes.

"Broek, you may have lost some anticipated income, but surely poverty is preferable to charges of murder and kidnapping?"

"Ignorant whelp. Some anticipated income, he says. As if we were talking of a week's work or some steady annuity. Fifty thousand pounds, Ridgemont. That is what you and this whore have stolen from me." His arm tightened around her neck and she grimaced, her hands clawing at his sleeve.

"Enough, Broek. If you let her go, I will reimburse you. Hurt her and you get nothing." It would take all the funds he'd set aside for repairs, fall planting, new equipment. The estates would suffer, but he could scrounge together what he needed. He felt a twinge at the thought that servants might have to be let go. But he wasn't lying. He would pay anything, do anything, sacrifice anything to get Hana free.

"Get out of my way! You don't have that kind of money." Broek edged toward the door, yanking Hana by the hair, dragging her off-balance.

"I assure you that I do," he replied calmly. He didn't move but held himself light on his feet, ready to pounce. "Not all gentlemen of means feel the need to flaunt their wealth or are as careless as my cousin in their disposal of it. But I am not purchasing possessions. I offer you this as a fee for their freedom. Fifty thousand pounds is more than you deserve, but it will be more than sufficient for you to live comfortably."

"A fine thing, when a hardworking man gets robbed twice over. Fifty thousand pounds was for Hanako, and you made sure her worth was destroyed. Now you think to grab the rest as a bargain." As he reached the doorway, Broek loosened his grip on Hana, greed gleaming in his eyes. "The rest aren't as fine as my little blossom here, but they have their talents and have earned me quite a pretty penny." Broek called out to the hallway in stilted Japanese. Whatever he had said made the women back away from the door. "When can you get me the money?"

He stared at Hana, willing himself to keep the disgust from showing on his face. That she'd suffered under this man's thumb for so long was incomprehensible. "Such a large transaction should be handled with our legal advisers present, so Monday morning would be the earliest."

"Unacceptable. What can you give me as—"

Broek reached the stairway. When he glanced down to the entry hall below, he recoiled and shot a hateful look at Skyler.

"There they are!" a female voice called from below. Mrs. Duchamp.

"Stay down there," Skyler called down to her. "Broek has Hana."

"Broek!" a male voice responded. "Authorities are posted at the exits. Cease and desist immediately." Devin.

He would never have imagined such bone-deep relief at the sound of his cousin's voice. A sense of calm settled over him. He turned to Broek and said, "You have no recourse. Release her. Release them all."

"No—" Broek's negative turned into a high-pitched scream as he stumbled backward, teetering at the edge of the stairs. Only then did Skyler notice the figure, clad in black, crouched low behind Broek's legs, a small and shiny knife in her hand. Broek howled in pain, unable to stay upright, reaching for his ankle with one hand while the other still twisted in Hana's hair. Hana tried to scratch his face and push him away. With a sharp cry, she heaved against him and twisted out of his grasp.

Skyler watched, frozen, as Broek tipped over, his arms pinwheeling, a combination of pain and panic warring on his face. His body pitched over the still-kneeling Takara, his legs tangling against her, dragging her with him. Hana caught the railing but gasped as she saw Takara being pulled toward the stairs. Without conscious thought, Skyler lunged forward, grunting as his chest hit the floor and he grabbed for Hana's sister. He'd just managed to hook the sleeve of her robe before Broek's momentum sent the man toppling down the stairway. With a sickening thud, the body landed in an unnatural, unmoving heap at the bottom.

CHAPTER 22

A Whirlwind

In the hours after the death of Mr. Broek, Skyler could not ignore how outlandish the circumstances appeared and how very fortunate he was to have Lord Devin and Mrs. Duchamp assisting with what turned out to be a massive undertaking. When they spoke with the coroner and other authorities, he could see the potential for a scandal, the kind of lascivious, outrageous scandal the ton and the penny magazines fed on. Mrs. Duchamp and the other Needlework for the Needy ladies burst into an impromptu and impassioned lecture on the nature of prostitution and the plight of women without other options, particularly these women, who were entrapped and stranded, strangers in a strange land. Hana's injuries supported the impression that Broek's death was defensive, that the women had fought to assist her. With Lord Devin's involvement, they were able to convince the police that they would arrange temporary shelter for the victims.

He wanted to be by Hana's side upstairs, tending to her wounds, but the Jade ladies would not allow it. While the women went upstairs to tend to her and gather whatever belongings they wanted to keep, he paced at the bottom of the stairs, his senses straining for any inkling of Hana's condition. Mrs. Duchamp and one of the other Needlework ladies began discussing how they might distribute the women among their households temporarily. Devin spoke of Sharling Worth, one of the Devin estates Skyler remembered fondly from his youth, but said it would take time to make arrangements for all of them.

With his ribs protesting his movements, Skyler sat on the lowest step, every inch of him aching. He felt foolish and powerless. Everyone was talking above him or around him, as if he were that boy in his father's study, dismissed from all the vital discussion of the adults, considered superfluous in the shadow of his older brother, the future earl. Enough. He had a simple solution.

"They shall stay at the Ridge," he said with conviction. Despite the pain radiating from various tender parts of his body, he pushed himself to stand and assume the weight of his title. Fate had placed the mantle of succession on his shoulders, and this moment was the first time he felt as if he rightfully belonged in the role. This decision was his.

Lord Devin looked at him sharply. "Is that wise?"

The memory of Hana kneeling with Broek looming over her, of the blood trickling from her mouth, of her doubling over—wisdom be damned, he would not be separated from her. "The house has more than enough space. Each woman could be assigned her own room, for heaven's sake. Why discommode so many of your homes when they could easily be sheltered in one place with minimal disturbance? It may seem out of the ordinary, but my greatest concern is for their safety. I can confirm with ease that they will be safe, secure, well treated, and together at the Ridge."

"Out of the ordinary? That is quite an impressive understatement." Devin's voice was even, but his brow arched. "Your own mother would go into hysterics, at the very least, and she would carry the rest of the ton in her affronted wake."

"I shall appeal to her sense of Christian charity."

Devin didn't answer, which was reply enough.

"And if she isn't in a charitable mood," Skyler added, "she can go live in the stables."

The picture of his mother in such rustic new lodgings was remarkably entertaining, and his cousin even chuckled before pointing out, "Your house is just out of mourning. Devin House would serve the purpose until they can retire to Sharling Worth."

"No!" The ferocity and immediacy of his response shocked him. Devin's jaw dropped, and a dim corner of his mind noted the historic event. Mrs. Duchamp looked at him curiously. There was no room for cold rationality in his brain. He needed Hana close. "The Ridge is their home for the foreseeable future."

"You would need at least one chaperone present," Devin replied, censure radiating from his stiff posture. "Perhaps my mother would be willing to stay with them. Perhaps one of these fine ladies would as well."

Although his cousin bowed to the Needlework ladies, he couldn't help but notice that the man would not meet Mrs. Duchamp's searching gaze. She flinched when she noticed that everyone except the object of her attention was watching her. Her face reddened, but she simply said, "The Ridge it is, then. We can certainly keep them company there."

Light, hurried footsteps sounded from the staircase, and they all turned to look. When little Takara rounded the rail post, her tense expression sent him bounding up to meet her.

"What is it, little one?" Skyler asked.

She frowned and said, "Do not call me that. Only Hana calls me that." It was an order, not a command. How strange for one so young to be so self-possessed. She stared at him. "Come, sir. She wishes to speak with you."

The child bowed to everyone and quickly ran back up the stairs. With a nod from Devin, he followed at a jog and caught up with her at the top of the landing. Her haste alarmed him, but no one had asked for a physician. That had to be reassuring, didn't it?

The room she led him to was small, much smaller than the one Hana had used before. The pallet took up most of the space, and a small crate sat next to it, adorned only with a candle and three small jade figurines. Takara gestured for him to enter and then closed the door gently behind him, leaving him alone with his heart's deepest desire, wrapped in blankets, staring up at him with those large golden eyes.

"I needed to confirm you were not injured," Hana said, without any greeting or prelude. She moved to sit up with her back against the wall and her knees pulled up to her chest. The blouse lent to her by Mrs. Duchamp had been replaced by an indigo kimono with fine embroidery along the sleeves. The darkness of the fabric contrasted sharply with her skin, and the swollen purple bruise on her cheek made his pulse pound in his ears. If he hadn't gotten to her when he did . . .

"I have been in torment downstairs, waiting to confirm your injuries and . . . to comfort you. The Jade ladies insisted that they see to your wounds and that you be shielded from public view until you decided you were ready."

She stood slowly, gingerly, and moved toward him, into him, and he could not help but wrap his arms around her. Her hand gently swept along his brow and down his cheek.

"Your nose is broken." She gently ran a finger along his upper lip. He caught it in his hand and turned her hand so he could kiss her wrist. "Did Broek do this to you?"

"You will likely have a blackened eye in the morning," he replied, savoring the sensation of stroking her hair, of all those strands of liquid midnight, softer than silk. "Your erstwhile winning bidder started the job. And Broek's guards built on his foundation."

"I could not bear being the cause of your pain," she said, frowning.

"You are not. I would do anything to keep you safe, to bring you happiness," he said. "The thought of Broek causing you harm infuriated me, but then seeing it, seeing you hurt by his hand, drove all sense from my brain. I wanted to tear him apart with my own hands."

"So did I, when I realized what he had done to you." She gripped his hand. "You're bleeding!"

"It is just a scratch."

"You stupid ox! Just a scratch! You need a physician's care." She reached past him for the door, flinching as she stretched, but he stilled her hand.

"All will be well, Hana. If I needed a physician, I would have sent for one. My concern is for you. How do you feel?" He raised a hand to cup her uninjured cheek, the softness of her skin a constant wonder to him.

"I am passable. I will live."

"Good," he said. He ran his thumb across her lower lip, felt it quiver, felt her slow exhalation.

"Still, this needs bandaging." she said, her determined tone cutting through the quiet intimacy of the moment. She pulled down the sheet covering her, untied her kimono, and began tearing at the bottom of her chemise.

"What on earth are you doing, Hana?" The sight of her bent low, her robe flowing open and allowing glimpses of her covered only by that thin chemise, sent his blood rushing from his head. He knelt in front of her, stifling a groan as his ribs protested. "Darling, there is no cause to destroy your clothing. It is just a scratch."

"No, Skyler. You are badly injured. At the very least, someone should set your nose and wrap your hands. You likely have broken ribs as well, but I doubt you have the sense of a tsetse fly at the moment."

"You are so charmingly domesticated like this."

He laughed when she answered with a decidedly uncharming grimace but stopped abruptly when she not so gently tightened a strip of fabric across his hand. This Hana was so different from the one he'd seen at the Exhibition, so direct and unguarded. She'd hidden away so much of herself, kept her words and thoughts in check. This Hana was already blossoming from the absence of Broek's tyranny, as if the real Hana had been biding her time, hoping and waiting for the opportunity to take control of her life.

"Assuming you and the other ladies are amenable to the arrangement, one of my properties informally called the Ridge has more than enough space for all of you. You and the Jade ladies may have a wing of the house to yourselves, and you would be welcome to stay for as long as necessary. Lord Devin and Mrs. Duchamp know of a property in the country that might serve as more of a home for all of you, but the Ridge could be your refuge until you are ready to make more definite plans for the future."

She paused in her ministrations and looked at him with shock.

"That would be . . . we could not possibly . . ."

"It would be no trouble at all. Most of the Ridge is currently unused. To leave it unoccupied while you all scramble for shelter is illogical."

"Surely it would not be proper."

"Mrs. Duchamp and her Needlework friends intend to chaperone on a rotating basis. And I will make myself scarce. If needed, I can rent an apartment temporarily." The thought of her in his house without him was bleak. But he would rather have her there, safe and secure and comfortable, even if he could not be with her. "Miss Tsubaki and Miss Bana are already leading the packing."

"You smell like happiness, too," Takara mumbled, tucking her face into Skyler's shoulder as he carried the exhausted child into his home. The women of the Jade Garden had unanimously agreed to stay at the Ridge until they could arrange more permanent lodgings. It was dusk before they finally crossed the threshold, and Takara had fallen asleep on the carriage ride. He led the troop of women through the house to the east wing, the guest bedrooms. Maids were hurriedly pulling the covers off furniture and trying to air out the stale rooms.

"What was that, little one?" What could she possibly mean?

Takara tightened her arms around his neck, pinching, until he gripped her more tightly, more securely to his chest. Then her whole body relaxed.

"Hana-san has been happier recently, not always so serious and bossy. When she comes home happy, she smells like you. I don't know what that is, but I like it. Not sour or so flowery it makes my head hurt. I always felt bad for the Jade ladies, having to put up with the stink of the visitors."

He paused in midstep as her revelation hit him, and then he moved ahead slowly, allowing himself to unwrap in his mind the gift that the child had just given him. When he glanced back, Hana was talking with one of the older women near the end of the line, her head down, her posture respectfully rigid, her hands held politely in front of her. The other woman's bearing was similar but—was that Tsubaki?—was not cowed, the way he had first seen her. The two seemed so engrossed in their conversation that it was unlikely Hana had heard her sister's words. Would she have contradicted it? She'd trusted him to accompany her, to protect her, but that didn't mean she cared for him. *She's been happier recently. That had to count for something.*

He jolted awake and sat up so fast his head spun for a moment. Something was wrong. Someone lurked there in the dark. His skin prickled with awareness. Futilely scanning the room, he reached for the matches and the candle on the bedside table, his nightshirt straining as he stretched his arm.

"Wait. Darkness is better." Hana. Close. Her voice pitched low and seductive as velvet. The whisper of her clothing said she was nearly by his side.

He bolted to stand on the opposite side of the bed and lit the lamp. She blinked rapidly, and disappointment flitted across her face before she resumed an expression that set his pulse racing. But things were not right. Powder masked the bruises on her face, and her eyes seemed more mysterious, her lips more full and welcoming. He'd never before seen the gown she wore. When he'd rescued her the night before, she wore an elaborate chemise, one designed to highlight her innocence. This sleek whisper of finery was a dessert for the senses, not at all innocent. Even from this distance, the sheen promised silk that was sinfully soft and warmed by her skin. Even in this dim light, the revealing shape and cling of the gown made clear there was nothing underneath it to interfere with the wearer's enjoyment of the fabric against that skin. At her sides, her hands opened and closed repeatedly, a movement at odds with the seductive vision she presented. It was something she did when she was nervous.

"What are you doing here, Hana?"

She looked at him with longing and a touch of defiance.

"I miss you," she replied.

"You should not be here."

"Everyone in the house is asleep. No one will know. Once was not enough, and there is no reason we cannot indulge ourselves now, as long as we are careful." She moved slowly around the bed, one hand stroking the bedding and the wood along her path. Her voice was convincing, but her eyes maintained a wariness that did not bode well. She knew he would deny her, and she knew as well as he that he should.

"Why are you here, Hana?" He crossed his arms in front of him.

She pouted, her mouth looking sweet as berries, but even that little gesture rankled. This was not Hana.

"Whatever you desire, in this moment you may have it," she promised, this siren in silk. "Last time was too hurried, too limited, but now you can do whatever you want. I can do whatever pleases you."

She reached for him and tried to pry his arms apart. When he would not budge, she leaned over his barrier, her body warm and tight against his, and pressed her lips just above the opening of his nightshirt. He groaned as the shocking warmth and softness of her lips sank into his chest, the heat settling in the vicinity of his groin. Still, as desire surged within, he could not shake the sense that this moment was not right.

"Why are you doing this, Hana?"

"Because I want to. Because I need to."

"You have been through a great deal of distress in the past few days. You do not know what you are doing, and it would be wrong of me to take advantage of your vulnerable state."

She blinked rapidly, her hands pulling at his arms in earnest, as she said, "But I am offering you whatever you might want. How can you not accept? Any man would!"

The change in her demeanor set alarms off in his head. He un-linked his arms to grab her shoulders and separate their bodies but did not let her go. "Only a base animal, without control over his bodily instincts, would. A thinking man, a reasonable man, would want more than just to engage in physical pleasures."

After struggling for a moment to close the gap between them, she quieted. A tear slid down her cheek, leaving a dark track in the white powder.

"Never touch me again in a lie, Hana."

"Admit to yourself, if not to me, that it was not a lie—it was a fantasy."

"Not mine," he said firmly. "Now why?"

"The women are afraid. All we knew was Broek. They do not know what to expect or how to survive here. Broek would not have hesitated to cut a girl loose if displeased. They want reassurance. They want a guarantee that we will not be scattered and abandoned. And I thought this would convince you."

"I have already guaranteed sanctuary to you and to all of them. For as long as you all need, you will be safe and want for nothing here."

"We need a place to *stay*. In the morning, when your world learns we are your houseguests, your resolve shall be sorely tested. A week from now, the pressure to remove us will be overwhelming.

The women need more assurance, and such certainty does not come without payment."

"It does from me. This is not the protection of courtesans, and I am not a pimp. You are guests here, welcome to all the hospitality due any Ridge guest, for as long as you need."

She stepped back out of his reach. He could see her mind working, turning his words over and around and inside out, looking for loopholes.

"Hana, the next time you visit my bedchamber, come in honest desire or not at all. Come out of passion for me, not for my title or my funds or my protection. I cannot deny that I want you badly, but I shall not touch you unless you truly want me from your heart."

Hana touched his hand, a fleeting whisper of her skin against his, the simplest of gestures. Then she reached up and pulled his head down to meet hers. This time, the touch of her lips against his was dizzying, overwhelming. She held nothing back. Her desire felt real and true. And he wallowed in it, wrapping his arms around her and lifting her off her feet to deepen the kiss. When she whimpered and tried to wrap her legs around him, his senses exploded. Yet one word burst through the chaotic passion: *stop*. So, despite everything in him that longed to keep going, to strip her of her gown and revel in her sweet bare skin and her breathy moans, to bury himself in her silken heat and make her scream with ecstasy, he gentled the kiss and eased her down. He had to swallow a groan as her body slid down his to touch the floor.

She looked up at him with resolve, her eyes bright with desire. "Was that honest enough, Skyler?"

He exhaled sharply, exasperated. "This is not a test. You owe me nothing. You and the others may stay here as long as you need without obligation. Now go back to your room."

"So you do not want me?"

It took a supreme effort not to explode. "Of course I want you! For heaven's sake, I want to make you my wife. I said as much at Mrs. Duchamp's bloody bookshop." At that, she gasped and her eyes nearly bulged out of her face.

What use was it to try to fool himself? He would marry her in whatever way he could get her, aside from coercion, and damn any member of the ton who tried to stop him. If she wanted the security of his estates, the prestige of his family line, the protection of his wealth and status, he would lay all of it at her feet in an instant. His mother would surely suffer apoplexy, perhaps even try to have him deemed unfit. None of that would matter if Hana accepted him as her husband. But he wanted her to choose him because she wanted him, only him, as much as he wanted her.

She gaped at him. So he took a deep breath and took a step back, mentally as well as physically.

"I wish to assure you, Miss Johannsen, that you and your companions may rely upon the house of Ridgemont for as long as you need to establish your independence. I have no doubt that you will find great opportunities for success in London."

A ghost of a smile swept across her face at his use of her actual surname, but then confusion lurked in her eyes, dark and shrouded. She stepped back but smiled tentatively.

"You have been most kind, Lord Ridgemont," she said with a bow of her head. "In fact, as you may know, Mrs. Duchamp has offered various supports, including her rooms above the shop and her contacts throughout London to assist us. Lord Devin has suggested a budding community called Sharling Worth as our new home. Some of the women hope to return to Japan, and there is a chance they will be welcomed by their families when the circumstances become clear."

"Are you certain about that? It does not sound as though . . ."

"Not all families would welcome such used women," she acknowledged, "even though these women had very little choice."

"You need not be afraid anymore, Miss Johannsen."

"I am not afraid, Lord Ridgemont," she replied, her chin jutting out defensively. "If I were, the Jade ladies and I would not have survived this long."

It was then that the pieces fell into place. She never showed fear. All these roles she played, all these masks, hid her fear effectively. She'd needed to be so strong for so many others and for so long that perhaps she'd convinced herself it wasn't there. But it was, possibly now more than ever, because now she faced a nebulous foe. She'd been able to craft strategies to deal with Mr. Broek, however ineffective those strategies had been. That enemy had been clear. This new one was a Hydra, with so many heads snarling and snapping from multiple directions.

"What we—I—what I need is a plan," she said.

Pain flared in his chest. It was amazing how much that little correction stabbed at him. Already she was trying to distance herself, to push him away.

"You need not do this alone."

Her hands trembled, but she only said, "They are my responsibility."

"They were Broek's responsibility." He tried to lay his hands over hers.

"You are not to blame."

She looked down at their hands and tried to pull away, but he wouldn't let her run from this.

"Hana, look at me." Then he dropped his tone to a whisper. "Look. At. Me."

Her silence unnerved him, as did the increasingly frantic tugging of her arms. He should let her go, but if he did, she would bolt and never face this. She needed to hear, needed to be absolved, needed to forgive herself.

"Hana," he whispered. Finally, her eyes met his. She stopped struggling but only just. Her body stood stiff, unyielding.

"You are not at fault here. Broek used you. He used your love for your sister and your sense of responsibility against you; you were as much his victim as any of the other women." He wrapped his arms around her and held her close, wishing truth could transfer from skin to skin. Her body shook as he continued to whisper words of comfort in her ear, words of understanding. As long moments passed, her arms slowly crept up between them and encircled his shoulders. Her tremors eased as her grip on him tightened.

She mumbled into his chest.

"What was that, darling?"

When she lifted her head to look up at him, her face conveyed a bleakness that chilled him.

"I cannot forgive myself until they are all safe. Yet, even with the assistance of Mrs. Duchamp and her friends, how can I afford to house them all, much less save enough money for their travel expenses? This is something I must do. It is a matter of honor, but what if it is a debt I am unable to pay?"

She looked like she could shatter at the slightest impact. Gently, so gently, he took her face in his hands.

"You are not alone. We shall do this together. Whatever you need can and shall be provided."

"Whatever I need . . ." She leaned into him, touched her lips to his, just a faint brushing, a feather. More potent than any of the kisses that had come before. She needed him. When she let him go, she stared up at him, undisguised desire glowing in her eyes. "I need so much," she admitted, "but what I need most is just to feel your arms around me . . . just to feel safe in this moment."

"You are safe, Hana, and so are the others. They acquitted themselves well, and my staff shall treat you and your Amazon army like the queens you are. Bear this in mind: they are here, safe and secure, because of you. If you blame yourself for their suffering, you should also credit yourself with their relief."

CHAPTER 23

An Objection

"Intolerable! The letters were true! My only remaining son courts scandal and ruin, and now I see for myself that the rumors are entirely founded." Ensconced in a cloud of black, Lady Ridgemont swept into Skyler's study with Lord Bartwell at her back. What an untimely coincidence that his dear cousin should come to call at this precise moment, a pivotal moment that could easily shape the future of the Ridgemont family. Untimely and unlikely. Bartwell was not finished with him yet.

"Welcome home, Mother." He stood and bowed to her without releasing Hana's hand. It was three days since Hana and the other Jade ladies had made the Ridge their temporary home. Three days in which the house had been filled with warmth and laughter the likes of which he hadn't experienced in years. And Hana had begun to laugh, too—not the bitter, sardonic chuckle or the artificially cheerful giggle, but rather the kind of laugh that caught her unawares and bubbled up without conscious decision. It was a beautiful sound, one he sought to tease out of her at every opportunity. She'd come in to deliver a vase of flowers, placed it on the corner of his desk and laid her hand on his shoulder. He'd made some quip and brought her fingers to his lips. The combination of their fresh lightness and her lifted spirits buoyed him amid all the paperwork. But now an ominous cloud had darkened the room.

"That is all you can say to me, Ridgemont? Welcome home? As you stand there brazenly touching that . . . that dirty savage? Are those from my garden? Of all the—! I shall not have it!" She stalked into the room, right up to them, forcibly crowding Hana so that she had to let go of his hand and move away.

"Mother!" He grabbed for his mother's arm, but she whirled toward him, setting him off balance as well.

"Your father would be appalled to see you consorting with the likes of this one," she said as she jabbed a finger into his shoulder. "I would never have expected your head to be turned by a skirt, especially one such as that . . . person. What a fool I was! I told Bartwell he was being ridiculous—that he must be fabricating this outrageousness out of whole cloth—because you, my son, my only remaining son, would never stoop so low."

His hands clenched into fists as he looked over at his cousin, whose attention was riveted on Hana. His expression rapacious, the weasel canted toward her, as if scenting his prey.

"Bartwell!" His cousin's head whipped to face him. "You wrote to my mother? What did you say to her? What possible business was it of yours to say anything to her at all?"

"As a close relation, I felt it was my duty to help protect the honor of the Ridgemont name. You must have known that there were whispers around town of your infatuation with that little dancing girl there, even before this week, ever since you were seen strolling together so charmingly at the Crystal Palace."

It took every ounce of self-control not to strike the smug expression off his cousin's slimy face. Standing behind Lady Ridgemont, Bartwell gave a twisted smile, dripping with menace and mendacity, that sickened him, as if the man hadn't tried to *purchase* Hana, his intentions far from honorable. Did his cousin think that putting his mother on the attack would make him put Hana and the rest of them out, defenseless, for his cousin to descend upon? His jaw clenched just to see the blackguard in his house.

"You should be on your knees thanking your cousin instead of interrogating him, Skyler," his mother said before he could compose a fitting response, considering the presence of ladies. "What

194 • *Amara Royce*

could you possibly be thinking? What spell has that Oriental witch cast upon you to turn your head so? To make you forget entirely who you are and what your responsibilities are? It's shameful!" At that, she burst into tears.

"Mother, shh." He led her to a couch and patted her hand. With a quick glance, he saw Hana edging toward the door. "I am sure you have had quite a taxing day. Travel in this heat is so wearisome. Let me have a tray brought up for you. You can take some sustenance and rest. Emotions are clearly running high, and I am as much to blame as anyone. Rest, and then we can discuss this when we all have clearer heads."

"Get that *woman* out of my house, son." He was accustomed to his mother's cold derision. But this vociferous fury transformed her into someone he didn't recognize, a grotesque.

He went to Hana and leaned in to whisper, "I am so sorry for her ugliness. This scene is going to get worse, and I do not want you to be subjected to it. Why don't you go to the sunroom for some quiet, or perhaps go find your sister?" When she nodded hesitantly, with a frown of concern, he added, "Nothing has changed between us—"

"Ridgemont! This deplorable fault in your manners is unacceptable. I know I raised you more civilly than to whisper at some . . . woman . . . in front of me."

"Mother, I shall speak with you momentarily. Until then, you have upset a guest of this house, and I am acting as any responsible host would by providing reassurance and an opportunity for said guest to be freed from this unpleasantness."

"She is *not* a guest in this house. I will not have it. Get her out of here. Now."

Lady Ridgemont's face turned an alarmingly deep red. Before he could stop her, Hana moved toward his mother as she said, "Lady Ridgemont, are you well? I fear that you may be at risk of a breathing attack or worse if you continue thusly."

His mother recoiled, almost climbing up the back of the couch.

"Do not dare touch me. Heaven only knows how much you have already polluted my home. Now get out. You are not welcome here. Leave now." She was shrieking, near hysteria.

"My dearest aunt, I shall remove her myself." Bartwell had slithered toward the couch and now patted his mother's hand.

Skyler snapped. Later, he would recall the sensations of that moment—the surge of fury that had his skin tingling and his ears ringing. As if a door had slammed in his skull, one moment he'd been reasonable, wanting to establish harmony between his mother and the woman he loved, and the next she ceased to be a part of his world. He simply could not care about any of the woman's wishes. She'd gone too far.

"In point of fact, Lady Ridgemont, this is my house. You have lived here as the widowed baroness, but you should make yourself accustomed to the idea that this house is not your sovereign state. And Bartwell, you would do well to remember that you have no authority here. If even the touch of your breath upon her causes Miss Johannsen any distress, you will regret it."

His mother sputtered and hurried to ring for a servant. "How dare you speak so! I shall have both you and your strumpet removed immediately!"

"Do not waste your energy, Mother. You know as well as I how things work. I am now the rightful head of this family and of this house, as well as the other estates and their manors and farms and villages. No one will be evicted without my say."

"I shall have you declared incompetent!"

At last he knew how little his mother regarded him. The sight of Bartwell patting her hand and murmuring soothing platitudes at her was sickening.

"My business dealings since returning to London are beyond reproach," Skyler said. "My sanity and capability have perhaps at no other point in my life been so clear. There are a number of highly respected members of society who would attest to this. I understand that recent developments may make you uncomfortable, but Miss Johannsen is utterly remarkable."

The glow on Hana's face as he said this made the rest of the world fall away. Even his mother's scowl as she looked from him to Hana could not touch them. His mother could not be reasoned with at this instant, only neutralized. At some later point—soon—he would insist that she apologize for insulting his love, for digging at her with such horrible precision. Granted, his mother could not have known how sensitive Hana was to accusations of immorality, yet she obviously participated in the simplistic narrow-mindedness that equated Eastern women with looseness. At the very least, he would protect Hana from his mother's venom. Later, he would determine how his mother should make amends, if willing, or at least be civil, if that was all she could manage.

"Charlotte! How good to see you! Why did you not send word that you were returning?" Lady Devin swept into the room blithely, seemingly unaware of the tension. She kissed his mother on the cheek and said, "If I had known, my son and I would have invited you to stay with us at Devin House while the Ridge is being used for sanctuary. Oh, these poor women. They have such tragic . . ."

Lady Devin trailed off and stared at his mother, who was ominously still and obviously fuming. No one capable of sight would miss the bright flush that rose from her throat and suffused her face as she listened to Lady Devin. His mother had only just calmed, and now the pink of her skin darkened to deep red as comprehension descended.

"What are you talking about? What do you mean by *sanctuary*, Rose?" His mother's shrill voice cut through the room. He winced.

"Mother, allow me to explain," Skyler interjected.

"Oh, indeed, please do. Begin with what your aunt could possibly mean about this house being used as a sanctuary for—what did she call them?—poor, tragic women. Has the Ridge become a seraglio? How many harlots are we housing at the moment?"

Hana winced as sharply as if his mother had slapped her. He wrestled with the primitive urge to lunge at what had caused her pain.

"First, Mother, please hear me: These are not harlots. They are fine, upstanding women who were torn from their homes and deceived into what amounts to slavery. They are good people."

"I seriously doubt that. What has happened to you? My son would never allow his head to be turned so easily by a woman, much less an uncivilized foreigner. I can only assume the other women you speak of are like *her*."

It was a wonder that Hana remained quiet at that. He would not have blamed her if she had thrown the nearest vase at his mother for so thoroughly insulting not only her but the women she loved and protected so fiercely. Still, she didn't mask the blaze in her eyes. It could incinerate stone.

Lady Devin interceded. "That is rather uncalled for, Lady Ridgemont. This is a fine young woman whose behavior has been unassailable. I wish I could say the same for yours at this moment."

"Do not dare to chastise me in my own home, Rose. Of course you would stand up blindly for such rabble. You have always been too softhearted, too lacking in proper decorum, too weak. So unconscionably liberal. You have no say here. I hear that you have gone so lax with the Devin name that your son is now ensorcelled by a common merchant. You, who were always so blind to your own husband's wanderings and indiscretions—it is no wonder you would support such degradation for my son when you so readily accepted them into your own husband's bed."

The sharp crack of a slap echoed through the room. Lady Devin must have bolted across the room in the blink of an eye. He'd never seen her so infuriated, and he could not fault her for it. Yes, he'd heard the rumors, mainly from his own parents, but his uncle had obviously adored Lady Devin. His mother held a hand to her cheek, her mouth agape, her eyes wide. He pushed Bartwell aside and knelt before her. When he laid a hand on her arm, though, she pushed him away and rose stiffly.

"How dare you, Rose!"

"You shall address me as Lady Devin or not at all. I am still due all the respect of my husband's title, even from you."

"Lady Devin." His mother's voice was laced with spite and venom. "You dare lay a hand on me. That only proves your baseness. It is no wonder your husband reveled in filth."

Lady Devin's voice was dangerously low. "You shall cease these slanderous claims about my husband. Immediately. I had no idea you harbored such terrible and absolutely false beliefs about the elder Lord Devin, a man so far superior in word and thought and deed that you should be ashamed to even consider such lies. My husband never betrayed my trust. I do not know how you could think him capable of infidelity."

"Everyone knew. Why else would he travel abroad so much? You were not enough for him, and he could indulge his perversions with the likes of her." At this, his mother gestured wildly at Hana. He caught her hand in motion.

"Mother!" He felt helpless to stop the vitriol spewing from her mouth.

"Oh, it was widely known, Lady Devin. The ladies pitied you for your husband's flagrantly exotic predilections. We always wondered how you suffered through your marital duties when he was in resi-

198 • *Amara Royce*

dence. You were lucky not to catch some nasty disease from his ad-
ventures."

"Enough, Mother."

"Yes, Ridgemont, it is enough." His mother faced him, her head
high and her posture imperious. Despite the bright handprint on her
cheek, she wore the mantle of authority. "Get these women out of
my house. I have had more than enough of their distasteful company."

He saw now that there was no other way. She would not be
swayed or cajoled. He coughed delicately before responding, his
voice low enough that only she would hear. "I realize that your
emotions are quite agitated at the moment, so your memory may be
affected. As I said just a few moments ago, you would do well to remember, Mother, that this is my house now. I have deemed that
Lady Devin and Miss Johannsen are welcome to stay for as long as
necessary. Lady Devin has graciously offered to accompany Miss
Johannsen and her companions to Sharling Worth. This house is open
to them for their preparations. The servants have instructions to assist
in any way possible, and I recommend you stay out of their way."

"How dare you? How could you treat me with such contempt?
Your father would be horrified. Your brother—your dear, sweet
brother—would never, never have behaved so shamefully. I cannot
begin to imagine what sorcery this little witch is using to corrupt
you." Her eyes glittered, whether from unshed tears or from fury, he
could not tell. Her gestures grew increasingly erratic, her face increasingly red and blotchy as she looked around and found no support. "You cannot evict me from my own home, Skyler, and you
certainly cannot dictate how I treat strangers who trespass on my
property! These whores are not welcome here, and I have no
qualms about calling the authorities to have them forcibly evicted.
The Devin line may sink itself into disgrace as it pleases—in as
many ways as its family members choose to wallow—but the
Ridgemont name is above reproach."

"Please, Mother, do not make this situation more onerous than
you already have. There is no need for ugliness. This is my property
now, as are all the entailments. There are plenty of Ridgemont holdings that would make pleasant homes for you." He moved slowly
toward her, keeping his voice low and even. "You could have your
pick of houses, mansions." When he stood within arm's reach of

her, he dipped down to catch her eye. "You would be so much happier at Bath—or perhaps Brighton. The clean air and the ocean. It's so peaceful there."

Her gaze turned hard. *Damn.* She would not go quietly.

"I am not an old brood mare to be put out to pasture when her usefulness is done. And I shall not allow you to sully the name of your forefathers. You may think the law would side with you, but I can assure you that good society will know right is on my side. You have seen with your own eyes how some have turned their backs on your aunt with all her loose, undiscriminating associations. It is a wonder anyone still receives her. We are above that. Now get rid of that girl."

He glared at his mother, fury scrambling his brain and locking his tongue. When he looked over at Hana, a heavy weight settled in the pit of his stomach. All her usual bravado was gone. She was twisting her hands together in front of her and staring blankly at the floor. She'd retreated into herself. Even when Broek had forced her subjection, she'd had a core of steel and fire. There was no evidence of that now. Alarm overtook his anger.

"My deepest apologies, Lady Ridgemont. It is not my wish to cause disharmony," Hana said quietly, and then quickly added, "The Jade ladies and I do not have many belongings." Her tone matched her swift movement toward the door. He felt her slipping away, and not just physically. The moment his mother had entered the room, she had caused a fissure. He'd been too focused on his mother to see it. And in the space of one conversation, it had yawned into a canyon. He could hear it in her defeated, submissive voice. "With so little to pack, I am sure we could depart within the next hour. We will leave as soon as possible. Lady Devin's gracious—"

"Hana," he whispered.

She glanced up at him for a second, only a second, before she reached for the knob and pulled the door open.

"No!" The syllable—the command, really—was out of his mouth before he even consciously thought the word. Without conscious decision, he blocked her exit. Even after everything he'd said, everything they meant to each other, she thought he would simply send her away. His gut roiled. "No, you need not rush away on my mother's account. You and the other ladies shall stay here as long as you like."

His mother sputtered and ranted, kept at bay by Lady Devin. Under other circumstances, the very thought of Lady Devin corralling his mother like a stable boy with an errant colt would set him chuckling. Instead, distantly embarrassed at his mother's crudeness, he ignored them both and instead focused all his attention on the dark, forlorn beauty who still refused to look him in the eye.

"I—*we* cannot cause a rift between you and your mother. There is no reason for me and the others to linger here."

He stroked her cheek, and she froze. The explosive gasp from his mother made clear she hadn't missed the action and knew precisely what it meant.

"There is every reason," he said. "There is the most important reason—you love me and I love you."

Finally—finally!—she looked up at him. The fear and doubt in her eyes demolished him.

"I will not have it, Skyler!" His mother's shrill voice cut across the room, and Hana jolted away.

"Enough!" He whirled to face his mother. "Because I am your son, I would not dream of insulting you. I shall not, however, allow you to treat Miss Johannsen so unconscionably. If she will have me, I mean to marry her. I advise you not to test my loyalties."

Miracle of miracles, the woman shut her mouth, but such a divine gift wouldn't last long.

When he turned to speak with Hana, all that remained was the gaping doorway. She was gone. Lady Devin hurried to follow. "There is much to be done. I shall ensure that the ladies have what they need."

To her great credit, her demeanor did not falter when Lady Ridgemont repeated, "Ladies! Ha!"

His aunt paused as she passed him and whispered in his ear, "Well done, Sky, but brace yourself. The war is far from over. Take heart. That young woman is stronger than you think. I am certain of it. If you stand together, nothing can stop you."

He gave her a quick peck on the cheek in thanks and then returned to the devastation.

"I am sure Lord Bartwell has other very important business to attend to elsewhere. We should not keep him as we sort through all this confusion."

Bartwell smirked but bowed to Lady Ridgemont nonetheless and allowed himself to be escorted out. Neither he nor his cousin spoke until Bartwell's phaeton arrived.

"This is not over, Sky. No one steals from me."

"Desist, Bartwell. We are no longer boys arguing over a wooden soldier or competing to be 'sent up for good.' There are people at stake, living, breathing people deserving of respect and honor."

His cousin's scoffing as he shook the reins was all the answer he received.

CHAPTER 24

A Decision

No longer facing an audience, his mother sank onto one of the sofas, her hand tracing the carvings on the armrest. She looked tired.

"Your trip must have been quite an ordeal, Mother. After tea, perhaps you would like to retire to the Lavender Room for some reading or other relaxation."

She nodded, every movement slow and drawn out. For the first time, he noticed how worn she looked.

"You must understand, Skyler, that I have only your best interests in mind." Her paleness worried him. He sat and took her hand, cold and slightly damp. She gave no resistance; it was like holding an eel that had gone bad. She didn't seem to notice. "Your brother made the same mistake and suffered terribly for it."

"What do you mean, Mother?"

"Surely you recall that debacle with the Italian opera singer."

"I am sorry to say I do not."

"Of course you do. He made an absolute fool of himself over a nitwit in the chorus. An Italian! He couldn't even be discreet about it. I could not show myself in public for months. Eventually, as these things go, she came to our door claiming he'd gotten her with child and insisting he make her his wife. The little strumpet! Everyone knew what she was, except your poor, ensorcelled brother. He saw her true nature clearly enough when she took the prize we offered to leave him be. She took the money and disappeared. For all I know, there was no child. And even if there was, it was a dreadful mistake on his part. We were so afraid he would compound his error by marrying her and possibly making that mistake an heir." She shuddered as she stared out of the window,

"Mother, when would you say this took place?" Dread tiptoed through him. He'd been caught up in his studies, but Father had always kept him abreast of family news. How could a situation this momentous have slipped by?

She waved a hand carelessly. "Last year, in the spring. Your father was so fraught with anxiety."

"I was in Philadelphia then. No one ever wrote to me about it. Why would Father not tell me?"

"It matters not."

How often had he heard that from her? *It matters not.* When Father lectured Lionel about some reform law or another and he tried to interject with questions, she always said, "It matters not." Such an all-purpose response, instead of saying *you are too young, too unprepared, too frivolous, too curious, too much in the way.* For the first time, he feared that what his mother truly meant was not *it does not matter* but rather *you do not matter.* She'd always favored Lionel, the first son, the golden child, the heir, but he'd never realized how much lower she regarded him.

She raised her head and took his hand in both of hers. "What matters is that you must not allow yourself to risk so much based on something as mercurial as passion. While it would pain me to see you heartbroken now, it would tear my heart asunder to watch you be used and disillusioned by marrying a woman who is not right for you."

He wanted to object. He wanted to be affronted. But this time he saw the mother he once knew. She didn't rail, didn't command. She looked much like she had when she'd found him dangling high up in a tree or chastised him for riding Tempest too hard, too fast. He must have been thirteen or fourteen at the time, not bothering with the stirrups, reveling in their heady flight. Yes, that was her face now. Pinched and weary. And concerned. Or perhaps just too inconvenienced.

"You have just met her," he replied gently, trying to keep the tenuous peace of the moment. "In point of fact, you have not had any opportunity to converse with her thus far."

She closed her eyes and stiffly leaned back against the cushions. "I know enough about her to determine that she is not of our station. Entirely unsuitable. Could you prove me wrong?"

"No. She has no claim to nobility, not in England and not in Japan. Her father was Dutch—"

"A half-breed? Have you no shame?"

"Mother!"

"Has she anything to recommend her?"

My heart. She most certainly has that.

"She has a great talent for languages and is rather a remarkable mimic. She can carry herself as regally and demurely as Her Majesty."

"Those are *not* characteristics to her credit, and you know it. No matter how convincingly she could speak and pour tea, she would still be a foreigner. Even with Lady Devin fawning over her, she would not be accepted by polite society. You would doom this family's name, this family's grand history to disgrace and ostracism. You. Could you destroy centuries of this family line over a woman?"

In for a penny . . . her position was not likely to change anyway. "You should know, Mother, that she is a performer at the Great Exhibition. I made her acquaintance through my work with the Royal Society."

"*What?*" His mother stood abruptly, her expression suddenly sharp and focused, her eyes narrowed to slits. "You mean she is a common *actress*?" She spat out the word. "Do not, Ridgemont, do *not* tell me she is a *circus* performer! Have you gone mad?" He had never seen her so incensed. "I would not have allowed such a dalliance before, but I was at least beginning to pity you for your affectionate nature. But this—this is beyond the pale!"

His mother rushed out of the room and toward the stairs. She bellowed at the servants in the hall. She, who never, ever raised her voice above a level suited for conversation, screeched, "Get them out of my house! Get them out immediately! Toss that rubbish into the street! Whatever linens they've used, burn them all!"

To their credit, Tyler and Mrs. Durst presented themselves with all the decorum of their positions and looked to him for further directions. He shook his head silently, and Tyler returned to his duties. They'd been in service for as long as he could remember. Now, when they could have sided with his mother, they openly deferred to his authority. Perhaps he could fill this role after all.

"My lady, may I take you to your rooms?" Mrs. Durst offered. "All this turmoil cannot be good for your health."

"Oh, Mrs. Durst, you cannot begin to imagine. You will see that my house is set to rights, will you not?"

The housekeeper's eyes went to him again, and again he shook his head once. She bowed her head to him and simply replied, "Leave everything to me, my lady. Your things will be unpacked with all due haste to make you comfortable."

Mother patted the woman's shoulder. "I can always count on you to be the sensible one in this house."

As his mother made her way up the grand staircase, Mrs. Durst remained in the hall. "If I may speak plainly, sir?"

"Of course, Mrs. Durst. Your perspective is always welcome."

"Those women don't belong in this house."

He looked at her sharply. "Is that so?"

"It is, sir. This is scandalous on a massive scale."

"And why should I care about the scandal?"

"I am not saying that you should, my lord. Yet this situation is damaging to everyone involved. It's not just about what your mother thinks or what society people may think. I don't suppose you've seen them, Miss Johannsen's companions? They are terrified and hurt, and this place is too much for them, if you don't mind my saying."

"I had not considered that. But what would you suggest? What alternatives do they have? I could not relegate them to a horrid workhouse."

The housekeeper shivered. "No, by all means, no. But there must be some other place where they could make a more permanent home, where they could feel less exposed and out of place."

"They will depart for the Devins' Sharling Worth manor in a

matter of days. Surely, in that short a time, they can safely remain here."

"Given your mother's . . . state of mind, I doubt that, sir. But I defer to your judgment."

"No matter, Mrs. Durst. Please make sure everyone is comfortable. To preserve the peace for the time being, perhaps our guests should be served meals in the east wing."

"Very good, my lord."

Now to find Hana.

Hana paced along the aisles of the conservatory. All the hateful things Lady Ridgemont had said were so familiar. *Gaikokujin.* Foreigner. Never welcome. Just like her mother's father had said. Despite herself, images of her mother flashed before her. She buried her hands in one of the flowerpots, digging her fingers into the earth, to keep herself in this time, this place, but to no avail. The horrors of that day long ago, of her mother sure and unwavering in her self-immolation, bombarded her. The coldness of the stone floor beneath her barely registered as she knelt amid the plants and flowers and sobbed. For how long, she did not know.

"Hana! What are you doing down there? I almost did not see you."

Sky. Just the sound of his voice made her ache, made her focus, made her hope. But that was exactly what she should not do. Her mother had shown her that.

"Lord Ridgemont," she said as she rose.

He looked at her in confusion.

"Am I not Sky to you, Hana?"

You are the sky and the stars and the moon to me. She trembled with the agony of what she was about to say. "Your assistance has been commendable, Lord Ridgemont, and deeply appreciated, but the Jade ladies and I have obviously overstayed our welcome. They should be ready to leave before supper, and Lady Devin has kindly offered to house us until Sharling Worth is ready. So we shall not inconvenience your house any further."

"Hana, do not do this. You know my feelings for you. Do not let my mother's narrow-mindedness upset you. There is no power behind her words. It is only bluster."

"Even the wind has the power to level houses."

"Hana, please, let me in. Light may dispel the shadows." His hands landed gently on her shoulders.

She could have held it in, kept it all to herself, if only he hadn't touched her. Once she felt the warmth of him, she sank. Once she felt the strength of his arms surrounding her, enveloping her, shielding her from the world, it slipped out.

"My mother killed herself. She disavowed me and my father and Takara in order to restore her family's honor after the disgrace of marrying an outsider, of bearing half-breed children." She nearly choked on the words. His entire body convulsed, but he didn't let go. Thank the stars he didn't let go.

"We were visiting her parents for the first time since my birth. Before we arrived, my father objected, said it would be a mistake. My mother said something about how they would change their minds when they saw me and Takara." She almost couldn't breathe as the memory hit her, the coldness of the man and woman who were introduced as *ojiisan* and *obaasan,* their hard faces in permanent frowns. That primal fear at the back of her skull rose as if they were again staring down at her, glaring as she performed the greeting her mother had taught her.

"They weren't happy with us. I didn't know what that meant. Then, there was supposed to be an important ceremony. But children were not welcome. My parents argued in a distant room. So loudly. My father yelled and cried, and my mother did, too. All I heard clearly was that she made him promise her he would not interfere," she continued quickly, as if afraid to stop. "I pretended to fall asleep and piled cushions under the blanket so it would look like I was still in bed. Everyone was facing away from the door, so no one noticed me slipping into the room. My father sat at the very front, next to my mother's father. I cannot even call that man my relation. That his blood flows through me still makes me ill. He refused to accept me and tore apart all I held dear, so there is no reason for me to recognize any connection with him beyond the accident of biology. I don't know how Papa bore it, sitting there, staring at my mother as she plunged the knife . . . through her throat." Bitter saliva flooded her mouth. For a moment she couldn't speak, could only cling to him. Drowning as all the horror and confusion flooded into her again, Sky was the only solid thing anchoring her.

"How did you bear it?" he asked softly. "How did you avoid notice?"

"I think I was too shocked to react. When her body . . ." She trailed off and shoved her face into his shoulder. His arms tightened around her, infusing her with a feeling of security, protection. Finally, she lifted her head again. "When she was gone, her father went up to her and put his hand on her head. When he turned to leave the room, I could see he finally looked pleased. Others filed behind him to honor her passing. *My* father just sat there like a statue. I hid behind a screen at the back until the room was empty. Mama was left laid out on the mat; I suppose now they were giving her spirit time to move on. Alone with her, I couldn't cry. It's a wonder I even breathed. My father eventually realized I wasn't in my pallet and found me asleep next to her, curled around her head."

"My God, Hana! That is too much for a child to bear."

She was no longer that child, and she had to make him see.

"My mother had to make that choice—between her people and her lover, her children. She chose poorly. Or maybe no choice would have been good. I will not make you face that impossibility. I will not tempt you away from honoring your family."

"Hana, I am not your mother. Yes, my world prizes honor as much as your mother's, but I have no intention of sacrificing my life, nor would I be expected to. Do you know the shape ostracism takes here?" When she shook her head silently, he explained, "We would not be invited to parties and balls, we would not receive social calls, acquaintances we met in the course of our daily lives would give us the cut—not a literal cut, dearest, but a public snub— and yet we could easily continue to live our lives without suffering."

"What of your business affairs? What of the people for whom you are responsible? What if they object? Or . . . what if they suffer because their lord is snubbed?"

He stroked her hair fondly. "Whom I marry is none of their concern. Whether they object, all they need to know is that I fulfill the duties associated with my title. Whatever society thinks of me, those responsibilities can be fulfilled, those estates maintained." He tapped a finger under her chin and caught her eye. "I wish you to be my family. You do not tempt me away from honor . . . it would be my honor to marry you."

CHAPTER 25

A Plan

The lush, green expanse surrounding Sharling Worth was deceptive. It gave the impression that this was a pocket universe, its own sovereign entity, an idyllic oasis untouched by society. As he stood on the terrace overlooking the gardens, Skyler grinned at the notion of this little independent state run entirely by women. A few of the women were tending the vegetable garden, filling their baskets with ripe cucumbers and lettuce and such, pulling out weeds along the way. Miss Ume and Miss Tsubaki were cutting chrysanthemums and laughing as they conversed. It was remarkable to see them all so sedate and content.

When he heard the heavy clacking of male boots approaching, he said, "You know, a central figure is missing from this pastoral scene: your Mrs. Duchamp. I was surprised to learn that she has not visited and can only assume that you have not been suitably persuasive. So, my poor coz, when do you think Mrs. Duchamp will succumb to your manly wiles, cease her rabble-rousing, and settle into her role as your mother's successor?"

"Ha!" Devin responded. "I wondered how long it would take for you to jab at me. I was surprised you did not take an opportunity at lunch and thought you might be ill." His cousin clapped him on the shoulder and scanned the scene before them. "Cease her rabble-rousing . . . She shall stop when there is no more breath left in her body. To suppress her efforts would be criminal. She is amazing." As Devin's hands moved to grip the railing, the tense set of his jaw and shoulders belied his jovial response.

"What about marriage, Devin? You cannot deny you want her as your own. Having seen you in her presence and having seen you deprived of her presence, I suspect we would all be much better off with her nearby. And do not forget, I have met the woman several times. She is just as consumed by you. If you both cannot find your way to each other, I should draw a damned map and drag you through it." He ought not to press the issue, but it so closely mirrored his own situation that he wanted, needed, to voice his position, testing its edges.

With a sigh—he never heard the old Devin sigh, for heaven's sake—his cousin responded, "Ridgemont, you know as well as I what obstacles such a union would face. My mother's role as an eccentric patron of the masses is merely tolerated. Marriage would be a very different beast. I would not wish to put Mrs. Duchamp through the scrutiny and disdain that would undoubtedly fall upon her. The last time I saw her, she argued that the work I have been doing, the progress I am making to limit the commerce of obscenity, would be eclipsed by even the slightest scandal. I would not care for my own sake, but I cannot, I will not, allow Honoria to be affected by any of that muck."

"Says the do-gooder. What have you to fear when you are championing righteousness?"

"Do not mock me. Any repercussions should fall upon my head alone. She remains above reproach."

"Becoming a viscountess might put her even farther above reproach."

"Do you think I have not tried?" Devin's voice had tightened and risen nearly an octave. It was as near as Skyler had ever seen him to loss of control. "She will not have me. I even . . . Sky, for heaven's sake, I even went to my own mother for romantic advice. I am the very picture of abject desperation. She will not see me, and I cannot risk her reputation any more than I already have."

He tried to suppress a grimace. Lady Devin was a sympathetic audience to everyone, but even he balked at the notion of asking her for romantic advice.

"Mrs. Duchamp is a widow. You are a viscount. You could only improve her social standing, not damage it."

"The scandal would be severe. Do you think I care whether society accepts us? Those vultures can go hang. What matters to me is that she be treated with respect, that she continue to be seen as the admirable, capable woman she is. I would not have anyone think less of her for any reason."

"You, Alex, are an idiot. If you feel thus, why have you not taken her to wife?"

"Do you not hear me? I have tried! You have no idea, no idea in the slightest what has gone on between us. I can but hope her heart opens to me eventually."

At that, Skyler turned to him and said wryly, "Oh, I think I have *some* idea. I think I have a very clear and vivid idea, in fact, of what it feels like to want more than anything to marry the one woman who lights up your soul but be blocked at every turn by the qualifications of our station."

"She is a lovely woman, your Miss Johannsen."

"She is not *my* Miss Johannsen yet. Between us, I despair that she ever shall be." He studied passing clouds, the sight of all the productive women below only adding to his frustration. "How have we two come to such a nadir? Besotted and despairing. Surely we are among the most eligible bachelors in England."

"Would you want anyone else?"

He scrubbed his face with one hand before looking at Devin. He couldn't answer, but he also couldn't bear the thought of leaving Sharling Worth at week's end. He didn't just want Hana; he needed her. He couldn't stomach the thought of anyone else.

"Neither would I, Skyler. Neither would I."

Light, purposeful footsteps made them turn toward the glass doors leading into the house. A maid he did not recognize made a quick curtsy and said, "My lords, there is a visitor. Miss Hearsch asked me to fetch you both. The gentleman is unknown to her, but he said he is a friend of yours. They are in the drawing room."

Devin nodded. "Did you get his name, Jenny?"

"A Lord Bingwell or Bagwell . . . Bratwell?"

Skyler cursed under his breath, and the maid's eyes went wide.

Without looking at him, Devin said, "Lord Bartwell? Tall? Boorish?"

A nervous giggle escaped before the girl clapped a hand over her mouth and nodded.

"We shall meet them immediately. Thank you, Jenny. Please inform Miss Johannsen of our visitor and assure her that Lord Ridgemont and I shall entertain him. Then inform the cook to prepare tea. Do you have all that?"

She nodded solemnly and then took her leave. Devin turned to him, frowning and agitated.

"What do you think he wants, Ridgemont? Money?"

"I imagine he still wants Hana, or at least her equivalent," he said with disgust. "He has the impudence to come here!"

"Given all you have said about him, I do not wish for Miss Hearsch to suffer his presence any longer than necessary. She has been through too much already."

He nodded. Before his first visit to this little haven, his cousin had explained as delicately as possible how Sharling Worth became the home of more than a dozen women, some with children, who had been freed from a pornography ring. Amazing, really, how quickly innovations in photography had already been put to such depraved use. These were some of the women who'd led to his vociferous insistence in Lords on stricter obscenity laws and investigations. Miss Hearsch, while not the oldest of the women, had been raised in Mrs. Duchamp's household and had a knack for managing, so she became the de facto leader of the house. And, while Devin had been too gentlemanly to broach the subject, Mrs. Duchamp had decided that Skyler needed to know that Miss Hearsch was not only her former housekeeper and lifelong friend but that the young woman had also been duped by one of the pornographers and left in a delicate condition. That was perhaps one of the most uncomfortable conversations he'd ever had.

As they neared the drawing room, he heard his cousin's voice, raised but muffled. They quickened their pace, and he crossed the threshold in time to hear Bartwell demand, "Where is she, you little trollop? Tell me now!"

Miss Hearsch sat on the edge of the sofa, hunched over, struggling to free her arm from Bartwell's grasp. The man backed away abruptly as he and Devin entered, and Devin threw Bartwell a quelling look before kneeling in front of the distraught woman.

"You have no right to barge in here, Bartwell, and demand anything of anyone. Have you no shame, bullying a young woman like that? Have you no respect?"

Devin's composure and authority grounded Skyler, who was so full of rage that he couldn't find the words to speak. He wanted Bartwell gone now, sooner than now.

And then, to make things worse, Bartwell opened his mouth. "My respect belongs to upstanding ladies, not to flagrant whores. I know who she is. From all those pictures I saw of her, I would recognize her anywhere, even with her clothes on."

Skyler clenched his teeth and counted. Then he said, "You would do well to treat all the women in this household as if they were Her Majesty's daughters. You would also do well to explain how you came to be here, since I am certain no one extended you an invitation."

"I thought Devin was having a house party and my invitation had been waylaid." The dolt chuckled at his own poor attempt at wit. Everyone knew Devin did not throw house parties—ever. Lady Devin was known for balls and dinner parties in town, but the Devins never entertained at their country houses. Devin would have a moat dug around Sharling Worth first.

Unwilling to tolerate Bartwell's snideness another moment, Skyler said flatly, "There is nothing for you here, Bartwell."

Devin caught his eye while leading Miss Hearsch out of the drawing room. Good. He could rely on Devin to keep Hana safely away. He hadn't even seen her since he'd arrived midday, and he would be damned if Hana would be subjected to this degenerate. They would need to send some reliable footmen from their London houses to guard the house in the future.

"Miss Sumaki belongs to me, Ridgemont. You stole from me! I want what I am owed."

"The young woman in question has reverted to her real name, which is Miss Johannsen. As I thought I made clear before, you cannot buy or own another person. If Broek did not refund your payment, that was between the two of you. Hana—Miss Johannsen does not factor into your transaction."

Fool his cousin might be, but the man caught his slip. He'd used Hana's given name. His cousin's rage flared with comprehension.

"I knew it! I knew you had her, but I didn't want to believe it." The man howled before launching at him. "She was my prize! My sweet peach! Now you've defiled her. And your ridiculous attempt to mask her with a European name does not hide who she is, what she is."

He wrenched his cousin's hands off of him and pushed the lout back.

"I intend to marry her, Bartwell. Would you have done the same with your *prize*?"

Bartwell's face contorted into that of a stranger, lined with jealousy and anger . . . and perhaps a bit of hatred.

"Marry her? Ridiculous. Marry a savage whore like that? She belongs to me, my property as much as one of my stallions or those marble busts I had commissioned last year. I would sooner marry one of them than an immoral slut like her." He sneered, and then his eyes glittered with intent. "Tell me one thing, coz. Was she as talented as promised? Did she make you explode with lust? Did she do unspeakably delicious things to you and let you do them to her in return?"

Skyler literally saw red. Red flashing and pulsing in front of him. Red crashing in his ears. Red filling his lungs. He was slamming Bartwell into the stone wall by the fireplace. He couldn't speak, couldn't hear the thuds of Bartwell's skull against the stones. But in one sharp moment, he could feel again—something cold and pointed was jabbing into the soft area under his jaw. Bartwell had grabbed the poker.

"Get out, Lord Bartwell," Skyler said, despite the metal at his throat. "This is your only warning. Leave now. Do not ever disturb Miss Johannsen's peace again. If she agrees to be my wife, you shall have to answer to me unless you cease this behavior immediately."

"Your wife," his cousin barked, followed by a harsh laugh and a sharper jab with the poker, forcing him to move backward. "Your mother shall be livid. She suspected your weakness; now I am certain that is why she told me where to find Miss Sumaki. She will never agree to such debasement of the Ridgemont line."

"What my mother wants or agrees to makes no difference. If Hana will have me, I shall make her my wife," he said, softly, calmly. Even Bartwell's histrionics meant nothing, if only Hana would have him. If only this lunatic would leave her alone.

Bartwell practically spat. "You are a fool. She is not worth destroying the history of Ridgemont. Don't bother to marry her. Just pass her along to me when you become tired of her. I can wait, even though—"

A distinct whistling sound was followed quickly by the *shhh* of slicing fabric.

Bartwell immediately spun to face his new attacker. Skyler saw the long diagonal rent in the back of his cousin's jacket. Long, direct, and shallow. Just enough to cut the jacket but leave the layers beneath untouched. Then he saw the assailant, and his breath disappeared. Hana stood dressed in a short robe and wide-legged pants, the costume of the juggling Izo, but her hair was pulled back simply and her face was undisguised. She had smudges of dirt on her face and dusty spots on her knees, and she was the most glorious sight he'd ever seen. Her wide-legged stance and fierce expression suggested she had experience wielding this sword, a gleaming short sword with a wrapped hilt. Bartwell paled and dropped the poker.

"Bartwell, I believe this is Miss Johannsen's way of saying your interest in her is not welcome. I recommend you recall what I said a few moments ago and return to London. There is nothing for you here."

"Allow me to be even clearer, Lord Bartwell," Hana said, her voice ringing out. "I belong to no one, least of all to you. If you try to come for me again, I will cut off any part of you that touches me."

He could have cheered. This was the woman he adored, this fierce warrior goddess. This was the woman who commandeered his dreams and who made him want to carve out a life he'd never imagined before. A woman who made him feel anything in the world was possible.

Red-faced, Bartwell stormed out, calling, "Your mother shall see that this marriage never takes place!"

CHAPTER 26

A Promise

"You look quite serious," Hana said as she approached. She laid down the sword on a display table, but the tension in her body remained. She looked up at him tentatively. "You sounded quite serious as well. Nothing is worth this amount of strife."

You, he thought. *Only you.*

"You are worth all of it, Hana. When I saw you there, like your own avenging angel, you overwhelmed me. Together we have nothing to fear, not from Bartwell or my mother or whatever silly, judgmental buffoons come along. Especially with that weapon in your hands. Wherever did that come from?"

As he spoke, she'd started to shake her head. When he took her hand, she stared at him, her lips parting as she took shallow breaths. Her golden eyes glowed, stirring an answering heat within him.

"It was among the goods Broek kept under lock and key. The quick-thinking Tsubaki insisted we take it with us, along with a few other trinkets she found. I didn't believe we would have need of it, but I am so very glad we brought it."

"You are magnificent. There is a power in you I have never witnessed before. You have no idea how very strong you are, how well you have protected your friends and continue to protect them."

She bloomed in front of him, her shoulders relaxing, pleasure suffusing her. She smiled up at him brightly, openly, as if she finally had unfurled all of herself to him.

"That look," he said. "Tell me I am the only man you have ever looked upon like that."

Her mouth quirked as she tilted her head and replied, "You realize, I hope, that there is no way for me to know how I looked to you? There is no possible way I could make that statement with any guarantee of truth."

"I know. I still want it. I want so much of you. Everything. Just for me." He stepped away, as if overwhelmed by his confession. "This possessiveness terrifies me. I have known nothing like this, this insistent desire. Absolute and exclusive. Me and no one else. Ever."

"That . . . is impossible," she said quietly. "I am sure you could not give me the same."

"Yes, I absolutely could," he said, firmly.

She stared into his eyes, her brows furrowed, as if she wasn't sure exactly what he meant. He watched comprehension settle upon her, followed gradually by belief.

"Yes," he repeated. "I already have. You and only you."

She shivered and moved closer, keeping her eyes connected with his.

"Here is what I can give to you. Here is how much of myself I have." She closed her eyes and took a deep shaky breath. "The way I feel with you, I have never felt with anyone else. This intensity of feeling, this overwhelming eclipse that blocks out the rest of the world—I only feel this with you." She went to him. "This"—She wrapped her arms around his waist and pressed her body fully against his—"this completeness I have only shared with you."

He stilled, and a storm of emotions whipped across his face in a matter of seconds . . . fierce triumph, joy, shock, fury, and, finally, a steely determination. His body tightened around her.

"Only me," he said, low and fierce and possessive. "Only you. And there shall not be another."

*　*　*

A bruised and fragile thing, hope inched toward her, meandering and retreating and darting in lightning bursts until it settled in a corner close by yet just out of reach. She wanted to believe him. All this time, she'd been accustomed to taking responsibility. Again and again he defended her. Again and again he demonstrated his devotion to her well-being. Sharing some of that control, some of that weight, trusting someone else to have her interests as close to his heart as they were to her own—for the first time, this seemed possible. Those broad shoulders could carry some of her burdens. That straight spine and firm jaw could stand up for her. Those powerful arms could protect her, would wrap her in a cocoon of muscle and bone. And that smile. Surely he could see into her mind because that smile lit her soul.

It took every ounce of Hana's patience to drag him up to her rooms. Gods preserve them, Skyler could be stubborn. When she first caught sight of him stepping down from his vehicle, the surge of longing had made her dizzy. She'd leaned against the windowpanes, relishing their coolness, as weighty emotions charged through her. She'd thought of him often as she and the Jade ladies made Sharling Worth their home, but stark yearning coalesced into a white-hot flame when she saw him, when the possibility of being in his vicinity—of possibly even touching him—became real. There was desire, yes, but more than that. The promise of being near him felt . . . comforting.

When she heard him arguing with Bartwell and saw the blackguard attack him with the poker, she couldn't rein in her emotions.

As she led him up the stairs and through the vacant hallway, his hand in hers, that passion flared again, at once chaotic and calming. This moment made sense to her, made her feel whole.

"We should not, Hana. The whole house is awake. It would be improper, indecent." His objections would have been more believable if they weren't at the door of her bedroom.

"No one will disturb us," she said quietly. When she smiled up at him, his eyes moved down to her lips. She smiled even more, sensing his capitulation. And then she said what she knew would seal his fate. "If we are engaged to be married, what could be the harm?"

He blinked, as if needing a moment to process her words, and then his eyes met hers. He all but exploded out of his skin as he swept her up in his arms and met her mouth.

"Are we, darling? Are we engaged to be married? You would not answer me downstairs."

"There was one small matter, a detail you overlooked." She smiled against his lips and felt, rather than saw, his hesitation.

"What?"

"You have not asked me. You have declared your interest and intentions several times, but you have not, in fact, asked if I agree."

"Well, do you?" he prodded. He pulled his head back and squinted at her. She couldn't help but notice that he had not released his grip one bit. "Agree, that is?"

"Yes, decidedly yes."

"Then we are engaged." That was all. No questions. No need for an explanation. His open, easy grin sent warmth shooting along her spine. He made it sound so simple. Heaven knew she'd heard enough empty words over the past few years to doubt their validity. This harmony of feeling didn't need a grand declaration or invitation . . . it simply *was*.

She did not respond with words, but her mouth enthusiastically affirmed his conclusion as she tucked her head against his shoulder and gently tasted his neck. His breathing quickened encouragingly. The muscles of his shoulders went taut beneath her hands, and he hitched her up more solidly in his arms.

"Please," she said. "I have missed you, missed feeling whole."

He shuddered and loosened his grip enough for her to slide slowly down his body. When her feet touched the ground, she leaned fully into him, resting her head against his chest, reveling in the solid feel of him all around her. She reached behind him, opened the door, and gently pushed.

"Lady Devin has been a truly remarkable hostess," she said as she walked him into the room and closed the door behind her. "It stuns me that she has opened this mansion not only to us but to the other women her son and Mrs. Duchamp rescued. Miss Hearsch told me about the pictures taken of them, the horrors to which they were subjected. Their experiences so strongly echo our own; I believe that is one reason the Jade ladies have settled here so easily.

Even though they still struggle to communicate, they all share that knowledge."

He stroked her cheek as he looked at her fondly. She could stay there forever, basking in his gaze, breathing in his presence.

"As pleased as I am that they are all doing well, I do not wish to speak of them right now. There are other things that command my attention at the moment." He leaned down and touched his lips to hers softly. "In fact, all my attention . . . is centered on . . . the wonder before me," he added, punctuating his words with delicate kisses.

The tenderness radiated through her, sparking a passion that she'd been suppressing, hiding even from herself. Before, her desire was born of desperation, that one moment of decadent freedom no one would be able to take from her. This time, there was no threat of loss, no hourglass stealing the seconds away from her. This time, she could luxuriate in every delicate sensation. She could savor every touch, every look, every sigh. She huffed as she struggled to push his coat off his shoulders. With his cooperation, the close-fitting jacket was soon draped over a chaise in the corner and was swiftly followed by his waistcoat. She paused to appreciate the warmth of him through the fine cotton lawn of his shirt.

As she wrapped her arms around his waist and inhaled deeply, she felt his torso shift as he looked over at her massive bed. Even at home with her parents, she'd only ever slept on a low pallet near the floor. The only bed that could be at all comparable to this was the one Broek had installed the night her innocence was to be claimed by Lord Bartwell, and that was so much kindling compared with this large, elevated, and ornately carved island of a bed. She needed the wooden steps at the bed's base to climb up onto this monstrosity that could have accommodated all the Jade ladies simultaneously. Instead, each woman had her own, along with her own bedroom and sitting room. The first night, Takara had sneaked into her bed, fearing the massive emptiness of her own. Soon, they'd all adjusted. This time, when she glimpsed the expanse of pristine sheets and enveloping feather mattresses, she welcomed it as a blank canvas on which she and Skyler would build their future.

His efforts to disrobe her refocused her attention. He shook with laughter as he tugged at her obi, unable to release the knot. "Could you please explain to me why you are dressed as a boy? What mischief were you perpetrating before I arrived?"

"It is actually a combination of pieces, all the most comfortable ones. The *hakama* enables me to ride on horseback and generally move much more easily than all those skirts and underthings. I was doing some repairs, and this was more suitable than my delicate silks." She dropped her voice as she added, "I believe some of the Englishwomen find our kimonos very appealing, if a bit scandalous. Our clothes are so much more comfortable, even our *tabi* and *zori*," she said, as she stuck out her foot and displayed the simple sock and sandal. The amusement on his face transmuted into something quite different, something intense and perhaps even possessive.

"Scandalous, indeed," he said, his voice thick with emotion. He cleared his throat before adding, "You might not know this, but it is quite improper for a gentlewoman to show her ankles in public, much less wiggle an exposed leg provocatively."

Yet the look on his face showed anything but disapproval. If anything, her actions seemed to motivate him. She brushed his hands away and easily untied the obi, letting it fall to the floor. She likewise made quick work of untying her *hakama* and shedding her kimono and undergarments as well. When she finally stood before him completely unclothed, she was pleased to see he had spent the time wisely, divesting himself of the rest of his clothing as well.

She barely registered the keen lust emanating from him as she looked upon all of him, hungry to see every inch of his glorious skin, his lithe musculature, like some of the statues at the Exhibition. Entranced by the sight and greedy for more, she dropped to her knees, ignoring all but the insistent desire to taste him, to savor him.

As she felt him approach his crisis, she slowed her motions. When his hips bucked to prompt her, she stopped completely and sat back on her heels.

"Dear God," he said, as he took deep gulps of air. When he finally looked at her, guilt suffused his features. "I am so sorry. I would not ask anything so crass or disrespectful of you."

"Do not be silly. You did not ask. I offered. In fact, I insisted. And I am not finished."

"No! I cannot allow you to continue. Have the other women not explained what happens when you do such a thing?"

"Of course. That is why I wished to."

"But . . ."

She took his hands in hers and rested their intertwined fingers against his thighs.

"It is true that they describe the act rather unpleasantly. They would all prefer not to service a man so, or at least all except Ume. But there are differences. First and foremost, they did not have a choice. I do."

She felt bereft when he disentangled his hands from hers and pulled her up to stand before him.

"Yes, you do."

"I choose you. I do this not to please you." She laughed at his raised brow. "Your enjoyment is incidental. I do this because I want to know you. I want to explore every inch of you. I want to delve into every corner, every dark secret. I crave every bit of you. I have already had my hands on so much of you, and it was not enough."

His lips felt hot, so hot, and demanding as they landed on hers. The commanding sweep of his tongue against hers sent a shiver through her. She had never wanted anything with more fervor, more agony. She gripped his shoulders and suddenly found herself beneath him, their mouths still locked together. His hands roamed as he finally gave her a moment to breathe.

"Lord, I want you, too," he said. "I cannot get close enough to you, and I want so much more than just your one-sided attentions. What, pray tell, did the Jade ladies say about a man providing reciprocating attention?"

She froze. Her hands stilled in his hair.

"Heavens, the women said it happened occasionally. Mostly, they disliked it. As rare as it was, it felt too intimate. They were able to distance themselves mentally from acts of sexual congress, but such directed attentions were often unwelcome. Except perhaps for Ume."

"I find that tragic. I think we can do better." His eyes gleamed with determination. "You said yourself that putting your mouth on me was very different from what they described. I suspect you shall find the same is true when we reverse our roles. Now climb up onto the bed, darling Hana, and lie down near the edge. I mean to feast on you."

She could not bring herself to speak and followed his instructions. As he kissed the rise of her breast softly, she was mesmerized. *Mother of the Heavens, preserve us.* A moan escaped her when his lips brushed her nipple. Even as she arched to push her breast against his mouth, he slid inexorably downward, refusing her tacit demand.

"I want to bury myself deep inside you," he whispered against her skin.

She lifted her hips against him. "Then do it. Please! Now!"

"Not yet, my sweet," he said, calm, controlled. "No, now it is my turn to explore." As his mouth traveled slowly down, meandering, detouring, exploring, she pleaded. To no avail. When his mouth finally touched her core, her entire body convulsed. His chuckle echoed in her sensitive flesh before his hands spread her wide in his firm grip, and then there was no more talk, no more laughter. There was only pleasure so intense she shook and cried out and thrashed until her universe exploded. And still his lips and tongue delved, pushing her on.

Finally, she lay back, spent and covered in a fine layer of perspiration. Her mind reeled from the earth-shattering sensations he'd driven her to, and still she craved him. Still, she felt incomplete. With her eyes closed, she focused on breathing deeply, rhythmically, to calm her scattered senses. The stroke of his hand along her side felt like it should be soothing, but it only served to stoke the banked flames of her desire. She needed to be one with him. Now.

As if sensing the fraying edge of her control, he laid himself down next to her. As his lips traveled up her neck, he whispered, "I am yours. I took what I wanted, and now it is your turn."

His words unleashed a tantalizing vision behind her eyelids, a vision of irresistible power and control. She rose on her hands and knees to straddle him, smiling at the surprise on his face. Then he winked. That was all the prompting she needed. She guided him into her and sank down, taking him in slowly. With each rise and fall, her body accepted more of him. The intimate friction, the unbelievably profound sensation of him sliding against her, inside her, sent her emotions whirling yet again. She paused once with him fully within her and stared down at him, tears brimming in her eyes.

"I love you, Skyler," she whispered. His hips bucked, causing her head to loll back as she moaned and gasped for breath.

"Why? Why do you love me? Why did you finally agree?"

"Because I was made for you. And you for me. I see that now. I see it in your kindness, in your determination, in the way you see me, truly see me. You make me believe you, believe *in* you."

"I do see you, love. I see how talented you are, how beautifully capable you are. You are everything I could ever want. And together we can surmount the insurmountable, I know it."

She kissed him, overwhelmed with a sharp desire to somehow fuse with him in a fundamental way, even beyond how their bodies intertwined at that moment.

"I love you, too, Hana," he replied. He pushed up his torso to meet her eye to eye, and she grabbed his shoulders to steady herself as his movements sent jolts of pleasure through her.

Finally—finally!—she felt whole. Together, they strove toward their culmination with increasing frenzy. Each demand her body made on his was met with a fierce, almost fevered response, each of them driving the other higher, hotter, farther. At her peak, she bit his shoulder and screamed into his skin. He groaned and shook and then pulled her body up off his. She protested the loss of him until her mind caught up, and she felt the liquid heat of him against her bottom.

As their breathing and heart rates returned to normal, they remained intertwined, whispering sweet words to each other. She could not get enough of his enveloping presence, his embrace not just physical but mental and emotional. He'd seen all of her, he knew all of her, and he welcomed her for everything she was.

"Again?" he asked, his hard body making clear exactly what he was asking.

"Always," she said. Always would be wonderful.

EPILOGUE

1854

Laughter danced across the lake as Hana and her little sister played with the toddlers at the water's edge. When the picnic lunch was laid out, all the children scampered over. They settled into remarkable silence, interrupted only by the occasional "That's mine!" and "My piece is smaller than hers!" Any disputes were easily resolved by the expertly soothing mediation of Miss Hearsch, at whose patience Hana could only marvel.

Little Miko, Yuki's daughter, born eight months after their rescue, tried to toss a ripe plum to young Chase, Miss Hearsch's son. The adoration in the girl's eyes was hard to miss, but her offering landed far short of its target and burst open against the stones covering the shore. With an endearing precociousness, given how close they were in age, Chase comforted her, reassuring her that it was the thought that mattered and sharing his own peach with her instead.

Throughout their visit to Temple Haven, Hana had witnessed many such small kindnesses, such expressions of camaraderie among the children, among their mothers, among all the women who'd chosen to remain there.

Temple Haven. A few years earlier, the women had unanimously decided to rechristen Sharling Worth, and the new name was more than apt. Temple Haven was more than just a shelter. For so many of them, it was a place of spiritual rebirth. And their exuberant self-sufficiency was a testament to the home's nurturing properties.

Hana was especially relieved that the children of the former Jade ladies were so warmly embraced, although she supposed that some people in the world beyond the estate would always see the Temple Haven children simply as bastards. Resting against a tree, she whispered to Lady Honoria Devin, "Have the complaints from the village truly stopped?"

"Mostly," Honoria said. "There are still a few residents who continue to associate Temple Haven with moral turpitude, but most of the store owners and their families would attest to how upstanding these women are. Once the villagers saw for themselves that Temple Haven's occupants did not put a strain on their resources or send the area into decline, they became more sympathetic to what these ladies have suffered."

"And how are the two most beautiful women in the world today?" Skyler asked as he deposited a basket of fresh peaches next to them on the blanket. He offered one to Honoria, who took it with a smile.

"Thank you, kind sir." Then she snatched two more from the basket. "If you will excuse me, Lady Ridgemont, Lord Ridgemont, the Devin men seem to be up to no good." She made her way to the stone table where Devin was trying to corral their adventurous son. It was charming to see the faces of both father and son transformed by happily mischievous grins when Honoria approached them.

"Everything about this moment feels right," Hana said. "Especially now that you have arrived."

Skyler touched her cheek, his fingertips brushing along her skin as gently as a rose petal. "Perhaps we can arrange to stay here for the holidays, my lady, if we return in time."

Now that Japan was open to trade with Britain and America, travel and communication were possible. Some of the women had managed to contact their families back in Japan, and Tsubaki and Ume both had decided to return as soon as the weather and transportation allowed. When Skyler suggested they escort the women home, she had launched herself into his arms with such exuberance that they tripped and landed across the sofa in his study. Then she'd demonstrated her appreciation most ardently. She didn't want her friends to return alone. "We will make certain they are truly welcomed by their families," Skyler promised. "If they have any doubts, they can return with us."

Not alone. Not abandoned.

"That is a lovely thought," she said as her mind returned to the present, "but I shall be happy to spend the holidays anywhere, as long as I am with you."

The fondness in his gaze evolved into something more heated and intense. Before he could speak, she shared a revelation she knew would stoke the flames exponentially higher.

"Watching everyone together like this, I can see for the first time why a couple might want to add to all this joy with a new life."

"What are you saying, Hana?"

"Nothing definite, my love, only that I can see more possibilities than I could before, that I see a world where acceptance and kinship are possible. For once, I can hope that, if I one day agree to have a child, ours would not be treated as some freak or mistake but as yet another beautiful, wonderful soul in this world."

It was a good thing that none of the adults in attendance were easily shocked. For Skyler kissed her with a depth and expressiveness that would have made a staid society mum, including most certainly his mother, faint dead away. The Dowager Lady Ridgemont still refused to acknowledge her or the marriage, but the many Ridgemont properties made it easy to avoid her and relatively easy to endure the censure of her cohorts from a distance, until the furor dissipated.

"I will not push you," Skyler said, "but even the possibility pleases me more than I can say. It would be unjust of me not to share that with you."

That radiant smile of his told her just how overjoyed he was. She nodded as she leaned into him, reveling in the way his arms enfolded her so familiarly, so securely, that the rest of the world fell away temporarily.

"Before you," she whispered, "I did not realize how deeply I craved someone to share myself with, someone to see me—really see me—and I thank the heavens you did. With you, the world is full of welcome and promise."

His arms tightened around her as he whispered in return, "Always."

CPSIA information can be obtained at www.ICGtesting.com
Printed in the USA
LVOW12s2351301214

420843LV00001B/5/P

9 781601 832269